BOOK

OF

CALEB

E. W. JONES

BOOK
OF
CALEB
THE TIME TRIPPER

TATE PUBLISHING
AND ENTERPRISES, LLC

Published by Tate Publishing & Enterprises, LLC
127 E. Trade Center Terrace | Mustang, Oklahoma 73064 USA
1.888.361.9473 | www.tatepublishing.com

Tate Publishing is committed to excellence in the publishing industry. The company reflects the philosophy established by the founders, based on Psalm 68:11,
"The Lord gave the word and great was the company of those who published it."

Book design copyright © 2015 by Tate Publishing, LLC. All rights reserved.
Cover design by Nikolai Purpura
Interior design by Mary Jean Archival

Published in the United States of America

ISBN: 978-1-63418-051-1
1. Fiction / Religious
2. Fiction / Science Fiction / Time Travel
14.12.04

To Lois and Othello Gurnsey

Thank you for believing in me.

Without you, this book would not be.

Acknowledgements

I would like to thank our Lord for giving me not just this story, but also the opportunity to share it with all of you.

I would also like to thank Lois Gurnsey, Linda Pharr, Jack Sandie, Pastor Nick Stumbo, and Noel McRae for their theological contribution.

To My Readers

If you are looking for an exciting read about Christianity, this is it. Before you start though, I want you to understand that the main character knows nothing about the subject. The beginning of the book shows this. However, he grows more in faith as the book develops, becoming one of God's greatest soldiers.

It is still a wholesome read from cover to cover. Before the main character discovers religion, he is a scientist, and the book in time, turns from that of a scientific story to that of a battle for the very revival of Christianity.

You may not like science fiction, but I assure you that it is well worth it to get to the Christian part of the book. I believe it was necessary to the story line; the science sets up the background for the best part of the book.

You see, without the science, there would be no time machine, and without the time machine, there would be no story. So it is a vital part of what does make the story interesting and religious.

Enjoy!

Introduction

In the post-apocalyptic world war of 2466, religion in any form does not exist. A lone man sets forth on a biblical quest, which is unprecedented in its array and scope.

While doing research to build a time machine in the library at Washington State University, Dr. Caleb Bronson, a theoretical physicist, finds just a few tantalizing clues about the subject. The clues are just enough for him to decide a need to come to the twenty-first century and investigate further. When he arrives in the year 2010, his first acquaintance is a knowledgeable librarian named Pam Brown. She is not only somewhat familiar with the science that allows Dr. Bronson to transverse time; she is also exceedingly familiar with the

Bible, the book that does not exist in Dr. Bronson's time and exactly what he has come for.

When Dr. Bronson finally confides in Pam about his mission, she is of course shocked at his revelations. It doesn't take her long before she is on board with the doctor in his quest to reinstate religion in the future.

The future, the past, and the present can they be changed, or will man be condemned to a world without God?

Using a modified compact Hadron Collider as the base for his time machine, Dr. Bronson and his trusted companion/tutor Pam, transverse time together, righting the wrongs of the war and restoring God to his rightful place with man.

They face few perils but are always in fear of being found out for what they really are—time travelers. Their only sanctuary is when they go to Dr. Bronson's future, where a handful of trusted friends share their secret and aid in their quest.

Will time run out for the doctor? Only time will tell.

I

My name is Dr. Caleb Bronson. It may seem late in life to start keeping a journal; however the path I am embarking on, if I'm correct, could change not just history, but the very world we live in. Thus I did start keeping one.

What follows is an account of what took place, from this moment to my end, and then some.

My story is very technical in several aspects, so I believe it important to explain some of the science that allowed me to do the things I have been fortunate enough to do, before I get to the very real meat of the story of my life.

You see, the real story starts after the real science; however, the real science wouldn't mean much without the real story.

So please bear with me as I attempt to explain the science, and the story that allowed me to live the miraculous life I have been fortunate enough to have lived.

The CERN Large Hadron Collider in Switzerland, was in its time, the largest and the most advanced machine of its type; in fact it was the most advanced machine in existence. It rivaled even the complexity of the Space Shuttle.

The year is 2466, it has been about 380 years since a Large Hadron Collider, or LHC had operated. It would be the very heart of the machine I was already building to make my sojourns and longer trips.

It was theorized that the collision created by a collider, could show a glimpse of what the universe looked like right after the so called big bang, or the creation of the universe. Even in my time it was still just a theory.

Some feared the experiment could create a tear in the space-time continuum; this is what Einstein called the fabric of space. Others feared that it could create a black hole, swallowing the entire Earth, then the solar system, and, in time, the entire galaxy.

What caught my attention though, was some scientist theorized you could jump in time if they could only increase the speed of the protons past light speed.

The thought occurred to me that I could build a practical collider, which would exceed the earlier version, and possibly create a small controllable black hole.

I know this sounds a little crazy, but a black hole would be the only way to jump in time, as the ability to fold space was still an unknown quantity.

Einstein came up with two theories as to how one might be able to transverse time.

He theorized that if you could go faster than the speed of light, the hands on a clock would begin to spin backward, as well as time itself.

Einstein also visualized that space and time are not two separate things; instead, they are incontrovertibly intertwined into a flexible fabric he called space-time, a fabric that could be folded under the right gravitational conditions.

Those conditions hinged on unifying gravity with the Earth's electromagnetic field, and this is believed to be the key to folding space. No one, including Einstein has ever been able to do this.

He theorized, instead of traveling in a linearly manner through time, if a person could fold the fabric of space, they would simply be able to step across the fold, and travel to whatever time they wished.

So I began to build my time machine. In the beginning, I thought I would be a traveler to observer only. Knowing that interaction with people, or altering events could have catastrophic consequences, especially if I changed something in the past.

However, as I did research for the machine, I came across bits of information about our past, not very much, but enough for me to believe that I needed to investigate. What I would find would be a very dark and disturbing history of, it almost makes me want to choke on the word, humanity.

Now that I have explained the science, it's time to tell you about that dark time in man's history.

2

Although I never travelled to the time of the Great Attrition War, nor was I involved in the war, it still was one of the most significant events of my life, and if it had never happened, what follows would also never have happened.

The Great Attrition War was fought from 2171 to 2188 and was truly a world war—nothing like the world wars in the first half of the twentieth century.

There is nothing good about war of any kind; our ancestors found that out the hard way. Sometimes, it is unavoidable though, mainly because rich and powerful people start wars, and poor people have to fight them. If it were the other way around, things might be very different.

By the time the war started, we thought the human race had become so civilized that the thought of war was somewhat absurd. Most countries had abandoned their military or reduced it to a color guard for visiting dignitaries. However, the grass is always greener in someone else's field.

By 2166, the Chinese officially became the world superpower. America had dropped to third behind the Saudi United Arab Emirate coalition.

In late 2171, China started to make nonnegotiable demands to third-world countries. A few countries folded and paid tribute; those that did nothing were steamrolled, and became a possession of China almost overnight.

The Nazi's Blitzkrieg of World War II, paled in comparison to China's brisk aggression.

North Korea, China's one-time ally, was one of the first countries to capitulate. They erroneously believed having been their allies at one time, they could renew their partnership. They were woefully wrong; China wanted the whole world.

After that, China took on the Middle East, and then Europe. It only took them eighteen months to reach the west coast of France and the south coast of Spain. From there they crossed the English Channel, and Britain along with all the Scandinavian countries fell. Then they took South East Asia, and Australia. At this point, the war had been raging for a little over nine years.

In Earth's history, there have been several rulers who attempted world domination and nearly succeed. One thing all of them never considered was people usually don't want to have oppressive rules thrust upon them. These conquerors never considered this, and as they conquered more and more land, the people left behind to rule depleted the numbers of the conquering force. Another problem they had was, they were too far from supply lines.

Whatever the reason, they never considered that if they would have taken their time, they could have swayed the hearts of the masses. Win the hearts of the conquered, and you win the land.

This can be done by separating the young from the old. Then you treat the young very well while decreasing the numbers of the old who don't want the new rulers.

It is possible to do this in one generation. Cambodia's former Dictator Pol Pot proved this with the Khmer Rouge in the last half of the twentieth century.

When good things happen to you for following the rules, and bad things happen when you break rules, you soon forget your old life and accept the new one.

This takes time however, and if you want to dominate the world while you're alive, you have to go the distance.

This is the trouble with being a megalomaniac; they believe no one is as capable as they are. They are driven by the thought that, "If I don't do it, someone else will make a mess of the job." They are insane.

The Saudis were the first to give China a decent challenge. They put up a fierce battle for three years, but they finally fell with a thud heard around the free world, or what was left of the free world. The US realized it was just a matter of time before it was their turn.

The United States was somewhat helpless to do much of anything though.

Its military had become so depleted, and the world had been at peace for so long, no one thought it would happen. War—how absurd!

To their credit, the Chinese warned that, any country that opposed them would be crushed. China kept their promise and delivered devastating blows to several countries that stood up to them.

After the first ten years of the war and the fall of the United Saudi Arab Emirates, the rest of the African continent gave in. It became clear, China was edging toward world domination. They had the numbers to rule, and keep the conquered in line. Who could stop them now?

After that, all the countries in South America capitulated; they had no military to speak of. The war, for them, would have been sheer suicide.

China had not yet made threats to the United States, which had already annexed Canada, Mexico, and South America to the Panama Canal. They were only too glad to join us. This created the New United States of North America, or NUSNA. China was saving us for last. The canal was the point of troop buildup for the push through to the rest of South America, and into Mexico, then the former United States of America.

About twelve years into the war, China crossed the Russian border, and the NUSNA could no longer ignore the fact that they would be next. If we were going to make a stand against China, we would have to become allies with the Soviet Nations.

Fortunately, the one thing the United States had maintained was its stealth programs. The US had maintained a fleet of stealth navel ships, including the only two stealth aircraft carriers in the world.

There was a large mothball fleet of aircraft carriers, destroyers, and other assorted warships. They would not be of much help though. The Chinese fleet was less than twenty years old, while our mothballed fleet was eighty to one hundred years old. The ships that had not sunk had been scavenged a great deal. In other words, it was better to start from scratch than refit the old ships.

The same was true for our air force. We had maintained our stealth program, and had even taken it to the next level.

There was once a place, now only known as Skunk Works, which developed much of the existing stealth program. They had developed a paint that acted like a TV screen and a camera simultaneously. The new technology was dubbed Pic Paint. It was a military marvel. The paint was essentially made of Nanobots, that would take pictures at the rate of ten thousand frames a minute and route them to the corresponding Nanobots on the opposite side of the aircraft, thus making it seamless and invisible to the naked eye. They were of course, still invisible to radar. The U. S. planes were the very height of stealth.

The Soviet contingent had a few conventional stealth bombers and battleships. They also had a good amount of intercontinental ballistic missiles (ICBM). They also had the fastest, highest-flying conventional fighter/bombers ever developed, but these didn't have stealth capabilities.

So, although painted with PicPaint, that just made them invisible to the naked eye, not radar. However, the Soviets developed a different type of stealth. Instead of making the plane with sharp angles, bouncing the radar signal in a different direction, the skin of the plane absorbed and redirected the radar signal.

The skin was able to make the signal hug the plane. Then, instead of being bounced back, the signal would simply curve around the plane and go off into space; again, Nanobots were vital for this technology.

The only drawback to it was, if a plane went past supersonic speed, the paint would simply be torn away, and it would materialize for the radar.

Unfortunately, the Russians didn't know the Chinese had built a machine that was extremely sensitive to detecting heat signatures. The Russians had not been able to find a way to reduce the heat signature of the plane, without compromising the stability of the aircraft even with the use of computers.

The NUSNA attacked first, their planes heat signature was undetectable by the Chinese defense systems.

The first bombing runs made by the NUSNA did little to softening the Chinese defenses.

The Americans attacked first, the Chinese sat tight through that round and suffered heavy losses for this tactic; unfortunately though, not heavy enough.

Thinking that the United States had softened up the defenses of the Chinese, the Soviet fighter/bombers dove from the edge of space, where they thought they could fly with impunity. They were horribly wrong. The Chinese heat-seeking radar defenses were still active, and they were alerted that the Soviets were attacking.

The designers of the Soviet stealth fighter/bombers couldn't hide the engine heat well enough to conceal it from China's efficient heat-seeking infrared radar systems.

The Chinese had also developed a type of cannon that used super-compressed water as a propellant. It was very inexpensive to build and simple to operate.

The main component was a large air compressor. It was so simple a child could operate it. They were installed everywhere, and they shot a fifty-pound fragment bomb that could fly as high as fifteen kilometers. They destroyed everything within a one-kilometer radius and caused damage up to two kilometers.

By the time the Soviets realized the Chinese defenses were too strong, they had lost nearly one-third of their aircraft.

The president called the Russian Premier on the only landline still working, the red phone from the Cold War era.

He told the premier that the NUSNA was still committed to defeating the Chinese, but they would need the Soviets help to do so.

The premier said that they had so little left he didn't know how they could continue.

The president said, "We don't have much either. However, if you will allow us to locate our planes and ships at some of your bases, and operate them form there, we believe we can protect our front in Panama and still put up a front on your border. We have a little surprise for the Chinese too."

"What would that be, Mr. President?"

"In World War II, a man named Jeffery Pike mixed a solution of twenty percent sawdust and eighty percent water. Then he froze it. It was called pie create."

They had planned to take the fight to Japan with large aircraft carriers made from it. It would have been cheap to build, hard to destroy, and easy to repair. Also, like an iceberg, ninety percent of the vessel would be under water. This would give them a very low profile so they could get closer to Japan's coast without being detected, and the heat signature would be negligible because of the ice.

The president said, "We could attack as a conventional aircraft carrier within range of their coast, and perhaps even closer."

They were so large, two complete strike forces could be launched at one time.

"We can build them in Siberia and Alaska, and let the harsh winter do the initial freeze. We already have one under construction, and it is nearly finished," the president said.

"This sounds like salvation to me Mr. President," he then said. "We have bigger things to work on. Let us pass this matter to our aides. We can have them delegate the drawing of the plans, and the building of these icebergs."

The president agreed. That's how we joined the Soviets, and shipped them nearly two-thirds of our military assets.

The war lasted several more years, and although they were winning, the Chinese were tiring of the perpetual war. After all, what were they fighting for anymore? The damage to the world was so vast, it seemed irreversible.

Every country, except the countries that capitulated, had loses to their infrastructure to some extent. Recovery would be difficult, less than three billion people were still alive, and about half of those were Chinese.

By the end of the sixteen years of war, more than nine billion people had died. All cities, even those in Russia and the NUNSA, which had a population of one million people or more, were devastated. We were very fortunate that no nuclear weapons had been used, else the world would have ended; nothing would have lived.

The world as a whole, had lost a large amount of tech-savvy personnel. Also, due to the destruction of all satellites, the only method of world-wide communication left was the old shortwave radios. Hard-wired phones had become obsolete by 2050, and their infrastructure had been uprooted and recycled.

There were very few technological advances after the war started, and by 2180, the Chinese were the only people making any technological advancement, and there were few at that.

The world resembled the mid-twentieth century, technologically speaking.

As the years of the war passed, people lost members of their family from disease, old age, suicide, famine, and of course, war wounds. Almost all families suffered a loss of some kind. Many families had losses to the last member, ending that bloodline for all time.

Back in those days, life was very hard. Charitable organization had ceased to exist all together. The war had used up a lot of our natural resources, but had spared our agriculture lands and factories. However, getting supplies from place to place would be a daunting task.

Still the NUSNA, was more fortunate than other countries. We were self-sufficient; our energy and food stocks were enough to sustain the country for the time being.

Religion suffered a very large hit though. Instead of people being drawn to religion as something to hold on to, they were repulsed. The more people lost, and the longer the war went on, the more disenchanted people became with religion.

People no longer had faith. The free world was dying. Where was God, people asked?

Still, there were pockets of religious people scattered across the country. The loss of all communication satellites had made it very difficult to fellowship with Christians in other communities though.

Sometime during the twelfth year of the war, a movement was started. They were called The Organization for Realistic Concepts, (ORC). They blamed religious people for lulling the world into a false sense of security, and also for promoting nonviolence. This was viewed as unpatriotic by the group.

The ORC led mass book burnings, but the only books burned were Bibles, along with other religious artifacts, including priceless works of art, even the ceiling Michelangelo painted in the Sistine Chapel was not spared.

This ORC managed to make all religions illegal in less than three years. In another ten years, no one knew about the Bible or God. If they did, they denied it.

The gang disbanded after celebrating their twenty-third anniversary. They decided the organization itself was now the largest source of information on religion.

After they were gone, there were no reminders of religion left. It was as if it had never existed in any form. It was a dark time in the history of man.

3

As time passed, things did improve. Most communities opted for a matriarchal type of government instead of voting for their leaders. Usually, the leader was the most knowledgeable person or on the darker side, the toughest person in the town.

Not all towns were connected, but some had formed partnerships with other communities to promote trade and unity, and discourage raiders.

These were small bands of people who would invade small communities. In some ways, they were worse than the Chinese; they were doing this to their own people.

Years passed, and communities grew in this manner. Finally, about forty years after the end of the war, one community had grown strong enough that other communities decided to join them. From there, it snowballed. About sixty years after the war ended, things began to get back to some semblance of normality in the New United States of North America.

Normal though, was so far in the past, few could remember what normal was like.

Fortunately, the Library of Congress, although neglected for some twenty years, had somehow survived intact. This aided us greatly because we didn't have to start from scratch. Just getting things back to where they were before the war though, would be a huge undertaking.

Still, there were areas of the sciences that had few surviving teachers. Instead of being taught, people would have to learn, which is much more difficult to do. Having to learn alone, and not having a professor to answer questions, this proved to be a big stumbling block.

Then we needed to put communications back in place; this was a taller order. It meant we had to put the satellites back up.

Somebody found plans for a space elevator. The concept was basic—send up an orbiting platform by rockets. The orbit would be about twelve thousand miles high. All that would be needed to maintain a geocentric orbit would be a cable anchored to earth at the equator, to keep the platform in a static spot. Then you could simply hoist whatever you wanted into space.

The centrifugal force of the earth's rotation would hold the platform static in space. This would eliminate the importance of having every launch a success. It would also be much less expensive, saving untold amounts of rocket fuel.

The original plans called for a carbon fiber cable. However, the carbon fiber cable called for in the old plans could only lift about three hundred pounds at a time, the weight of the cable itself and the elevator platform alone would take up almost all of its lifting ability.

It would take almost seven and a half weeks per round trip to reach the geocentric orbiting platform. The slow speed was necessary to prevent strain on the cable; snapping it would be a two-year setback. This means it would take an inordinate amount of time to lift one satellite into orbit.

The trip would be impossible for a human to make. The weight of the person and his space suit alone would exceed the platforms weight lift limit. Not to mention the weight of the oxygen, food, and water that would be needed to make the trip.

Around the same time however, a scientist modified Aerogel. This is the lightest solid known to man. A space platform one hundred by fifty feet and four inches thick made of Areogel, would weigh about sixty-thousand pounds. If it were made of aluminum, it would weigh two-hundred-eleven-thousand-five-hundred pounds, saving one-hundred-fifty-one-thousand-five-hundred pounds of payload.

He found that by combining newly developed Nanobots with the gel, and putting it through an extruder, he could fashion the gel into a tube with a mesh-like pattern. It was thirty times lighter than the carbon fiber cable would be. Because it was so much stronger, it would only need to be about one-tenth the diameter of the carbon cable. It was also about eighty-five times stronger.

When you put weight on it, it would stretch the matrix a very small amount. This made the cable become even stronger, similar to the way that an arch becomes stronger the more weight you put on it.

With this improvement, not only could you lift three satellites at a time, you could make the round trip to the platform in about ten days. With astronauts riding along with them, it was only a two day round trip to drop of a satellite, even at the maximum height of nine-hundred-fifty miles. Still the elevator platform would have to be put in orbit by rockets. Fuel was a hard commodity to come by. Scientist gathered at a conference and came up with a solution though. Helium was not as hard to get as rocket fuel was.

They constructed a helium balloon in the shape of a large ring; it resembled a huge doughnut when filled. They mounted the space platform under it and several other balloons over the top of the structure. The balloons lifted the platform nearly twenty miles before rockets took over for the rest of the trip, saving one-billion-two-hundred-thousand pounds of fuel.

It was an ingenious solution. Astronauts could also ride up with the platform.

The platform and its living quarters were also constructed using the modified aerogel, covered in a type of Mylar. It would not survive a workload in earth's gravity, but it would be fine in the zero gravity of space.

A lone rocket requires about one thousand pounds of fuel per pound of payload to achieve a low earth orbit, or about 200 to 950 miles for a satellite. After that, it requires about 5 percent or fifty pounds per payload pound, to achieve a geocentric earth orbit, which is about twenty-two thousand miles. With the cable anchored to the earth though, scientist had calculated that an altitude of only twelve thousand miles was needed to achieve the static earth orbit planned for the platform.

This was because the combination of the centrifugal force of the earth, with the cable anchored to the earth, would exert enough force to maintain the geocentric orbit.

The satellites would be dropped off at between 200 to 950 miles because that was all they needed to maintain their orbit, and a signal beamed back to earth from twelve-thousand miles away, would take so long that there would be a large gap between a data return.

After some of the satellites were replaced, progress sped up and actually multiplied at a very swift rate.

Things eventually became a little stable. Society started the process of getting back on track. The big one though, was when they got the first six satellites up. These were all communication satellites.

The internet was back online. In the first six weeks use of the system, it was so overloaded that it crashed over 125 times.

People trying to communicate, trying to see how others lived, most hoping life was better where someone else lived.

Another problem the war caused was, people who were young during the war, never got an advanced degree. They were lucky to finish primary school and survive the war. The warriors who used to be teachers were mostly dead.

When the NUSNA originally entered the war, if you were considered essential personnel you could avoid the draft. However, we lost so many people that first year that the government opened the draft to anyone sixteen or older.

They drafted single women with no children, even some of the disabled and retired. They also removed the rule about being essential personnel.

Most teachers were killed in battles. Engineers and doctors, along with other essential skills, were lost. Professions that people didn't consider to be important until a need arose for that skill, were lost too.

It's true; you never know what you have until it's gone. It would prove to be a poor and costly decision to send the teachers into battle, but at the time, what choice did they have?

With all the losses, it wasn't surprising that religion took a large hit. There were a few pockets of religious people scattered around the country. The ORC hunted them down unmercifully though. The organization had the power of judge, jury, and executioner.

If you didn't freely agree to rebuke God and the Bible, you would first be tortured. If you still refused to convert, they would kill you. It was reminiscent of the Spanish Inquisitions and Torquemada, only in reverse.

They ransacked houses looking for anything religious, especially Bibles and crosses. When they were through with a religious community, they told the people to pack the possessions they could carry in one backpack.

The ORC would search each backpack for contraband, or anything religious. If they caught you trying to skirt this part, they would kill you on the spot.

Then the final heartbreak; if you were religious, and you agreed to rebuke God and religion, everyone in that family would be forced to separate, and be shipped out to different communities, never to see one another again.

Children, their parents, and married couples, were moved to different regions of the country if it was deemed they had been religious.

Some people became bounty hunters, finding religious villages or individuals, and informing the ORC. There was a reward of one-quarter ounce of gold for turning in a whole village, and one-quarter gram for turning in a single family.

Basically, these people were treated like they were not even chattel. As if they were something to throw away—useless, worthless—instead of the loving, caring, harmless people they were.

In the history of man you would have to go back to that terrible time when white people enslaved black people. The big difference between slave owners and the ORC was, slave owners didn't kill their slaves very often. They were treated very poorly, but they had value, and it would be like throwing away gold. Not that slaves were never killed in the old south, but the ORC was relentless in their search and destruction of the innocent.

As for the rest of the world, China did the work of the ORC. China for along time had looked at religion as a thorn in their side. They were more merciless than the ORC. They would go into a community and kill everyone and then burn the community to the ground after it was scavenged. When they were through, you couldn't find a trace of the town, or the people who lived there. Also, free religious people were not allowed in any countries that China controlled.

After Russia teamed up with the NUSNA, they adopted the ORC practices and dealt just as harshly with the treatment to religious people as China did.

4

By the time I was born, the war had been over for about two-hundred-seventy-five years. Things were not only back to the way they were before the war, but some huge scientific advancements had also been made. Some referred to it as the Fourth Renaissance.

That happens when humans have their backs against the wall. We are a resilient and creative species.

Yes, things got back to normal; but unlike before the war, charity and compassion had been lost. If you were unfortunate enough to run out of food, there were few individual or organized groups to help you.

Charity was quite unorganized. It wasn't unusual to happen upon a corps, even in the middle of a town. Humanity seemed to have lost its compassion. How can a person ignore a basic need like that? Unfortunately, humanitarian advances never caught up to the prewar standards that had been achieved.

I viewed this as unacceptable. I went to town hall meetings to make my concerns about this known. My concerns fell on deaf ears though. Their answer was always the same. "What can we do? There are no funds or volunteers."

Dejected, I started to read law books to find precedence that could possibly change the counsels' minds. It was a daunting task. The big problem was staying awake while reading them—so boring.

One day, I had lost all interest in reading law books and decided to look for information on particle colliders. I found a book and while reading it, came across a word that was totally unfamiliar to me, it was God.

It seems when colliders were being operated, they were looking for a particle called the Higgs Boson particle, nicknamed the *God particle*. They believed it to be the first particle that existed right after the big bang.

I am a theoretical physicist. I thought, "Why have I not heard of this before?" I found an old unabridged dictionary and found the word's definition. It was confusing to me. It explained,

God: The being perfect in power, wisdom, and glory, whom men worship as creator and ruler of the universe, man, and the heavens. A deity. For more information, see the Bible.

I looked up the word "Bible." It explained the book was about the early history of man on Earth, with an emphasis on a person named Jesus, and another reference to God.

I looked up deity as it was also a new word. I found it just meant a god, as if there were several. I was able to deduce that the Bible only had one deity—the Lord, or God.

I was baffled, I had never heard of the Bible, Jesus, God, or deity. I looked up Jesus in the dictionary and could not find it. Who was this man featured so prominently in a book about man's early history, and how was it that the book didn't exist anymore? Why were there no copies of the Bible even in this vast library?

I thought, "If this book was so important, why weren't there any to be found?" My curiosity piqued, I abandoned my efforts to change the way man treated each other with indifference, and yes, this made me choose to be indifferent too. Still, I began focusing my efforts on finding one of these Bibles. It was an intriguing mystery.

I returned to the library at the university the next day. I figured if I were going to find a Bible, the library would be the place to look. I searched for a week and could only find bits and pieces, nothing like I had hoped to find.

Then I stumbled on some documents about a group that had been formed during the Great Attrition War. They called themselves the ORC. I found they had been responsible for the disappearance of the Bible. Apparently, they had done a good job of wiping out any trace of the Bible. Even their papers didn't disclose very much about the book. I guessed that was what they were after—the erasure of the Bible, and an entire way of life, a genocide.

While walking down the stairs of the library, it dawned on me that I possibly held the key to find the holes in human history covering that period. I could build a time machine!

If I could build a Hadron Collider that could propel protons to exceed the speed of light, it could be possible to time travel. I already had a portable star in a jar reactor that could produce a burst of up to five hundred megawatts.

This would power the Small Hadron Collider I had designed as a child—yes, as a child. I have an IQ of 212 and an eidetic memory, I can also read over four thousand words per minute with full comprehension.

Most people who have an eidetic memory are somewhat like idiot savants, in the sense that savants can be brilliant at something like playing the piano as if they were concert virtuoso, with never even having seen a piano.

People with eidetic memories for the most part can read for example, a book on physics, then they are able to accurately regurgitate everything they had read, but even so, they can't comprehend what they had read, or apply it in a real world situation. A lot of them end up at everyday jobs.

I am one of the rare ones who can comprehend everything I read. This does make some people a little unnerved at times. Sometimes, it is the better part of valor to hold your tongue, and not blurt out the answer every time, even if you know it. After being beat up several times at a young age, I learned this.

I turned around and went back to the library. This time however, I was looking for something else.

I was seeking information about black holes and folding space. I was able to find quite a bit of information on the subjects. Still, they were just theory, I could find no research from anyone who was either able to fold space, or create a black hole.

With what I had found out so far, I felt a black hole was the way my machine would work.

5

Constructing the machine would be very expensive. That would not be a factor however. Shortly after I received my degree from Hanford, my parents were killed in a botched home burglary.

Father and Mother had both been very successful medical doctors. Father was a renowned heart surgeon, and mother was one of the most famous brain surgeons in the world. Their hospital was always full, and sometimes they worked a hundred hours or more in a six day week.

Being an only child, I inherited everything. Mother and Father were also only children, and both of their parents were also very wealthy. So my inheritance was very large. I understandable went into a deep depression. I couldn't work for some time, and when I came out of it, I decided to fund my own research. I didn't want to have to answer to anybody.

I was still a man of some notability though in the scientific community, and had many acquaintances in various fields of science. From time to time, I would ask advice from these people on things I was unfamiliar with, on various projects I would be working on.

I began modifying my old plans for the time machine. I already had the Star in a Jar power plant constructed. Star in a Jar was developed in the early part of the twenty-first century, and perfected by the mid-twenty-first century. The jar was a layperson's way of describing the warping magnetic containment fields. The star is a fuel called Tritium. Tritium is a radioactive isotope that has one proton and two neutrons. It replaced the old nuclear power plants that were built in between the nineteen-fifty's to approximately two-thousand-fifty.

The main difference between the two power sources was, you could control a nuclear reaction by simply raising and lowering metal alloy rods that contained the uranium pellets, into the water of the reactor. However, if the core is exposed to air, the uranium will begin a comparatively slow meltdown to that of a star in a jar, and disaster would ensue.

With a star in a jar, it was necessary to keep an electric load on it constantly. If the load was cut off, there would be an instantaneous meltdown. This made the star in a jar less stable when first developed. However, by about two-thousand-fifty, any problem with the loss of electric load had been solved. It became the preferred method of a clean power source, and took over for the old nuclear power plants, which were much more dangerous, took up hundreds of acres of land, and metric tons of water to operate.

A star in a jar could produce the same amount of energy as an old nuclear power plant, but they are only about the size of a two-thousand-square-foot house to produce the same amount of energy, and required no water.

Next, I needed to make a platform. The tubes of the Small Hadron Collider would serve as the base for the platform.

I needed the Small Hadron Collider to get that instant burst of energy at the point that the protons collide to create a black hole. The star in a jar was necessary to deliver an additional boost of energy to the magnets just before the collision, to create even more speed. This was vital; without the boost, the neutrons would not reach the required speed.

I calculated that it was necessary to combine both energy sources to create not just the extra boost of energy for the collider, but also to power the super cooling lasers.

Four computer servers would be necessary to control the time machine. There were so many calculations, and a near immeasurable short time to complete them. The servers would also route the energy to the right magnets, and lasers at the right moment. This made the servers more than just an essential piece of equipment. Without them, the whole project would be for naught. It would be the very heart of the machine.

A Tesla coil was necessary to absorb any escaping electricity. There would be such a large amount of electricity that would escape from the magnets, because the magnets required so much power to get the protons up to the required speed. There would be bolts of electricity darting around the magnet field of the entire vessel. It would be a spectacular show.

The Tesla coil would capture any loose energy darting about, then a transformer would disperse it into the silicon-based, high-induction/high-dispersal battery. This stored extra energy would be simultaneously distributed back to the magnets.

All these power sources would need to be combined to propel the protons past light speed. This would result in a proton collision, creating a gamma-ray burst.

That gamma-ray burst would create the necessary amount of energy to create the black hole for time travel.

A black hole, a gamma ray burst, both quite deadly, and neither had ever been artificially developed.

I was entering unknown territory. I had only theorized that's what would happen, I was taking a very large risk. If my calculations were off by just a one or zero of written code, disaster would surely ensue.

If successful, it would open a small, and hopefully controllable black hole. The servers were essential to control the timing, and the amount of energy released by the gamma-ray burst. The amount of energy released by the gamma ray burst, collated directly to the amount of time I would travel.

It was however, a relatively simple matter whether you wanted to go backward or forward in time. Reversing the directions of the speeding protons in the collider was all that was necessary to travel back in time. A few keystrokes on the computer and the changes were completed.

I formed the collider tubes using depleted uranium-infused spacecraft-grade aluminum. It was very expensive. If I had not received such a large inheritance, this whole story would never have been told, and the machine would never have been built.

The magnets were super-cooled induction magnets. I used super-cooling lasers to keep the magnets from overheating. They would be much colder than liquid nitrogen, and obviously less dangerous. They would be ideal for the task of cooling the magnets.

However, if the collider's magnets were allowed to overheat the resulting explosion would be a 2.3 megaton event. That would be an unacceptable disaster.

Since I didn't tell anyone about it, I had no help building it. I wanted it that way though. I wanted to know every inch of the machine, and the only way I could do that was to build it solo.

The price tag was more than I want to remember. I invited four of my associates, who were also some of the best theoretical scientists of the time, for the unveiling of the machine.

6

The doctors who I had invited were from varying fields of sciences. I had left instructions with Donna, my housekeeper, to serve refreshments in my absence, and to serve dinner at 6:00 p.m. and to give them a letter I had written as an explanation if I had not returned by then.

The doctors new each other mainly by their reputations, but they had also met at dinner parties, award ceremonies, and various other fund-raising events. They were all speculating as to why they had been summoned together. None of them could have imagined what he or she were about to witness.

Donna came into the front room and announced that dinner was served.

Dr. Kinsey asked, "Has Dr. Bronson arrived?"

Donna said, "No, the doctor said to seat you gentlemen, and he was sure he would be back soon."

Just then, the door burst open. I said, "Greetings ladies and gentlemen."

Dr. Kinsey asked, "Where on earth have you been Caleb?"

Dr. Kinsey and I had known each other since our days at the Institute for Advanced Theoretical Physics in Hanford, Washington. I smiled and said, "Ah, where I've been is not nearly as important as when I've been."

Dr. Jason Simmons spoke first. "What do you mean, 'when you've been'?"

The rest chimed in excitedly asking different questions, and not waiting for an answer before asking the next. I got control of the chatter and said, "Let me brief you first, and I'll answer questions when I'm done if you're still puzzled." The guest agreed.

My guests were Drs. Mike Kinsey, theoretical physicist, Jason Simmons, theoretical astrophysicist, Kim Osaka, theoretical Engineer, and Ali Asana, alternative energy physicist. All sat quietly waiting to hear what my next words would be.

"There is so much to tell. Let me see where to begin. Gentlemen, what is the fastest thing known to man? Light speed, is it not Jason?"

"Yes," he answered, "the speed of light, anyone knows that Caleb."

"Yes, but that doesn't mean they're right, does it?"

"Unless you're going to say that man has been wrong about that for all these centuries," Jason said.

I gave a dramatic pause and then said, "Yes, we have been wrong." They all looked stunned for a moment, then I broke the silence.

"Man believed for several centuries that Sir Isaac Newton was completely correct with his mathematics, even though his math could not account for the elliptical orbit of Mercury."

Dr. Simmons said, "Yes, Newton failed to account for the gravitational pull of the sun, which Einstein corrected with his theory of relativity, but what does that have to do with the speed of light?"

"Nothing, and everything at once," I said.

"Caleb," Dr. Kinsey chimed in, "if you're going to tell us you have found something that is faster than the speed of light, will you tell us at least at the speed of light, if not faster." Everyone chuckled.

I said, "We have all known the answer. It has been in front of us all these centuries!"

"I don't know about the rest of you, but I'm stumped," Kim said.

I asked Kim, "If you have something that exerts a certain amount of energy, and you have something else that exerts an opposing force that is stronger, when you put them up against each other, what will happen?"

Kim answered, "the stronger force will cancel out the weaker force, and the weaker force will be drawn to the stronger force."

"That is correct. Jason, can you tell us what the strongest force in the universe is?"

A black hole was the answer. "That is also correct. What happens when light crosses the path of a black hole's event horizon?" I asked.

"The black hole would draw the light in," Jason replied.

"Correct again." I then said, "does light have any mass?" Almost in unison, they all said no. I asked, "If light has no mass and it travels at the speed one-hundred-eighty-six-thousand miles per second, why can it not escape the pull of a black hole?"

"The gravitational pull is too strong," Ali said.

I said, "how can something that has no mass be affected by gravity? Then I put it to you gentlemen, if the force from a black hole can bend light and pull it into itself, changing its direction. Then not just light, but everything that passes the event horizon, will exceed the speed of light.

I purpose the gravitational pull that a black hole exerts, exceeds that of light speed. The difference between the two is, light is pushed. On the other hand, if the gravitational field of a black hole is strong enough, it can bend light and pull it into itself. However, since light is pushed, without an external power source to push it or pull it faster, light should remain at a constant speed in space. The gravitational pull of a black hole however, increases the further something is pulled in. If this is so, light speed must also increase.

I believe that light would go so fast, that it would stretch the photons to the point that light would dissipate, and at some point, become invisible, if you could see inside the black hole."

I smiled as my guest sat in stunned silence digesting what I had just purposed.

Finally Kim said, "I can't think of an argument against it."

Jason mumbled, "Nor can I."

Mike and Ali were also at a loss. They kept staring at each other as if they were trying to elicit some kind of rebuttal from one another.

None came though, and these were all men and women at the top of their respective fields. If there was a rebuttal, it wasn't coming from this group.

"I have something to show all of you, trust me you don't want to miss this." We all hopped on our hover-boards, an antigravity board for transportation proposes.

The hover-board was an amazing development. It produced a force field around you and redirected the gravitational field, thus making you weightless.

The boards would have never been developed if the world hadn't come so close to the planet-level extinction event of 2289.

An asteroid came from behind the sun, and was heading right for earth. When it was first sighted it was too late to do anything about it other than saying good-bye to your loved ones.

It was about the size of Lake Michigan. This would not just be an extinction-level event, the planet itself would be vaporized, not even a rock would be left.

We had about twenty-three hours from the time of discovery, to time of impact in the Atlantic Ocean, off the coast of New Brunswick.

As it entered the atmosphere, astronomers realized that it was slowing a great deal. When it was about five miles from impact, it was only going about five hundred miles an hour and still slowing.

Of course, this slowing of the asteroid puzzled scientists. One mile from impact, its speed had slowed to a tolerable one-hundred-fifty miles per hour. At about fifty feet from impact, it just stopped. It did create a tsunami from the air it was compressing in front of it though, but the highest wave recorded was on the New England coast, at a height of five feet.

No one died because everyone had fled the area. The asteroid settled down, and floated at a height of about ten feet above the surface of the water. Then floated slowly to the Eastern seaboard where it stayed.

It was studied for months. Then one day, a thirteen-year-old boy got a chunk of it, pulverized it, and mixed it with paint. Then he painted a snowboard with the concoction, and the first hover-board was born.

Scientist still can't figure out what makes the rock hover, but they know that it redirects the atmosphere and gravity around you and the board.

The group followed Caleb to an old aircraft hangar at a nearby abandoned airport. Inside they saw the machine. After looking it over for a while, Mike asked, "Well, just what are we looking at?"

Caleb said, "Gentlemen, this is a machine for travel."

"What is it, some kind of large hover-board?" Kim asked.

I said, "It is a craft for travel, I never said it was for traveling through space." They had puzzled looks on their faces.

"Are you trying to tell us that this machine travels through time?" Mike queried.

"That is exactly what I'm telling you." They all came back at the same time, protesting the absurdity of it, postulating in a jumbled, garbled mixture of voices that made it impossible to make out one single question. I tried to get the gang to settle down, and finally had to whistle very loud to wrest control of the discussion. "Gentlemen, gentlemen, please, there is so much to talk about tonight, let's try to stay on track shall we?"

I went about the task of explaining my machine. As I pointed out different components, they asked questions.

They knew what the Star in a Jar Power Plant was, and what the Tesla coil did. They also knew what the transformer would do. No one could figure out what the tubes were that supported the apparatus though.

"Jason, do you remember a rumor when we were attending Hanford about an attempt to collide protons at near light speed?"

"Yes, they were trying to create what the big bang looked like a microseconds after it occurred. The machine was referred to as the Large Hadron Collider."

"Yes," I said.

Five years after they secretly built the one under the university, a company named CERN built what they called a Large Hadron Super Collider.

He stammered for a moment and then said, "Caleb, this isn't a collider is it?"

I just smiled.

Mike said, "You didn't build one, did you?"

I asked him if he was afraid.

"Yes, a little bit. Have you tested it?"

"I have, don't worry, it's still here and I am too."

"You do understand that when the protons collide there is a tremendous explosion for a microsecond?" Said Ali.

"Yes, and that was the problem. In the past, they didn't have the power plants, the powerful magnets, the super-cooling lasers, or the newer metals we have today.

They could only achieve a speed of 99.9999991% that of light speed with the protons, so they could not complete their experiments."

Ali said, "Is that what the Tesla coil and the transformer are for?"

"Yes," I said.

On closer inspection, Ali noticed the silicon-based battery mat, that was the floor of the machine.

"This is an excellent choice for a battery. It has the dual feature of being able to handle fast uptake, and equally fast dispersal of energy. I can only assume that the extra burst of energy goes to the superconducting magnets, releasing a super burst of energy, making the protons go past light speed."

"That is correct," I said, "It will also power the super-cooling lasers."

Kim asked, "Why do you need the Tesla coil?"

"It will collect any escaping energy available, and redirects it to the transformer, which will disperse it to the silicon batteries. The battery also works just as efficiently in reverse. This way it can release a large burst of energy for time travel, and in addition, prevents the battery from overcharging and exploding."

Kim asked, "Why do you need the living quarters?"

"With the amount of electricity the machine will produce, there needed to be an insulated place to protect myself, the servers, and the controls from static shock."

Mike said, "Well, this is very interesting, in a science fiction sort of way, but does it work? After all, you have made some pretty outrageous statements."

"I already told you that I used it. Do you need a demonstration Mike?"

He said, "Well, yes, it's not that I don't believe you, but I am a man of science, and it would be…oh just get on with it."

"My cat Cinnamon will be the second time traveler. I'll set the machine to go, say thirty seconds into the future." They all agreed. Who has a phone? I asked. Kim gave me hers. I reached into my pocket and said, "Here is my phone. I'll set the timers on both of them and engage the machine. When the machine starts up, the timers will both start. I have set the return time for thirty seconds from the start of the event."

We all got behind a protective barrier I had constructed, and donned welding goggles. I engaged the collider with a remote. There was an escalating whirring noise, and a breeze for a moment, and it was gone. Words like *magic*, *fantastic stunt*, and *unbelievable* were bandied about. By this time, the machine returned.

On its return, there was a more violent wind, and you could see the black hole as the machine reappeared thirty seconds later.

Kim said, "It took thirty seconds."

Cinnamon was on the bed purring as if nothing had happened. They tried to say it wasn't real. I told Ali to get Kim's phone and the camera that was mounted on the wall. "But don't shut it off. I want you to see the congruity of the film and the timers, so you can't say I faked that also."

They watched the video, and could see the cat didn't move around at all. Also in the background, we were not visible. I pointed this out and told them. "That's because we were here in a different time than the camera." I also pointed out the time stamp on the video. It had moved only ten seconds. By the time we looked at Kim's phone, only thirteen seconds had elapsed, while my timer had advanced forty-three seconds.

It was some time before anyone said anything. They all had a shocked look on their face. Mike spoke first.

"Well, when are you going, and *when* are you going to?"

I just smiled and said, "That's what we will decide through our upcoming discussions."

We met the next night, and every night after that to plan the protocol for usage of the machine. After all, there could be unintended repercussions from contact with people from the future or the past.

As the days passed, we installed more and more equipment in my protective shelter. There was a biological decontamination chamber, personal environmental monitors, and numerous and varied recording devices, the list was long. One night I said, "We have done enough."

There were some protest, but it soon died down. We all wanted to leap in time. It would be an adventure comparable to that of an astronaut going to some far off planet. The first person to travel in time—it would be an historical event of astronomical proportions.

7

That night, we closed the shop early and withdrew to my home. Donna served the gang and I coffee when we reached the house. Donna was very discreet about my work, and by the first night, I had told my friends about the machine, she had known of it for some time, but kept my secret just as a trusted friend would.

I asked her if she would be so kind as to sit in on our discussions. She, understandably, was a little surprised, but nonetheless joined us. I said I wanted someone who has a practical mind, instead of just a scientific mind to sit in on our discussions. "We can sometimes become caught up in the moment of discovery all too easily," I said, almost childlike.

"This will take a while, and we won't find all the answers we are looking for, so there will be holes in the story.

"It started when I decided to build the machine. The idea came to me in a flood. I went to the college library to get information I would need to build the machine. While I was collecting this information, I came across an outline of the expectations for a Large Hadron Collider.

"At the point of collision, there was an unbelievably large and diverse amounts of particles created that only existed for a short time, immediately following the big bang. They theorized it was possible to recreate some of these particles that may have been present after the big bang took place. They believed a particle named the Higgs Boson particle, sometimes referred to as the *God particle*, was the first particle created.

"At the time, the term *God* confused me. I picked up a very old unabridged dictionary and looked up God. It said, and this really floored me, God, the being perfect in power, wisdom, and goodness, whom men worship as creator and ruler of the universe, man, and the heavens. A deity. Then it said, 'Read the Bible for more information.'"

"What did this Bible say?" asked Jason.

"I couldn't find one, but I searched other books, and I found mention of the Bible, and of God sporadically, but nothing completely explained the questions I had." I reminded them of how desperate people had become during the Great Attrition War. Then I told them about the Organization for

Realistic Concepts. I had found out about them when I first started looking for a Bible. When I finished telling them about the practices of the ORC they were stunned. Book burnings? I reminded them about the lawlessness that sprung forth during the war.

"Leaders of this group thought this God person, or deity as he was also referred to, offered false hope to the weak-minded. The practice of believing in God and the Bible were perceived by the ORC as a deterrent to forward thinking. People that believed in God were deemed unproductive, and therefore did not support the war effort."

Then I told them what happened to those who refused to rebuke God. They were aghast at how civilized people could do those things to one another. Then again, how could this type of conduct be considered civilized? We were fighting a war that wiped out more than three-quarters of the people on the face of the earth, which was far from civilized.

Donna finally spoke up. "Dr. Bronson, this seems to be a conversation for you scientists, not for a housekeeper."

I said, "Come now, you must have some concerns."

She thought for a moment and then said shyly, "I suppose you gentlemen have heard of the butterfly effect?"

We were all stumped. It had been centuries since anyone had thought about time travel, believing it an impossibility. I said, "Please, tell us what this butterfly effect is."

She began, "We were assigned a book to read in high school, it was fiction of course. It told about people that traveled back in time to the age of dinosaurs. They could not stray from a certain path. If they did, they risked the possibility of stepping on an insect whose evolutionary decedents, humans may eventually have spring forth from, and then we would never have been."

We all sat there stunned. Could this happen? We discussed the possibilities.

Finally, we decided that Donna had something concrete. This was a possibility! I could go back in time, and kill one of my grandparents, then I would never have been born. Time travel could be rife with all kinds of variables.

The next day we met at the university library to find anything we could about the Bible, Jesus, and God, or what life was like before the war. This would be a daunting challenge. The library was so large, but we dove into our task with great intensity.

8

When we arrived at the university library, I assigned each member of the gang certain documents to look for. I had determined that Jesus was Gods' son.

I had also concluded that the Bible was some sort of book that was considered by some people before the war, to be the indisputable guide as to how people should conduct themselves, and live their lives according to Gods' Word, whatever that was.

We discovered that there was much more written about Jesus in Roman history, than any other written history, including the Hebrews. The ORC had fallen down on the job when it came to expunging Roman history though.

Another thing we noticed was, there was very little history left about the Hebrews. We concluded that Hebrews got a bad deal for many years from the Romans and the Egyptians. Why then was there little written about Hebrews in those years?

We had been taught at a young age, that BC stood for before civilization, and AD stood for after development. I had always thought there was something odd about the abbreviations. I found the true meaning of the symbols while I was going through Roman history.

AD actually means anno domini, which is Latin for, "year of our Lord." BC stands for, Before Christ. Both are used in connection with the Julian, or Gregorian calendar, and both are correct for whichever calendar you use.

As I became more educated about the erased past, I found that Before Christ meant, the years before Christ was born. Obviously then, AD meant the world after Christ was born.

Since this was such a significant event that it was etched in history for all time throughout the world, I thought, "Jesus had to have weighed heavy in man's past." My quest for further knowledge of him intensified.

After we had spent a few days at the library, we decided to return to my home and discuss our findings. We had gathered a good amount of information, and felt we could come to some kind of conclusion about the Bible, Jesus, and God. We also wanted to find out if there was a basis to investigate the subjects.

At first, we tried to collate all the materials into the three main subjects: the Bible, Jesus, and God.

This proved to be a nearly impossible task. The three subjects were clearly intertwined. We soon found that we needed a fourth pile, which included all three subjects in relationship with each other.

When we had finished, we found the original three piles we had gathered were very skimpy, and the fourth pile we had deemed necessary was so much higher than the other three piles, that we concluded one pile was all that was needed.

We had wasted a good amount of time trying to collate the material. However, we did read quite a bit of it while doing this, so it wasn't a total waste.

Now we knew that all three subjects were inextricably intertwined. The records that the Romans kept were quite thorough, and were verifiable with ancient writings from other civilizations.

Pontius Pilate was the governor of Judea, and a main figure in Rome's ruling of the area in the time of Jesus. We had found a passage in Roman writings were Pilate had tried to give Jesus a break, when he sentenced Jesus, a man of peace to death. There was another man named Barabbas, who was sentenced along with Jesus.

Barabbas was a man convicted of some very serious crimes including murder. Pontius Pilate had the two men stand on a raised platform and told the crowd, "Here you have two men accused of different crimes. This man (Barabbas) has committed various crimes including murder, and has been found guilty.

This man Jesus, is guilty of being a Christian."

Christian—another new word that we determined was a derivative of Christ, the last name of Jesus, or so we thought at the time. Pilate tried to make the murderer Barabbas look bad, and tried to make Jesus look harmless. Then he told the crowed, "One man will get his freedom today, and one will be crucified." He then said to the crowd, "Choose who will go free, and who will die."

Crucified was a new word to us, so we looked for it in the dictionary. As I read what the term meant, my colleges and I were appalled at the definition.

How could people be that cruel, even if they were not as evolved as we are? It was quite apparent to us, that this was a cruel form of execution.

A cross consisted of two large wooden beams, sturdy enough to hold the weight of a man. The cross was shaped, so the length was about three times as long as the breadth of the crossbeam.

The cross was first laid on the ground, and the convicted person was forced to lay down on it. Then their wrist and feet were nailed to the cross. Next they raised it up with the long end of the cross inserted in a hole on a hillside. Then dirt was backfilled around it to hold it up. After that, they were left to die, this could take as long as two days. Spectators would throw rotten fruits, vegetables, and feces at them.

We were shocked that the crowed overwhelmingly chose Jesus to die, and set the murderer free. Even though Pilate, who had no vested interest in Jesus, pleaded three times to the blood-thirsty crowed to change their minds, the crowed still wanted Jesus crucified.

We would come to find that three was a number that we would encounter often, as well as seven, both numbers are prominent in the bible.

We concluded that Christianity must have some negativity connected to it. We couldn't find anything though. However, we did find that the Pharisees, yet another new word, did not like the way Jesus would associate with the poor and downtrodden for some reason that wasn't clear just yet. They were even more appalled that he would sit with them for meals. We knew about prejudiced people in our time, so this was not completely shocking to us.

We were perplexed though, Christians didn't seem like a threat to the masses in fact quite the opposite. From what we could find, we determined that for the most part, they were a loving, peaceful people. Yes, they did try to convert people to their way of belief, but as scientist, we are open to new ideas and changes. We always believe there is a better way to do things, those ways just haven't been thought of as yet. Was this the same sort of situation?

If so, why set a known murderer free while condemning a man who promoted compassion, tolerance, and love? Were people that underdeveloped twenty-five hundred years ago?

This could be the reason the ORC was so brutal and thorough. Being a scientist, I hated having so many questions and so few answers. I said, "Gentlemen, I have concluded that we must correct this injustice. We owe it to the world, and we owe it to Jesus."

Kim said, "Yes, but how will you go about doing it?"

"Simple," I replied. "I'll go back to that time and"—I hesitated for a moment—"I'll solve it, or maybe I'll keep it from happening altogether."

"We have already talked about changing the past," Jason said. "Remember the butterfly effect? What if you go back to that time and save this man Jesus. He might have decedents that may do something."

He was searching for a finish to his sentence when I finished it for him. "Something like prevent the Great Attrition War?"

"You know I meant something bad."

"Well, would it be that bad?"

"Would what be that bad?"

"No war, billions of people spared, no stagnation of the worlds everything, as if it never happened," I said.

"This will be a lengthy discussion, and I think it's important that, once we start, we should stay with it until we finish. We can pick up this discussion tomorrow."

Everyone agreed and gathered their coats, and said their good-nights as they shuffled out the door. This left Donna and I with all sorts of thoughts swimming through our minds. I can only guess what the others were thinking.

I told Donna, "You do know I value you, not just for keeping us well fed on top of keeping the house clean, but also for your contribution to our discussions. You are an absolute marvel. I appreciate everything you do. I think all of this would not be possible were it not for you. Thank you."

She smiled and said, "Doctor, I don't know what my life would be like, had you not hired me."

I said, "The same goes for me. I would probably have piles of books and papers stacked all over, from the floor to the ceiling. That being said, I would like to discuss something with you of a serious nature."

"Doctor excuse me, but haven't all of our conversations of late been of a serious nature?"

I said, "That is true, our discussions of late have been a bit heady. Nevertheless, this has to do with you. Donna, this is about my estate."

I opened the top drawer of my desk and retrieved some papers from it. "Come over here Donna, please have a seat. As you know Donna, I have no relatives alive. You have been my constant companion and confidant for almost ten years now. You cook, clean, and most of all, you keep my secrets.

"As of late, you have been much more than that. You have done all these things for five people instead of one. You have also made valuable contributions toward our goal of time travel. That said, should we be successful in our undertakings, you will receive a full share of credit for your contribution toward this scientific endeavor."

She was stunned. "Doctor," she said, "I can't accept that. What about the others?"

"We all discussed it today while you were shopping. There was little discussion about the subject. We all agreed we would be at least two, and possible four weeks behind where we are now without you. Not only have you been feeding us, making coffee, and straightening up after us—I'm sure there is something I'm missing—yes, of course, there's your scientific contribution, the butterfly effect, which we all deemed as very significant. Yes Donna, you deserve full credit along with the rest of us."

"Well, I don't know what to say Doctor."

"Wait, there's more, I had my will rewritten. If for some reason the worst happens, I have left everything to you."

Donna was caught off guard. "I don't know what to say."

"There is nothing to say. I need you to take care of my house and all that comes with it. I'm increasing your salary from two grams of gold, to one-quarter ounces a week." Her eye's opened wide.

"You will move into my house and live here as you like. I have had my lawyer write a codicil to my will, saying if I go missing for a month, he is to execute the will. You will then receive one-third an ounce of gold a week for life, and receive a cost of living raise every year. In addition, there is an allotment for taxes and home repairs. On execution of the will, you will receive five ounces of gold right away."

When she fainted, I managed to catch her before she hit the floor. I carried her to the couch and made her as comfortable as possible. She awoke a few moments later, and I told her that if I didn't return, she was to hold a dinner for the other four doctors every night.

"They will each give you a half gram of gold a week. In addition, you must never sell the house. It is to stay in your family forever." Still a little dazed, she simply said, "Yes Doctor, I will take care of the place for you if you should go missing."

9

There really was no question as to who would be the time tripper. Since our mission was to save Jesus, there was really no question; I would be the time traveler. I had learned how to speak Aramaic, the language of the day rather well. In addition, I had a working knowledge of the customs of the time. Also, I was the only one with an eidetic memory. Although we were extremely interested in the past, we all agreed that the future held more interest for us. We all wanted to find out if the future was worth knowing about. I would first travel to the future, then to the past to learn about the Bible. After that, my plan was to go to the time of Jesus, to right the wrong of his crucifixion.

It took twice the energy to travel to the future, as it did to the travel back in time. I took a lead-lined suitcase filled with fresh tritium pellets. This was so I could refresh my fuel supply, and travel as much as I wished. I would find that there were limits to the machine's time traveling capabilities though.

First, I could regulate whether I traveled to the past or future, simply by the direction I programmed the computer to propel the neutrons. I could travel to almost any time, depending on the amount of energy expended.

The further in time I traveled, correlated directly to the amount of energy required by the time machine. The energy expended multiplied expediently. In other words, whether I went forward or backward in time, the further I went in either direction, the more fuel I would expend. The machine would shut down when it reaches its power limit. This ended up being about two-hundred-fifty years into the future, and about five-hundred years into the past.

The reason it took twice the energy to travel to the future was a mystery. We could only hypothesize the reason for this was, the future hadn't happened yet.

Does this mean that we would be creating the future if we ventured there? We could not answer that question either, but it did seem to be very possible.

We had discussed where in time to go, and agreed on starting by going one hundred years in the future. This required a slight adjustment in the programming, which consisted of just a few keystrokes on the computer.

Going to the future would let us know if we had made any mistakes by going to the past. You would know simply by the fact that if it was changed in the past, then it should be changed in the future.

This is because, even though I had not yet gone to the past, I would be going there. If I did change something, it would be changed in the future. I already knew what the original past was, so I would know the difference, but I alone would know.

The problem is, if you were the one to make the time trip, you would also be the only one to know the difference. Other than recording some part of the event, it would be your word against the whole worlds'. If you changed something in the past then traveled to the future, you would have a different memory of the past than everyone else.

Yes, this whole explanation is somewhat convoluted, but if you think about it for a moment, it does make sense.

We all agreed that it would be safer to trip into the future, something that I would find to not be true. I took some clothing, food, and water to last a week.

We had one last meeting before I tripped. We discussed how I should approach people should someone bump into the machine when it was cloaked. This would not only be a physical contact, it would also make the machine partially pixelate, meaning the machine would momentarily and partially materialize. The Pic Paint could do only so much.

The date was November 16, 2466. There were cameras set up in eight locations to record several different aspects of the time jump. Some of the cameras we used were super high-speed. We already knew the visual transfer outside the machine lasted just a microsecond, so the cameras' speed was set at forty thousand frames per second.

I programmed the vessel to advance one hundred years into the future. All that was left to do was press the Enter button and I would be gone. I had programmed the machine to return after a one-week trip in case something happened to me. Then at least my associates would have the machine to search for me. To my associates, it would seem that I would only be gone for a few minutes.

The bunker I built had walls that were lined with four inches of lead, and had a six-inch-thick lead-impregnated, Plexiglas window. Then for eye protection, we wore acetylene torch goggles. There would be a blinding light at the point of transference, and that would be the end of our eyesight without the goggles.

We were all in our places with our protective gear on. I asked to go through the pre-trip checklist. There were twenty-six gauges to read, and eighteen were for the star in a jar reactor.

When it was time, I nodded to my friends. They waved back, not with smiles, but with a look of trepidation of the unknown. The possibilities of what could happen if things went wrong were unfathomable. The fear of the unknown shone on their faces. Not that of the amazing discovery they were about to witness, which I had hoped to see. I know if I had been on the other side of the bunker, I would have been apprehensive too. However, I had so much to think of, I didn't have time to be afraid, but I was still a little scared.

I pressed the Enter button, and the machine began to make the whirring noise we had heard on the trial run.

At this time in the test, the machine had vanished for my colleagues. I was still time traveling though. The whole platform began buffeting from the stress. The tornado of the black hole engulfed the entire vessel, however, I felt no breeze. It started from the bottom of the craft and climbed up to a peak about fifteen feet above the machine where it came together. This took less than a second into the trip. It had completely engulfed the craft like a protective cocoon. The noise was so deafening I believed I would lose my hearing if it didn't stop soon.

About three seconds into the trip, the veil of the black hole began to fade. The whole trip lasted less than four seconds. I had arrived. The year was 2556, one hundred years into the future.

I was surprised to see that the airport hangar that I had been using was not only still standing, it was also in good repair. Donna of course, had kept the hangar rented and in good shape, so I would have a safe place to appear in the future. The hangar entry door was locked, and there was a note hanging on it. The note said, "I thought it might be prudent to rent the hangar so you could have a place to insert yourself into the time you selected without being noticed. I have missed you so much over these years Doctor. I know I will see you again, when that will be, who knows."

The note was brown and brittle. It must have been hanging on the door for years.

There was an additional note in someone else's handwriting.

"Hello Doctor, If you are reading this, I can only assume that you were successful in your venture to the future. We know you went to other times, and I want you to know you are going to go on a magnificent adventure. Unfortunately, my future holds very little. My name is Jack Carlson. My mother was Donna, your housekeeper. She kept your house in immaculate shape over these years. I inherited the house from mother, and have been waiting anxiously for your return. I will come to see if you successfully made it to our time one hundred years to the day, at 8:00 o'clock p.m."

The clock on the wall was broken. Then I looked at my cell phone. It was 7:57.

Not knowing what society may have crumbled into, I decided to wait and see if Jack would show up.

Moments later the door opened. A thin, spry-looking man in his late eighties walked in. He entered slowly, looking intently, and with awe at the time machine. He circled the craft until he overcame his amazement. He spotted me in the corner and approached me, slowly extending his hand.

"Dr. Bronson, I presume?"

I nodded in agreement. "My name is Jack Carlson. I am Donna Carlson's oldest son. How do you do, Doctor?"

"To be quite honest, Mr. Carlson, I'm not sure. It has only been five minutes since I last saw your mother, and she had no children then."

"Well, to be honest, she never did have children. She never did marry, but through your generosity to Mother in your will, she was able to adopt four children. I was the first one. May I shake your hand sir?"

He reached down and took my hand before I could even react.

He shook my hand with great vigor. As he did, I could see tears welling up in his eyes.

I questioned this emotion, and he explained how Donna had contacted his biological mother shortly after she became pregnant with him, and how they had made a deal.

"She moved Mother into the house, and took care of her during the pregnancy. So Donna got the child she so badly wanted, and Mother was put at ease that I would be well cared for. Had she not done that, I doubt I would still be alive. So you see Dr. Bronson, if not for your benevolence, I would most likely be dead.

"After my birth, my biological mother was packing her things when Donna passed her open door. She could see tears rolling down her cheeks. Mother asked her if she was going to be all right. She replied she had some money but it wouldn't last long.

"Mother thought about this for a short while, and concluded a few things. The house is very large, she and Jodi got along fairly well, and you sir, left so much gold, it would last a large family for a long time. Mother went back to Jodie's room and said, 'I have an offer for you.' Mother told her that she wanted three more children. She said that she knew Jodi would like living here, and they seemed to get along all right. Jodi replied that she did like the home, and that she thought they did get along.

She told her, 'I have thought we have become good friends, so here is the offer.' She said she would like three more children. She said, 'I would like them to be about two to three years apart. You may marry, but I want you to give me the courtesy to discuss whether he is a good man or not. There is a lot to parenting, but you handled your pregnancy very well. I trust you will cope with parenting just as well. We will raise the children together. I will, of course, pay for everything. I will give you an allowance. I haven't given this a lot of thought, but I'm sure we will be able to come to some agreement.' Jodi gave mother a big hug and said thank you over and over again."

'This couldn't have worked out any better if I wanted it to,' Donna said. 'We will be wonderful parents and the greatest of friend.' "And they were for about fifty years. Then Donna died from a stroke about thirty years ago."

Even though I knew Donna would be gone, as well as the members of the gang, it still was a shock to hear it.

"By the way, what about Jodi? What happened to her?"

"She ran the house for the next ten years, and then slipped away one night in her sleep."

"Your brothers and sisters, where are they?"

"I have one sister who is married and lives here in town. My brothers live here also. One is married, the other, widowed. We keep in constant contact, and you are the subject of discussion a great deal of the time. It's as if you're a member of the family and present at all times. They are at your home as we speak. They are dying to meet you."

I asked, "How many people know about me?"

"Only myself and the immediate family know the real truth."

"Do you trust that all of them will keep the secret?"

He chuckled a little and said, "To be honest, your story has been told often, and they are somewhat of a staple in local folklore."

I inquired, "You say I am going on a great adventure. What did you mean, and what does the future hold for you?"

He smiled slyly and said, "Doctor, it's your rule, if you learn something about the past while you are in the future, you could either change it willingly, or put yourself in a position that may cause you to accidentally change the past. That is one of your big rules. Besides, it would spoil the many surprises of your great adventure. Isn't the moment of discovery the most exciting thing about being a scientist?"

"Yes, of course, you are right. Still, as a scientist, I have a great deal of curiosity."

Jack just smiled and said, "You won't get anything out of me except this. Your life will soon have a magnificent, and unexplainable change for the better."

He put his hand on my shoulder and said, "Caleb, I know you don't have a clue at the moment as to what I am alluding to, and although I do appreciate how you took care of Mother, what I am going to say has nothing to do with your financial contribution. I'll just say this to you now. Meeting you has been, and always will be, the greatest honor of my life."

I continued to shake his hand with what must have been a bewildered look on my face because, well, I was perplexed!

"I know that you want to know what is going to happen, but that day will come soon enough for you. Know this Caleb, people have spoken your name for very many decades, and they still do."

"You said people laugh at your stories about me."

"Yes, but they think we're lying about having any kind of association with you. I'm talking about your life in the past, and how you single-handedly shaped the way the world is today."

I have to say I was completely dumbfounded by this last statement. How could I change the world? I would have to wait to live my future in the past, to find out what he meant.

I suddenly noticed a certain sadness come over his face. I asked if something was bothering him.

He said, "Of course, you were time tripping when it began, The Second Attrition war."

I was appalled, I asked him, "How could they do it again."

He simply said, "When the past is forgotten, man is doomed to repeat the past.

China had become so ashamed of the war, that they quit teaching it in their public school system about eighty years ago. They had forgotten the war, and how devastating it was. About thirty-five years ago, they decided to try for world domination again.

"One of their scientists invented a water-based solution that made women sterile. They inserted agents in several countries, and they contaminated water systems in those countries. The Chinese had finally won the war. All they had to do was sit back and wait for everyone to die, and the world would have been their oyster.

Sometimes though, the simplest of things are overlooked by the smartest people. They neglected to think about the single, simplest problem with their plan."

"What was that," I asked?

"Evaporation and rain; they never considered nature. Heating the contaminated water to almost four hundred degrees is the only way to destroy the biological contaminant, and natural evaporation is not nearly that hot.

Within about thirteen years of its initial distribution, the last baby was born, ironically in China. By the time they realized what was happening, it was too late. Now, the youngest person on earth is something like twenty-seven years old.

That reminds me Dr. Bronson, your stay here has to remain short. If you drink something while here, it won't hurt you, but you will take it to whenever you go from here, and a glass of water will be enough to sterilize a fifty thousand women."

I said, "I must leave right away then.

There is moisture in the air. I'm ingesting that toxin just by breathing. It's also getting in me by osmosis!"

"Then you must leave before you take it back with you. I never thought of the consequences of you mixing with our environment."

Jack shook my hand once more and then said, "I envy you Doctor. I wish I could join you. Good-bye forever Doctor. I will never forget you, and I will continue to pray for you."

I said, "What do you mean ' Good-bye forever,' and what is pray?"

He said, "The contaminate Doctor, you must not take it back with you, so you must never return."

"Pray, what is it to pray, I asked?"

He just smiled and said, "All in good time Doctor, all in good time."

He let go of my hand, I told him to retreat to the bunker and don the glasses.

I entered the biological decontamination chamber for about one minute, and I was decontaminated inside and out, or so I hoped.

I reprogrammed the computer, waved good-bye to him, and pushed the Enter button. The whirring noise began once more. The magic veil of the black hole engulfed me, and seconds later I was back with my contemporaries.

I climbed down the vessel's stairs, and the others came out from their protective compound. They were as usual, all talking at once, and very excitedly. I expected that they would be like this though. It took some doing as usual, but I finally got control of the conversation.

"I will tell you what I experienced, and if you still have questions, please wait for me to finish and I will answer them as best as I can." They were like children in a candy store.

"When I materialized, a man named Jackson greeted me." I looked at Donna and asked, "Does that name mean anything to you?"

She said, "An uncle, he was one of my favorites, why do you ask?"

"You will name your first child after him."

She looked shocked. I told her that we would have a private conversation later, and I would explain things.

"Gentlemen, we have some very serious problems to solve, or there will be no future!" I began to tell them of the impending doom for the human race. As the story progressed, I could see the sadness welling up in their eyes. They tried very hard not to cry, but they could not contain themselves.

You would have to be a pretty hard-hearted person to have no emotion at this news. After all, I was telling them that in less than two hundred years, the human race would be extinct.

Dr. Asana said, "What is the point?"

I said, "What do you mean?"

"Why try to make the world a better place to live in when no one will be here to enjoy it?"

"That's the beauty of the machine," I said. "If we know what's going to happen before it does, we can attempt to prevent it from ever happening at all."

Kim said, "What about the butterfly effect? If we change the future, won't that start a ripple effect?"

I said, "If there's no one left to suffer the consequences of our actions, the butterfly effect won't matter."

They realized I was correct right away. We would need to be very discerning as to the changes we would make.

"We need to keep in mind that we can't change the war, ever since the war, life has been much better than before the war," Donna said. "You must also keep in mind that the world was overpopulated. There were not enough natural resources, or food. People died from starvation. Some died even from lack of water. I have heard it's not a very pleasant way to die. The earth was dying before the war. I hate to say it, but the war made living different from before, but it also made it possible for people to live. I believe the war was a necessary evil.

"At least after the war, there was food and water enough for everyone. If you prevent the war, some nine billion people would not die, and then they would have off-springs and so on. The population would probably be over fifteen, maybe even twenty billion by now. Can't you see what kind of a ripple effect that could create?"

I said, "Donna is right, we need to proceed with great caution. We have the chance to alter anything. It's quite a heady though. I will go back in time, and be more of an observer than a participant. However, preventing the demise of the human race will be a matter for another time."

We met two nights later. I was amazed at the amount of information about the past they had compiled in such a short time. They gave me information about customs, science, and mannerisms of the early twenty-first century. It took me four long days to digest the information they had compiled. We all met that night to discuss what protocols to establish.

Kim said, "I know, we can paint the machine with Pic Paint so no one can see it!"

"That still won't keep people from physically running into it," I said.

"Yes, what can we do about that?" Jason said.

Kim said, "I have the solution. When I thought about it, I knew what a problem it could be, so I did research of caves in the area, and I think I have found a cave that we could utilize."

I asked, "Do you intended for us to move the machine into this cave?"

"That is exactly what I am proposing. We will put heavy-lift hover-boards under it, and then we'll just walk it along."

"How far from the hangar is the cave?" I asked.

"The cave is about three miles from the hangar, and the topography is level. We can even use the old runway to take it part of the way."

"This cave, are you sure that it's large enough for the machine?" I asked.

She replied, "Large enough and deep enough that you won't be able to see the machine from the mouth of the cave when you un-cloak it."

After a short discussion, everyone agreed to move the machine. Then we started to discuss when to move the machine. Then I remembered, "It's simple, we'll do it right under everyone's nose. You act like you're not doing anything wrong, and walk it out with no fear."

It made sense to me, and it's insane at the same time. "That's what we will do, and besides, it's painted with Pic Paint. Yes, gentlemen, we'll take it to the cave right under everyone's noses. Should anyone happen upon us while were moving it, they'll just think were out for a walk."

The next day we all got together and proceeded to move the machine. One thing I did not think about when I was building it, was the possibility of having to move the machine. It weighed just over twelve tons, but I had not provided lift points for the machine while building it. It took some doing, but we were able to get the heavy-lift hover-boards in place. By the time we finished, it was dark. We all agreed to resume the next day. We were all quite exhausted from the task.

10

It was a cool sunny day, a nice day to move the machine. We all gathered in the hangar a little before noon. The move was quick and uneventful.

We left the hover-boards under the machine. It was such a pain to get them under it in the first place, and we figured that if a move was necessary in the future, we would be ready for it. We couldn't leave it floating, we tied it off to rocks though holes in the deck so the ropes couldn't be seen, to prevent it from floating away when unattended.

I postulated that we had just changed the future.

"How so," Kim asked?

"When I went to the future, the hangar is where I arrived, but now the machine is in the cave, so there won't be a reason to keep the hangar anymore."

They all agreed that I was correct, and Dr. Kinsey said, "The first butterfly effect, I wonder how this will affect the future."

I said, "Well one thing it will change is, Donna won't be paying rent there for the rest of her life." Everyone chuckled at this.

With the machine secured, we went back to my house to make plans. Some of the gang wanted to leap one hundred years into the past. There was a suggestion to go back to just before the Great Attrition War, but that idea was squashed per our previous discussion on the subject.

I said, "I have decided to leap to the year 2010."

"Why?" Jason said. "What could you do there as opposed to another place in time?"

I said, "That was around the time they began making what they called a supercomputer. I will be able to research deleted items from our programs, such as the Bible, Jesus, and God."

Donna asked if I would be home for dinner.

What she really meant was, would I go time tripping tonight. I told her that this trip would be a little longer, and all I wanted was a decent dinner, a warm bed, and a good breakfast in the morning. I smiled at Donna and said, "I had planned on going tomorrow afternoon." She excused herself and went to prepare my dinner.

After dinner I read some more of the ancient Roman writings. I was able to put enough bits and pieces together to realize that Jesus was the Son of God. However, his parents were listed as Joseph and Mary of Nazareth. This confused me, but I would soon discover the amazing truth.

If what I read about Jesus was true, why did the Romans have a problem with him? From what I could gather, Jesus was a peace-loving man, so why the persecution?

This led me to an interesting conclusion: the less-advanced people are the more superstitious, and the more superstitious they are, the easier they become scared of something they don't understand. This leads to a, *desire to destroy the unknown, before it harms you*, type of mentality.

I found from my readings, that people of that time would believe nearly any accusation that might be leveled against another. It seemed that Jesus had performed some miraculous healings, and there was no reason he should be able to do so. Some believed it was some sort of sorcery. People were very superstitious in those days. It was easy to say something, and people would join in out of fear, pack mentality, or just for something to do.

In the morning, I woke to a good breakfast as I requested. Donna wouldn't let me go anywhere on an empty stomach.

The rest of the gang arrived, and we went to the cave. We all had maintenance on the machine, so we all got busy on our individual task. Nothing was wrong with the machine. This was similar to a preflight test on an airplane.

After the check was completed, we gathered around the main console. I asked if anyone had anything to say or suggest before I left.

Mike said, "I think you should keep to yourself and especially stay away from any of our ancestors."

"Yes," said Kim. "Any contact with them, no matter however minuscule it may be, could be hazardous to our existence. Don't even seek our families out."

I assured them that I would do my best to blend in. I promised I would not be discovered. A promise I would soon break.

I set the machine's controls for the year 2010, as the others said their good-byes, and left me alone in the cave. As soon as they were out of sight, I put a chip in my pocket computer, turned it on, and the music started to play. I turned the volume up so my associates could hear it. I chose a song from the later twentieth century, David Bowie's Changes. I felt it was proper, considering the changes I would be going through, and the fact it was popular about the time I would be tripping to.

About halfway through the song, I pressed the Enter button on the machine's control panel. I heard the whirring of the machine start up. The black hole engulfed the craft once more. Again I was transported. This time, I went back almost four hundred fifty years in time.

Once again, the whirring noise of the machine began to quiet, and the thick veil of the black hole began to melt away. I took my time getting prepared since the cave concealed me completely.

Time—the word had a new connotation for me now. Suddenly, I realized that time really didn't matter. Yes, I would still age, but I could relive a moment in time over and over again. I could also skip something unpleasant should I desire.

One thing that played to my advantage was, fashions came and went over the years, but the everyday clothes people wore changed very little over the centuries. This meant I had no need to have clothes made for me, at least not for this trip.

I dismounted the machine and stepped away from it a few meters. I pressed the button on the remote control unit, which engaged and disengaged the cloaking paint; the machine disappeared.

It was about 1 p.m., I was very cautious about leaving the cave, I didn't want anyone to see me come out. They could look inside the cave, and while they couldn't see what I had been in there for, they could stumble upon the cloaked machine.

My plan was to go to the airport to get my bearings. I got to where I thought the old runway should be, but there was a pasture in its place. Then it dawned on me; the runway had not yet been built. It was time to implement plan B, only I didn't have a plan B.

Then I remembered the path that I used in my time. It had been there for centuries. I took a turn in the direction I thought it would be. After a few minutes, I came out on the path, and not far from where I thought I would.

The further I walked down the path, the wider the path became. Eventually, it became a much-wider path covered with asphalt. A white dotted line had been painted down the center of the path.

In a short time I came to raised paths that bordered either side of the asphalt strip. The paths were made of concrete.

Then there were rows of houses that were identical, except for the colors they were painted, and the landscaping for each home was different also.

Suddenly there was a horn blast directly behind me. I nearly jumped out of my shoes. I turned to see an adolescent driving a car. I was aware that it was a car because I had watched video chips of one. In this year, CD-ROM discs were the preferred method of recording; however, while still very new to the market, using microchips to record were quickly taking over for discs. Chips are erasable, and you can't scratch them either, making them ideal for the job.

I was shocked tough to see a boy who looked like he was no more than eighteen years of age driving a car. In my time, you could obtain a hover-board permit at age fourteen, but hover-boards are much more easily maneuvered than automobiles. That was my opinion though, not having driven an automobile. It was just a guess based on what I had seen and read. I had seen statistics for annual deaths caused by automobile accidents; they were staggering.

That was one of the perks of being a time traveler. I would get to do things that were nonexistent in my time, or were so rare that there were just no opportunities to do those things. I was looking forward to my first chance to drive a car. I was also looking forward to riding a horse.

The horn startled me again, and the boy said, "are you going to move off the road, or are you going to build a house there?"

I must have looked stunned; so much for blending in. I stepped on the raised concrete that bordered the asphalt. I found out later that the raised concrete was a walking path called a sidewalk. We had sidewalks in our time, but they were just rock paths. The asphalt with the dotted line was a road. It was used for car travel almost exclusively, I was perplexed, everything was so different from what I was used to, but what was I supposed to do? Even with all the research I had done, I was still not prepared for the world that I had just entered. I felt a little lost in time.

I continued to walk down the sidewalk until I came to a section of the road where another road crossed it. I was walking next to it at a ninety-degree angle. There was a red octagonal sign that had "Stop" printed on it; well, even I could figure that one out. So I stood by the sign for a few minutes. It never changed to "Go," so I deduced that it must be broken.

Another man drove up to the sign and stopped. It was a nice day, and he had his windows open. I said, "Excuse me sir, can you tell me how to get to the nearest library?"

He kindly started telling me, and then abruptly said, "Why don't you just hop in and I'll take you there, I'm going by it anyway."

I thanked him and walked to the car door and said, "Door open."

The only thing that happened was the man laughed and said, "This is a 92 Ford, mister. You must be used to some kind of newer and more-expensive car model."

I shyly said, "Yes, how silly of me." I fumbled at the door latch for a little bit and successfully opened the door. Then I went to close the door, and I pulled on the handle as I closed it. The door just bounced out of my hand and was still open.

The man stared at me and asked if I had just gotten out of a mental ward.

I thanked him for his concern, but I assured him that I was fine.

He looked at me, and in a hushed voice, he slowly said, "Just—Pull—It— Closed. Don't hold on to the handle."

Not wanting to upset the man, I thought it prudent to close the door. This time I held tight to the door with my arm on the outside, and put quite a bit of force into it to make sure I successfully closed the door this time.

Well, that was also the wrong way to do it. He chastised me for slamming the door too hard, and asked again if I was sure I hadn't escaped from a mental institution.

I was confused with his fixation with mental institutions, and I apologized, assuring him I wasn't use to this type of door latch, nor had I escaped from a mental institution. While not happy with me, the man still delivered me to the library.

The car ride was so much stiffer than that of a hover-board. A hover-board is more of a fluid ride, more like a snowboard, skateboard, or a surfboard.

In my time, these devices are used as training tools for getting a hover-board endorsement. I thought how odd it was that a car, having the most room, and seats that were comfortable, would be my least desired form of transportation.

It seemed confined and was restricted to roads. You couldn't go across certain geological features in a car. Yes, the other forms of transportation previously mentioned had restrictions also, but they were used as a training tool for a hover-board, and a hover-board will travel most any terrain, without restrictions.

Still, I longed to ride a horse. I had seen recordings of people riding a horse. It appeared as if the person and the horse were as one when at full gallop. I really believed that to be true. How woefully wrong a person could be, I came to find.

I thanked the man for taking me to the library and closed his car door just so, as not to raise his ire.

He smiled at me, and as he drove off he said, "Later, man."

I ran after him asking, "What was going to be happening later?" He apparently didn't hear me because he kept driving. Nonetheless, I was at the library. Now I could get some answers about the Bible, God, and Jesus!

The library was an impressive Gothic-styled building made of red bricks, white-painted wood trim, and black wrought-iron trim over stained glass windows.

I entered the building and went straight to what I thought looked like a computer. I sat down at the terminal and said, "Computer on." Nothing happened. I spoke up a little, "Computer on." my portable computer was in my pocket, it detected my command and answered, "Computer on."

My computer was much more advanced than the ones from this century. It was a disk, about one inch high and two and a one-half inches in diameter, and could be carried in your pocket. You could use either voice commands or a keyboard to type silently.

At the top middle of the disk was a lens that projected a three-dimensional hologram for a viewing screen, and on the side was another lens that projected a keyboard in front of it for manual typing.

There was a little girl at the monitor next to me. She appeared to be about six years old, and she heard it answer, "Computer on." Thankfully, I was able to shut it down without attracting any more attention.

The little girl looked at me, and then at my coat pocket. I tried to ignore her, but she said, "You have to push this button to make it come on."

I thanked her and thought how wonderful it was that such a young person could teach me. Later, I thought about this and believed I had been somewhat pompous thinking that way.

It seems I was no longer the smartest person, at least not in this time. I had to learn new things. I would need to learn how to learn in a new way.

I typed in Bible. When I pushed the Enter button, I got over sixty-eight million hits. I was simply amazed.

Since I didn't know what I was looking for, I clicked the first site. I expected the wordage of the Bible to come up. Instead, I got some facts about the book.

From what I had read, I deduced this was the site I was looking for, but all the site did was give bits and pieces of information.

I wanted to read the book, and then I saw a bit of information that really stunned me. It said that the Bible was the best-selling book of all time! Also, it was the first book printed on a printing press invented by a man named Gutenberg.

Before the invention of the printing press, all books were written by hand, a tedious task at best. The ORC did such a good job, that they even removed the name of the inventor of the first printing press from history, because he printed the first Bible. The first book ever printed, the best-selling book ever—this book was more important than I could have ever imagined.

Why then were there no Bibles in my time? Was the ORC that thorough? Then I thought, "If it's so well known in this time, there should be one in this library." I asked the little girl next to me how I would go about finding a certain book. She showed me how to access the list, and in a moment, there it was. I wrote the Dewey decimal number down, the system was still in use in my time. Some things transcend all time. I asked the girl if she knew where I could find this number.

While pointing at a woman behind a counter, she said I needed to ask a librarian.

I thanked her for her help.

She said, "No sweat."

"Odd," I thought. "Of course she wouldn't sweat. All she had done was impart some information." Then it dawned on me that she was using slang from this period.

I asked the woman whom the girl had pointed out where I might find a copy of the Bible. She pointed me to a section that was labeled "Religion," another new word. I went down one aisle, and after a few minutes I found it.

The only positive thing I could say about the ORC was, they were efficient. There were books over fifteen-hundred years old in my time, but still no Bibles.

I pulled it from the shelf and opened it. I marveled at how large it was. The print was somewhat small, and there were so many pages, to think, at some point in history a person probably sat at a table day after day, copying the book by hand. I thought the process must have taken years.

I began what would end up being the greatest adventure of my life, Jack was right. I opened it to the first page and began to read.

"In the beginning, God created the heavens and earth" (Genesis 1:1, NIV).

This was what I had been looking for. I devoured as much of it as I could. I didn't speed-read though, as I didn't want to stand out.

Sometime later, the librarian announced that the library would be closing in five minutes. I had read a lot, but it seemed that I had hardly made a dent. There was so much more to read.

While it spoke quite a bit about God and the first humans—Adam and Eve—there was still no mention of Jesus. I actually had more questions now than before I started to read the book. I thought that was to be expected though.

I put the Bible back on the shelf, and as I turned to leave, the librarian was standing at the end of the aisle.

She caught me by surprise and said, "Oh, I didn't mean to startle you."

I smiled and told her that it was okay, and that I scare easy, and then I chuckled.

She smiled and said, "I couldn't help noticing you reading the Bible all day."

I asked if she had read the book. She replied that she had probably read it five or six times.

I wondered how she couldn't remember how many times she had read such a large book. I found out later that you couldn't read the Bible like any other book. People did read the Bible, but also, people used it to give lessons from, or as a reference. I found most people would skip some of the books. This was similar to a chapter in a book and then skipping a few chapters. Only it makes sense with the Bible, because it was not written in chronological order.

She said, "I haven't noticed you in here before." I told her I was new in town; if she only knew how new. She introduced herself as Pam Brown.

I said, "I'm pleased to meet you. My name is Dr. Caleb Bronson."

She said, "Oh, a doctor." Then she asked me what branch of medicine I practiced.

I said, "I'm not a medical doctor. I'm a theoretical physicist."

She looked a little stunned. Finally, she said, "Isn't the Bible a little out of your field?"

I wasn't sure how to answer her. I replied, "It soothes me to read it."

Then she asked, "Have you picked out a church yet?" I had not found out about churches as of yet, but I figured it must have something to do with the Bible.

I said, "No, I haven't had a chance to look for one."

She offered her church as a good church, and gave me the address and directions, she then told me services begin at 10:30 Sunday morning.

"Now you have to leave," she said, and I have to lock up. I will see you Sunday."

I told her, "I'm coming back here tomorrow."

"Okay, I guess I'll see you tomorrow then," she said. She had a radiant smile. She looked very much at peace.

When I came out of the library, it was already dark. I was worried that I may not be able to find my way to the cave and the machine. I had some paper money from this period that a collector friend had given me. I did not know what a room would cost for a night, and I would need money to eat. It would be several months before I would study a dollar bill and see the phrase, "In God We Trust," printed on one.

I walked down a road that had lights on tall posts. At the roads' end was the path that led to the cave.

As I walked down the path, I reviewed in my mind the material I had read. At the time, I didn't know what God was, or how to classify him or her. I thought that God must be a male, because he made Adam first, and Adam was a male created in God's image according to the Bible. Therefore, God must be male like Adam.

However, I would find that the prevailing philosophy of the time did not necessarily agree with my assumption. At the time of my indoctrination to religion, the subject was a mystery. By how he was portrayed in the Bible, my scientific brain understood God to be male.

I came to the end of the road and found the path. It had been a busy day, and I was ready for a shower, some food, and a bed. Tomorrow would be a long day also.

12

I had brought 10,000 American dollars with me. The gang, as I had began to refer to my colleagues in the future, decided I should take that amount. We all figured that should be enough to last me at least a week, but we all believed that I still needed to be prudent with the money.

I decided to take a different route to the library and see what the city looked like. As I got closer to where I believed I would need to turn toward the library, I came upon what I would find to be the city center. I looked up and down the street to see what businesses were there.

Then I saw it. I had heard that such places used to exist, and now I was standing right in front of one. The name on the sign simply said, "Pancake House."

I went inside, and a cheerful woman greeted me and said, "Are you alone?"

I said I was, and she told me I could sit at the counter, or I could sit wherever I wished.

She then asked if I wanted coffee. I said, "That would be nice." I added I would like to sit at a table next to the window.

She said, "Okay, you go sit down, and I'll bring your coffee." Then she said, Oh, do you want that coffee leaded or unleaded?"

I just looked at her with a blank stare. Then she said, "You look tired. I'll get you some leaded."

She returned with the coffee and a menu which she set in front of me. I looked at her and asked if this was leaded coffee. She confirmed that it was. I just stared at it for a moment. Then she asked if there was something wrong.

I hesitated, then meekly said, "Lead is a heavy metal, and even taken in small dosage could cause irreversible brain damage or death."

She paused for a brief moment, then began to laugh out loud. She turned around, and as she walked away she said, "That was a good one. You said that with such sincerity. I'll be right back to take your order."

She continued to laugh as she walked off. I thought that was an odd reaction to such a serious subject.

I picked up the cup and smelled it. I noticed no metallic smell. In fact it smelled delightful. I noticed everyone else was drinking it, and it seemed that everyone was enjoying it.

I put the cup to my lips and took a small sip. I allowed it to sit on my palate for a moment and detected no metallic taste. In fact, it was the best cup of coffee I had ever had.

Then I heard another waitress who was carrying two pots of coffee ask a woman if she was drinking decaffeinated or regular. She took the regular, and the woman filled her cup. At the next table, a man said he wanted leaded.

So that's what it meant. It was slang! I felt a little stupid for believing they would be serving poison. I realized that getting the hang of slang would probably be something that would be an ongoing process.

I opened the menu. I was amazed and pleasantly surprised at the same time. There were so many selections, and the prices listed were—well let me say this, at that point, I realized that the 10,000 dollars I had brought would be more than enough to last the week.

I studied the menu for some time. It was so hard to decide what to order because of the large selection.

When the waitress came back for the fourth time, she said, "If you can't decide, why don't you just order something, and you can come back tomorrow and get something else?"

I said, "Yes, that is a good idea."

She looked at me strangely, almost like the man who gave me a ride to the library the day before.

The look he gave me when I slammed his door was as if I were from another planet, which basically was right. I shyly said, "I'll have a number one please."

In my time you could get most items on this menu, however, getting the ingredients together at one time was another thing.

Then I saw what I wanted. "Wait," I said. "I will have the complete breakfast instead."

"How do you want your eggs?"

I answered, "Scrambled," thinking that was a way they would be cooked in this time.

"Bacon, sausage, or ham?" she said.

"Oh, I haven't had ham in such a long time."

"Ham it is," she said. "Pancakes or toast?"

"Toast," I said.

She said, "Whole wheat or white?"

I thought for a moment. In my time, wheat only came as a whole grain. I had no idea what white bread was. "White wheat" I thought, "I'll try the white." I said it as if I was venturing to some unknown territory, and I was.

Everything was so different, but then I was in a different time. Then she asked if I wanted something to drink besides coffee. I said that I would like a large glass of orange juice.

"Do you want anything else?" she asked.

I said that would be all for now. She told me she would have that out for me in a couple of minutes.

When she came back with my food, she placed it in front of me and said she would be back with more coffee in a minute.

I picked up the plate and smelled the food. It was unbelievable. The eggs were so fresh. The aroma of the ham caused my mouth to salivate. The orange juice was so fresh. The white toast, well, I didn't understand why anyone would like it. It must be an acquired taste. I determined I did not want to acquire it.

By the time I finished, I thought I would burst. It was the best meal I could ever remember having. I paid my bill. It was less than eight dollars.

As I walked out, I felt a certain type of calmness that I couldn't identify. The food had something to do with it; that much I was sure of. The sun was shining, birds were chirping in the trees, and the trees, there were so many.

The one thing I didn't care for were the gasses emitted by the popular form of transportation of the day—automobiles. They were powered by an internal combustion engine that burned a petroleum product called gasoline. It was very offensive to my sinuses.

I only had to cross four streets to reach the library from the Pancake House. I would find that the space in between one cross street to the next cross streets were called blocks, possibly since, if you looked at them from the air, they were square.

Even though I got an early start, I had spent so much time eating that the library had already opened.

13

I didn't see Pam as I entered the library. I wondered if she had gotten sick, or maybe taken the day off, but she had said she would be here today. It was a big building though, she could be in another room. I went to the section of the library that contained the Bible, and much to my disappointment it wasn't there. I looked around. There were only three people in the building, and none of them had the book. I sat down, I was very disappointed and didn't know what to do.

I felt a tap on my shoulder. I looked up to see Pam standing there, holding the book in front of me.

She said, "Are you looking for something?" I thanked her, but I noticed the bible she handed me looked different from the one I was reading the day before.

I asked Pam if it was the same, or if it had a different slant on the story.

She smiled and said, "No, it was an NIV Bible."

I asked what the initials stood for.

She looked at me oddly and replied, "It stands for the New International Version." She said it was no different from the one I had been reading the day before.

I asked her why I didn't see this one yesterday.

She replied, "I bought it for you last night." She smiled as she handed it to me.

I said that I couldn't accept such a gift and added that I had money. "I'll pay you back."

She smiled and said, "Well, I am glad that you offered to repay me, but as a Christian, it is my duty to see that you have one if you would like."

I looked at the book as if I had just been handed the keys to the golden kingdom. Little did I know at the time, but that's exactly what I had been given.

Pam said, "Now you can read it in the comfort of your home, at your own pace."

She handed me a sheet of paper. It had all the books of the Bible listed on it.

The listings didn't seem to follow any particular order. It was a reading schedule for the Bible though. A reading of the Old Testament was paired with a passage from the New Testament.

Pam explained that reading it according to this plan would help me understand it better.

I thanked her for the Bible and the reading plan. I added that I liked reading at the library. "There are like-minded people here."

Pam said, "I don't know how like-minded they are, but you do what you want. Now you'll have it to read at your leisure, and you can take it to church also."

She excused herself and went to work.

I sat down at the closest table and studied the reading plan. It was geared so you would finish reading the Bible in one year. I was somewhat surprised that one year was needed to read the book, but then I had all the leisure time I needed.

I decided to start reading the New Testament part of the Bible, until I caught up with the corresponding part in the Old Testament I had read, so it would match the reading plan, and get on track with it. The New Testament is where Jesus was introduced in the book. I thought, "This is where the history of modern man begins, this is when AD started."

About one o'clock, Pam walked over to me and asked if I would like to go get some lunch. I said I had eaten a big breakfast, but I could eat something.

She said, "I have an hour for lunch, so let's go."

I followed her out a door to a paved open space where several stationary automobiles sat side by side. She went to one of the vehicles and opened the door. The door on my side was locked. She reached over and attempted to unlock my door. However, I tried to open it at the same time, but it wouldn't open. Pam tried again, and so did I. Nothing happened again. I said, "I believe it's broke."

I thought back to the man that had given me a ride to the library that first day, and the trouble I had with his door. Would something as simple as a car door be my undoing?

She looked at me a little flustered and said, "The only thing broken is your head." Then she said, "Let me open it."

I stood back, and Pam easily opened the door. I said, "It must have been stuck."

She looked at me for a short time and gave an exasperated laugh then said, "Yeah, that must have been the problem."

I knew sarcasm when I heard it, but I said nothing.

I got in, and she said, "Put on your belt."

I told her I had my belt on all day.

She laughed and said, "I mean your seat belt."

She reached over, pulled the strap over me, and locked it in place. Then she asked me what I wanted to eat.

I replied, "I'm not from here. You pick a place. She again said sarcastically, "Really, you're not from here, I would have never guessed."

After we went a few blocks she stopped in front of a café and said, "Here we are."

I fumbled with the seat belt as Pam undid hers, exited the car, and closed the door. By the time she made it to my side, she realized that I was still fumbling with the belt. She opened my door and deftly released the belt, saying, "I said I only have one hour for lunch." She didn't say it in a mean fashion as the young man did the day before when I tried to close his car door, but rather in a frustrated manner, as one might say to a child after repeatedly telling them how something was done. I felt my face becoming flush from embarrassment.

We went inside and she asked where I wanted to sit.

I said that I liked to sit by the window.

She said, "Me too."

The restaurant served Italian food, and they had what was called a salad bar. It was a self-serve table, which had all sorts of vegetables, grated cheese, along with dressings to top off your salad. In my time, you would be lucky to see a quarter of the items on this salad bar at the same time.

The waitress handed us our menus and began to tell us about the specialty of the day—stuffed bell peppers with unlimited salad bar. Pam ordered that. I knew what I wanted, but wanted to see the cost. The salad bar by itself was only seven dollars, and you could fill your plate as many times as you liked, so I ordered it.

Pam asked if I wanted to say grace.

I hesitated and then said, "I'm not very good at it. Why don't you do it."

She agreed and closed her eyes, bent her head, and then she spoke, "Gracious Lord, thank you for providing this wonderful food to nourish our bodies, minds, and souls. All the glory goes to you Lord. Amen."

Pam opened her eyes and said, "This smells good."

I agreed, and added I hadn't had a salad for a long time. We ate, and Pam asked where I was in my reading of the Bible. I told her I had gotten to Leviticus 6 in the Old Testaments, and I had just finished reading Matthew 26:35 in the New Testaments.

"Those are interesting places to pause, the guilt offering, and Jesus prophesying Peter's betrayal. The first was an offering to please God. The later, a betrayal of Jesus for thirty pieces of silver."

"What are you talking about? I'm not that far yet."

She apologized for revealing what I would be reading that afternoon. She added, "It's not like a mystery. It's not like I'm spoiling the ending. After all, everyone knows what happens to Jesus in the end."

"Everyone but me," I thought.

I finished my second plate of salad and started to go back for another.

Then Pam said, "You can stay and eat until you burst, but I have to get back to work."

I said, "I didn't realize what time it was. I'll go with you."

She reached into her purse to pay for lunch. I said I would pay for lunch as I reached in my pocket and pulled out a handful of bills.

She said, "Put that away." In a hushed, vexed voice, she added, "Do you want to get mugged?"

I asked what was wrong.

She said, "What are you doing with all that cash?"

I said, "If I want to buy something, I have to have enough money to pay for it."

She just shook her head and said, "Have you ever heard of a bank or a checking account?"

I said, "Of course I have, but I just moved here and have not found a bank yet." She just shook her head again, picked up her purse, and went outside. I paid the bill and joined Pam outside.

She asked what kind of tip I had left the waitress. I stammered a bit, and she shook her head once more. She went back inside and gave the waitress a few bills.

I wondered why she had looked at me in the sullenly manner she did. The concept of tipping was new to me. In my time, it didn't exist. The restaurant owner would give their employees a bonus just before the renew celebration.

In the car, on our way back, Pam said, "Where are you from?"

I said I was from Hanford, Washington. It was all I could come up with on such short notice.

In a somewhat elated voice she said, "Really? So am I."

I thought this could be trouble, and I was right.

"Have you ever been to the Desert Movie Theater?" she inquired.

"Oh yes, I used to go there all the time when I was younger." I couldn't believe the luck. Hanford was a small community when I lived there in the future, but I knew little about the place in the year two-thousand-ten.

She pulled over abruptly and said, "Who are you, and where are you from, and don't give me that bologna about being from Hanford. I have never been there, and I doubt there is a Desert Movie Theater, is there?"

I just dropped my head in shame, the way a child would when caught in a lie.

"So tell me, who are you?" I had been found out. Well not found out, but Pam knew I was lying. What could I say?

I was brainstorming for something to say. Finally, I told her that I would come back to the library when she got off work, and explain everything to her then. I also promised that I wasn't doing anything illegal, after she inquired about that.

I got out of the car and she drove off. I began walking around town. I didn't know my way around yet, and thought it best that I knew my surroundings in case of some sort of emergency.

I left Pam with a pit in my stomach. What would I say? Would she believe the truth, or should I just time trip back to a further point in time and meet Pam all over again?

When it comes to book knowledge, I'm pretty hard to beat. When it comes to people though, especially from another time period, I was as clumsy as the proverbial bull in a China closet.

No, Pam already knew too much. To start over could be even worse. What would she think if we were reliving some event we both experienced, and I slipped up on something about to happen? What if she caught me predicting the future?

No, it could only make things worse; after all, she was still willing to talk to me. So I still had a chance to make things right. It might be hard to repair the damage, but starting over might end up even worse.

I was, for better or worse, stuck with having to tell Pam the truth. I was surprised when I found myself mutter, "Dear Lord, please help me." It was the first time I asked God to help, but it would not be the last time I asked for his help.

14

I returned to the library just before six o'clock, when Pam's shift ended. I waited outside by her car.

When she reached the car, she said, "Well, Caleb, where is your car?"

I said I didn't have one.

She said, "I thought so. You can't drive one anyway, can you?"

I answered no, bowing my head to avoid eye contact. For some reason, she made me feel infantile. Again she asked me, "Who are you?" This time though, she said it more sternly, as if she was demanding an answer.

My mind raced. Was this the moment of truth, or should I just walk away?

I started, "Pam, what if you knew something, something that was the most important thing anyone had ever known? What if what you knew, would alter the history of the entire world for the better? What if you knew your story would be impossible to believe? I want to tell you who I am and where I come from, but you won't believe me."

Pam said, "How do you know?"

"Because, Pam, *I* wouldn't believe me."

"One thing you can count on though is, if you tell me nothing, I'll have nothing to believe or disbelieve, and I'll have nothing further to do with you."

"Okay," I said. "I'll tell you, but you have to swear no matter what I say, you will not only believe me, you will also promise to keep my secret."

She lifted her right hand and said in a mocking tone, "I swear, but if it's too unbelievable, you'll have to prove to me you're telling the truth."

I told her that I would show her irrefutable proof.

She simply said, "Okay, tell me your secret."

I took a deep breath and began to tell her when I came from, and how I got here. I could see the disbelief in her eyes as I wove my story. She was well read, and knew something about almost every component of the machine. She also knew something about how they operated. I could see that the story I was revealing was making her somewhat bewildered.

Then I told her what the future held, why I had come to this time, and what I intended to do.

When I finished she was shocked, and I believed a little stunned.

She said, "So you come from 450 years in the future."

"Yes."

"You built the machine yourself?"

I replied I had.

"So you have been able to build a compact Hadron Collider, a machine that creates a small black hole, which surrounds you, and transports you in time."

"Yes, that is the truth."

She had a blank look on her face for a short time, and then she said, "Prove it."

I said, "What?"

She repeated herself. "Show me the machine. You said you would prove it beyond a doubt."

I didn't think for a moment that she would ask to see the machine. What was I thinking? I had just revealed my secret, and now she wanted the proof I had promised. I was caught off guard for a moment.

She said, "I knew you were lying."

I said, "No, I'm not lying."

Again she said, "So show me, I'll keep your secret."

"We will have to walk about two miles to reach the machine." I said, "Do you trust me enough to do that?"

She replied, "I believe you. No one could be so in the dark about things as you, and be from this time. I just want to see the machine for myself."

We drove to the end of the road and walked the two miles down the path to the cave. When we got to the mouth of the cave Pam said, "I know this cave, you're hiding the machine inside it?"

"Yes, follow me into the cave. We need to walk all the way to the back."

Pam said that she was having trouble seeing. I pulled my cell phone out and turned on the light application.

Pam was quite surprised at the amount of light my cell phone produced. She even told me it was too bright, and may attract attention, so I turned down the luminescence.

I said, "So Pam, the light was too bright? Have you ever seen a cell phone with that bright of a light?"

She said, "No, but there are new phones coming out every day. For all I know, you could have just bought that phone."

I replied, "Yes, that is one explanation. Or you could believe that I am telling the truth."

She said, "For now, I'm going to believe the first explanation."

I said, "For now will be over soon, because seeing is believing."

When we got to within ten meters of the machine, Pam turned around and said angrily, "Did you lure me down here? What's your plan? Are you going to rape me?"

"Rape!" I said incredulously. "I would never do such a thing. Why the very thought goes against how I conduct my life. Turn around, and look at nothing become something incredible."

I turned off the cloaking Pic Paint, and the machine materialized before her. There was, as I expected, a moment of stunned silence.

While she stood there in amazement, I told her, "It's painted with Pic Paint." I explained how it worked. "It was originally a government secret. When it was released to the public, it was very expensive as I'm sure you can understand."

Finally she turned around and said, "It's true. You are from another time. Does it fly too?"

I told her, "No, but it does hover."

Then it hit her. "The future you told me of, was that true?"

"Yes, I'm afraid that was accurate."

She slowly sat on a rock, and then she looked at me with a tear in her eye and said, "It's the end of days."

I tried to comfort her by telling her that she would be long gone before the world begins to fall apart.

She began to cry. "If I have children though."

"Yes, I'm afraid that your descendants will face an uncertain future."

She cried for some time. I tried to comfort her, but the concept of there being no future was a little more of a shock than she could handle.

After about ten minutes, she was still crying. Then she had a sudden realization.

"You can travel in time. You can change the future."

I told her I was sorry, and that I couldn't change the future because of the butterfly effect. I explained to her what that meant.

She said, "Do you like this time in life, or would you rather return to your post-apocalyptic world?"

I told her I understood where she was coming from, but the risk that things could be worse was possible. She said she understood, but the thought of what the future held, still made her sad. I knew how she felt, but I needed to stay on course. If I deviated from the plan it could be even more disastrous for the future.

She understood I couldn't change certain things in the future, after all, why stop there? Why not go back and prevent Hitler from coming into power. Why not take out Saddam Hussein as a young boy and prevent his genocide, or stop any other despot from history. No, the ORC was certainly not for better, but defiantly was for the worse. It was a necessary evil.

Unfortunately, changing anything could create a ripple through the fabric of time, releasing who knows what kind of horror.

"Can you make it work?"

"You mean right now?"

"Yes."

"Well, I can, but it requires a great deal of energy. It would be a waste if not used for a specific purpose."

Then she surprised me and said, "Send me. If I went on a trip, that would prove so much to me."

I knew this would be a bad idea, but I agreed. I told Pam I would go with her. She said she wouldn't mind the company.

"When to shall we go?" I asked Pam.

She asked, "What would you suggest?"

"There are so many times and events that we could be witness to. Can you think of something in recent history that you would like to see? Or perhaps a short trip into the future?"

"We could watch the constitution being drafted and signed, or Columbus discovering the new world," she said.

I asked, "What is the constitution? Who is Columbus, and what is the new world?" The ORC had wiped out any information about these events because they both were so intertwined with God.

In the end, we decided to just go five minutes ahead. "We'll synchronize our cell phone timers, and leave one here and take one with us. When we finish, the timer we leave behind should be advanced five minutes, and the one we take with us should be advanced just the few seconds from the time we leave."

We did the test, and it proved to be true. Pam was convinced, and stunned at the same time.

She wanted to know more. I told her, "In due time. It's not prudent for you to know too much." It would take only a slip of the tongue, and people would be questioning her knowledge of the vessel. "They would probably question your sanity as well. It's not a matter of trusting you, which I obviously already do. It's just the less you know, the less chance of a slipup." She agreed, and that was the end of it.

I told Pam that it was getting late, that it was time for us to part, and that I would see her when she picked me up for church the following morning. I walked her to the car and waved good-bye as she drove off.

I wondered if I had done the right thing telling Pam my secret. I thought about the conversation that I had with the gang before I left—how, if I stopped the Great Attrition War, the world would not be able to support the population.

I imagined what the population would be in my time if I went farther back in time, and prevented all wars from happening.

It was unfortunately out of the question. The population would have gotten completely out of control. That would mean that somewhere in time, if I prevented one war, it would be sure to cause another war somewhere else in the future because of overpopulation. I would find out later, more wars have been fought in the name of God than any other cause. It shocked me to find this out. There was no stopping it, unless the world population could be controlled. This I believe is the key to ending all wars. If there is enough to go around, then there is no need to battle over provisions. War was, unfortunately, inevitable. "A sad realization to end the night with," I said aloud to myself.

"Lights off," I commanded, and I laid my head down, but sleep didn't come easy that night.

15

I waited at the end of the trail for Pam to pick me up at eight the next morning. We had made plans to have breakfast at the Pancake House. I was excited to be going there again. It was hard to contain myself, and I felt like a little kid on his birthday.

Yesterday's breakfast was the best I could ever remember eating. My mind swam around what I might have today.

When she got there, she turned the car around before stopping. When I climbed in, I asked her how she was doing.

She replied positively, but that she had difficulty getting to sleep, and also had a very fitful night's sleep. She knew that the implications could be very drastic if I changed the past, and concluded that it must be God's plan to let all those people die in wars. It was the only conclusion she could come to.

Pam asked me, "Since you grew up without Christianity, your knowledge of God is somewhat limited. I know all of this is very new to you. I have to ask, do you believe in God?"

"Well, if the Bible was all I had to go by, I would be very skeptical about the truth of the book and God. However, I can cross-reference so many parts of the Bible with the written history from other countries. Several stories from Roman history for example, not only coincide with the time line of the Bible, the stories mirrored each other. I am still not one-hundred percent swayed, but I must say, I believe I could make a good argument for the Bible's truth, and God's existence."

"I'm glad to hear you say that. It's unusual that someone with only a few days of exposure to the Bible would believe so quickly, especially someone from your profession. It's kind of like mixing water and oil. Well, it just goes to show you the power of the Lord's Word," she said.

I said, "It's much easier for me to grasp a concept with my memory. Other people tend to forget at least part of what they read, causing them to have a skewed concept of what they did read."

She said, "I guess that makes sense, after all, you are the scientist."

"Do you understand the structure of a church service?" she asked.

I said I did not.

"The pastor runs the whole service, and you are not to talk during the service either. Other than to praise the Lord, this is important."

I told her that I understood and promised not to speak up or interrupt. "I'm not one to break the rules."

Pam told me that the service normally proceeded this way. "First there will be a short opening by the pastor greeting everyone. Then we will sing three or four hymns, followed by the pastor giving a sermon. Then the worship group will play one or two more songs. Finally, the pastor will give the benediction, which is—"

I interrupted her and said, "I had read about the benediction."

She said, "Then you know that will be the end of the service?"

I said "Yes."

"We will get up, and since you are new in town, everyone will be asking me who you are. Others will come right up to you and introduce themselves. It's done with the best of intentions. The congregation will want to greet you and make you feel welcomed."

"You mean I will be the center of attention in other words."

"Yes, but in a good way, don't worry."

"What shall I tell them?"

"The truth, tell them you're not from around here, and you're visiting. Are you visiting?"

"No, I have a feeling I'll be staying for a while."

"Tell them you're a theoretical physicist. In fact I know the college president, she's a member of our church."

I said, "I'll be caught if I divulge information I know."

Pam replied, "Just dumb yourself down a little."

I didn't understand what she meant, so she explained herself. I replied that it was contrary to my logical side to do so.

She laughed and said, "Okay Mr. Spock, just try not to impress anyone."

I had never heard of this Mr. Spock, but he must be famous I thought. So I asked her, "Who is this Mr. Spock?"

She laughed and replied, "You'll find out soon enough."

We parked the car and entered the church. Right away, people were coming up to me. I cheerfully shook their hands and introduced myself, and they introduced theirselves in return. I could hear others asking Pam who I was, and how we met.

Pam and I sat together, and I joked that I thought they already knew me inside and out.

Pam replied, "Not everything."

We both chuckled. It reminded me a little of the night I revealed the machine to the gang, the way they asked questions, and not waiting for answers.

The service started. As promised, the pastor greeted us, and asked the worship group to come up to the stage and perform. As expected, they played three songs. Fortunately, they projected the words to the songs on the wall behind the worship group. For me, this was necessary; others knew the words by heart.

With the end of the three songs, the pastor stood up and addressed the congregation. He began by greeting the congregation and asking them if they had a good week. Most people spoke up positively.

He then said, "This week, we're going to talk about deliverance, salvation, redemption, and justification."

I knew what salvation, justification, and redemption meant, but my understanding of the words were different than the Bible's use of the words. This is the definition it listed:

> Redemption: deliverance from sin through Jesus Christ
> Deliverance: deliverance from sin or the consequences of sin through the sacrifice of Jesus Christ
> Salvation: the sacrifice of Jesus Christ on the cross for our sins
> Justification: Through the grace of God, we are all absolved of all our sins.

The pastor continued. "The blood of Jesus Christ on the cross washed our sins away. God sacrificed his one and only Son, so we imperfect souls could have redemption. For us to please God, we need to praise him in good times, as well as bad."

He asked, "Could you sacrifice your only son for the greater good? God had time to think about what was going to happen before it did. Still, he sacrificed his only Son. Just as I am asking you, could you sacrifice your only son for the greater good of humanity?

It's easy to answer yes to this question, because you won't have to make this choice. God did this though. I know there are those in the congregation that are squirming in their seats as I speak." He chuckled. "The prospect of having this done to one's only son, or any loved one is so heart-wrenching, that it is incomprehensible. I'm sure I don't need to ask what someone would do. They would say no. The rest of you would say the same. It's not shameful to feel this way. I'm talking about your own flesh and blood. Even Jesus had a moment of doubt on the cross.

My God, My God why have you forsaken me? (Matthew 27:46, NIV).

Think how God must have felt."

I had known about the crucifixion, but it had not dawned on me that God had allowed it to happen. How could a person do that? A person didn't do this though. Only God could do this. Only God could give us eternal salvation, through the body and blood of his only Son.

The pastor finished talking about salvation and started in on the subject of redemption.

16

When church ended, Pam held my hand and guided me through the crowed of people toward the stage.

I asked, "Where are we going? The service is over." I wanted to get out before people started to ask questions.

She said, "To talk with the pastor."

I stopped her right there and asked her why?

She said, "Did you like the service?"

I told her it was fine. She asked if I would be coming back next week.

"You mean to church?"

"Yes." I said, "I thought that the people were nice, and the pastor seemed to have a way of explaining things that made the subject material easier to understand and more interesting."

"Well that's exactly what he's supposed to do. This is just an introduction, not an interrogation."

"I understand, I just wanted to know what type of conversation I could expect."

"Expect something like, 'Where do you come from?' and 'What kind of work do you do?'"

"Oh, the easy questions," I said sarcastically.

Pam said, "You'll be fine."

"Pam," the pastor said as we approached.

Pam said, "Pastor Lind, this is Dr. Caleb Bronson. Caleb, this is Pastor Bill Lind."

"Well Dr. Bronson, just what type of doctor are you?"

"A good one I hope, but if you asked my peers, they would probably tell you I'm below average."

We all chuckled for a bit, and the pastor said to Pam, "At least he has a good sense of humor." He chuckled and said, "What is your field of expertise?"

I said I was a theoretical physicist.

"Ah," he said. "I don't want you to quit coming to our services, but isn't coming here a conflict of interest for your occupation?"

"I've heard that quite a bit lately. It is somewhat, but for some reason as of late, I have been drawn to the Bible."

The pastor and Pam smiled, and the pastor said, "I have an idea. I may be jumping the gun here, but I believe you have been summoned by our Lord."

I looked at Pam, and she was smiling, and nodding her head in agreement.

"Just why do you think I have been summoned?"

"Ah," the pastor began. "that is yet to be seen. The Lord works in mysterious ways. He will reveal his desires at the appropriate time. Would you like me to pray for you about it?"

I answered, "Yes, thank you."

He began, "Dear Father, you have seen fit to send Caleb, a man of reason, a man of science, to our flock. Our world and his world have very conflicting concepts. Help him as you guide him down your path of holiness and righteousness. I am sure you have something big in store for Caleb, and I feel that Caleb is more than ready for your plan. All the glory is yours Lord. In your name, amen." Then the pastor asked, "Are you looking for a job?"

I thought a moment and said, "I was hoping I could secure a position at the college."

"Well," the pastor said, "let me give you a little help." He called to the woman whom Pam had pointed out to me before the service. "Mary, could you come here for a moment?" She turned and came right over to us. "Mary, this young man is looking for a job at the college. His name is Dr. Caleb Bronson." Then he turned to me and said, "Caleb, this is the college president, Dr. Mary Johnson." He said, "Caleb is a theoretical physicist."

"Wonderful," Mary said, "we are actually looking for one. Are you interested?"

"Yes, I was going to apply after I got myself situated."

"Can you bring a resume and references from former employers to my office at say, one o'clock tomorrow, and we can discuss a position."

I told her, "I would love to do that. However, as I said, I need to get situated. I have to find a place to live, and I would like to make sure I get all my documentation together. It's still packed in some box somewhere. Could I come by Tuesday at one o'clock instead?"

She agreed and gave me a business card. After church Pam asked if I wanted to get some lunch.

I said, "Let's go, I'm hungry too."

When we were seated, Pam asked what I intended to use for documentation. There would be watermarks, embossments, and other identifiable things that could not be copied easily.

I said, "Calm down, I am an educated man. I just have to do some research, get the right paper for a diploma, copy some other person's degrees, print some glowing recommendations, and there you have it." I told Pam that I believe with the computer I have, those things will be easy to overcome, and that I could be finished by one o'clock tomorrow, but that would be pushing it. Then I asked, "What did the pastor mean when he said he didn't want to jump the gun?"

She explained that it meant he didn't want to get too far in front of himself. "He can't predict the future."

I was still puzzled. I asked, "How does one get ahead of their self? That would be physically impossible."

She let out an exasperated sigh and said, "Getting you up to speed on the slang of this time is going to be a tall order."

I replied, "How can an order be tall?"

She only said something that sounded like "ugh!" I felt that was a signal to drop the subject.

I asked where I could buy a laptop computer and office supplies. Pam said, "Don't you still have your disk computer?"

I explained to her that it didn't have the required ports to interface with the ones from this time, and I haven't been able to figure out how to get them to do so yet. I was also hoping I could find an adapter.

Besides, I would need a laptop for my job. My computer disk would elicit too many questions. She agreed that I was of course right.

She took me to an office-supply store where I purchased the laptop and some other supplies. The total was only a little over eighteen-hundred-dollars.

In the car, Pam asked how I expected to make the fake documents. She said, "You may be able to make good fakes with your computer, but the computer you bought will not be able to make documents of the quality you'll need to get a job. The documents won't look aged properly."

I told her that was not a problem. I would make the document and travel back twenty years, leave the documents in the cave, and return to this time, and there you have it—instant aging.

"That's brilliant," Pam said. "But that is you."

I said, "Thank you, it's what I do."

She said jokingly, "So you're not a physicist, you're a document forger."

I laughed and said, "Yes, you got me. Physicist by day, forger by night."

I told her that with this laptop, and the equipment I have at the machine, I should be able to achieve the interface needed to produce the documents.

"This is like cheating," Pam said.

I replied, "I am a real theoretical physicist. I could probably win several Nobel Prizes just because of my advanced knowledge of science in the future alone. After all, I did build a time machine which should be worth one by itself."

Pam thought about this for a moment and agreed, but added, "You can't make any discoveries. Otherwise you run the risk of throwing a ripple in the butterfly effect."

I agreed, I was glad to see she understood the effect that one person can have on the world. After all, look at what Jesus accomplished, and he didn't have a computer.

Pam helped me carry the items I had purchased to the machine. We got back to the machine and began setting up the interface. I had the foresight to bring cords from my time to splice with cords I had just bought to complete the interface.

Once we had done that, we looked online for paper that would match a diploma from Harvard and MIT.

My printer was unlike anything Pam had ever seen. If I wanted to, I could have gotten into a lucrative forgery business.

The computer I had bought also had a DVD player. I would need it because my computer didn't play DVDs. You simply plugged a microchip into a port instead of a disk.

I had asked Pam to bring a four-hour physics lecture from the library. It was from one of the day's leading theoretical physicists.

Pam asked why I wanted to watch those.

I replied, "I need an idea of how much I can show. Remember, you told me I needed to dumb myself down. I know so much more about physics than my contemporaries' do; I don't want to blow my cover."

"This lecture sounds quite boring." Then she said she was going home.

I walked her back to her car and said that I probably would be too busy to stop by the library the next day.

She smiled and said, "That's all right, if you get bored with the lecture, you can always read the good book."

I must have looked bewildered, because the next thing she said was, "The good book is the Bible."

I simply said, "Oh."

She looked at me and said, "I don't know if you'll make it here. You stand out simply because you keep acting as if you don't get what's going on. I'm going to come here tomorrow after I get off work. I'll try to find slang jargon that is up to date and pertinent."

I thanked her and said, "Here." I handed her fifty dollars.

"What's this for?" she said.

"When you come tomorrow, could you stop at that fried chicken restaurant and get us some fried chicken, mashed potatoes, and gravy with biscuits and corn on the cob please?"

"Yes, I'll take care of it," she said with a laugh. "What kind of pop do you want?"

"Orange," I said, not knowing what might be available.

Pam said she would see me around six-thirty or seven.

I got back to the machine, and although I was very tired I still had so much to learn. There was also the Bible. I believed I would be able to learn enough about the culture, and the Bible, to make people think that at the worst, I was odd.

I started to read a textbook, but I began to get sleepy almost at once. Even though I wanted to learn as much as I could before my meeting with President Johnson at the college, it seemed like I heard a voice say, "Rest, you can do this after a good night's sleep."

It was odd, the voice in my head seemed to come to me like a thought, but at the same time, it sounded like it was outside my head and audible. It was sort of eerie.

I gave way to the thought and laid my head on the pillow, but sleep still did not come. I was facing the nightstand and saw the Bible sitting on it.

I decided to pick it up and do some reading. I had stopped reading at Deuteronomy 3. Deuteronomy translates into Second Law. Moses wrote it shortly before his death, about 405 BC, after leading his people through the desert for forty years. It deals mostly with obedience and following commands. Deuteronomy 8:10 caught my eye.

"When you have eaten and are satisfied, praise the Lord your God, and thank him for the good land he has given you" (Deuteronomy 8:10, NIV).

That's why Pam prayed before we ate. I was beginning to understand that God was *it*. Total dedication was a mandate. There is *no* wiggle room. It's God or nothing at all.

17

I felt quite rested the next morning. It was about nine o'clock by the time I finished doing the breakfast dishes. I opened the DVD drive, dropped the first disk in and pushed the close button.

It took a little more time than I was used to for the menu to open. These computers were so slow compared to what I was used to. Even my little portable disk computer was much faster. It even had the premonition program. This program allows the computer to predict what my next command would be.

If you were writing about a subject, by the time you were two to three paragraphs into the paper, the program would take over, and you could sit back and just read as the program wrote the paper for you. If it made a rare mistake, you would just have to stop it, correct the mistake, and continue.

It also had a research application. When it came to a portion of the document where it was unsure which direction you wanted the paper to go, it would stop and present options for you to pick from. Once you made your choice, the program would resume. It wrote at about ninety words a minute, and was from ninety-nine, to as much as one-hundred percent correct.

The program finally opened. An index listed each lecture by subject, chapter length, as well as related reading material. I took a break after about three hours. The knowledge of the day was, for the most part, unimpressive.

I used this break to read the Bible. I read it for several hours, then I turned the physics DVD back on.

I finished reviewing the information on theoretical physics, just in time to help Pam carry our fried-chicken dinner back to the machine. I was already salivating thinking about the taste of the chicken and gravy.

I tried to engage her in conversation about her day.

She responded, "I work at a library. The most exciting thing that's happened to me since I started working there is meeting you! Still, it's pretty boring working there."

"Well, meeting you and being able to be so honest with you has been quite refreshing for me," I said. "I detest having to keep a secret by myself. Having someone to share it with is like having a pressure-relief valve. I'm sorry Pam, you probably would like to have your own pressure-relief valve I imagine."

"Yes, there are times I wish I had someone else to confide in, another woman perhaps, someone who could better relate to what I'm going through. It is nice to talk to you about this, but with you it's not new, it's review. Please don't take that badly."

"Oh my goodness, no," I replied. "I understand for you it's discovery, while for me, as you said, it's review. People naturally would rather talk about new than review. I appreciate you being secretive about me."

"Well, it's not as if I can introduce you to everyone as my friend the time traveler."

"No, they would probably lock you up."

"And throw away the key," Pam said, finishing my sentence.

We laughed a little, but it was true. Yes, people would think she was loony.

We arrived at the machine and put the meal on the small table I had made for myself. I said, "I never imagined I would have company."

Pam said, "That's all right, I never imagined I would be eating dinner on a time machine with a man that was born about four hundred years after I die."

I said, "You're not ever going to die."

We both laughed, and Pam asked me to say grace. I said I couldn't, "I'll make a mess of it."

She told me I needed to learn. "Besides, God will appreciate you trying, and he will help you to find the right things to say. You'll improve with practice."

We held hands and I began, "Lord, we thank you for this wonderful bounty of food you have laid before us. We give you all the glory and praise. Thank you for guiding me to Pam. She has been such a help. I just can't imagine being where I am in my search to find out about you, without her help. I thirst to know you better. All we are is what you command. In the Father's name, amen."

Pam said, "That was pretty good. Have you been practicing?"

"No, I really don't know where all that came from."

"Well, you seem to be a natural, or maybe God did guide you."

Then it dawned on me those must have been God's words. "All we are is what you command." I had not heard this phrase before, but I would hear it in other people's prayers eventually.

I said, "Let's dig in." Pam handed me a plate, and we began to serve ourselves. As we ate, we engaged in small talk. Mostly, she tried to get me caught up on the day's world events, and slang. We also talked a little about my day, finding out about where this generation was at, in regards to theoretical physics.

At one point, Pam looked at me and said, "Boring. It isn't the most exciting of subjects, is it?

I'm sorry, I just wanted to have a pleasant meal with you," she said. "I meant no disrespect."

I said, "None taken, it is a boring subject for most people."

She changed the subject back to the present. "How long do you plan on staying here?"

I hadn't thought about it. I would need to stay for some time if I were to learn the Bible.

"It shouldn't take me more than a year to learn it," I said.

Pam said dryly, "I know, you have an eidetic mind."

Pam said that I was going to meet too many people, to stay as private as I had been so far.

"Also," she said, "you'll need to rent an apartment or a home. Being a professor, you should have a home suitable to your station in life."

I can't believe I hadn't thought of that. If I stayed here and met people, I would need to have a base of operation that would be acceptable to the people with whom I would interact. Bringing them to the time machine was, of course, out of the question.

Pam was right, in order for me to blend in, I would need a place to stay that would be close to the college, and not a secret to keep.

Pam said, "Since your appointment is tomorrow afternoon, you should rent a hotel room for the night. After I get off work tomorrow we'll start looking for a home, and yes, you have enough money for one."

"Thank you Pam. You are such a help to me, I honestly don't know what I would do without you." I joked with her, "You and that little girl that showed me how to turn the computer on."

We both laughed. Suddenly, my thoughts were of Donna. Pam was, for all intent and purpose, my twenty-first-century Donna.

Pam brought me back around and said, "If I ever meet your friends, I'm going to tell them how a five-year-old girl taught you how to start a computer."

I defended myself by correcting her. "She was six."

I said, "My friends would fall to the ground from laughing so hard."

We didn't say anything for several minutes. It was odd, we hadn't had a moment of silence that long between the two of us since we had first met.

I broke the silence. "Would you like to meet them?"

"Meet who?" she said, then she looked into my eyes, and without me saying anything she continued, "You mean meet your friends in the future?"

I said, "Yes. Would you like to see my world?"

Pam looked at me in stunned silence. Finally, she said, "I couldn't, I'll be missed. How would I explain my absence?"

I laughed. "We have a time machine, and we can set it to return to any time. It's 7:25 now, and it can be set to return to five minutes from the time we leave. No one will even notice that we were ever gone. We won't be missed at all."

"The future," Pam said.

You could see it in her eyes, she was dreaming about what it would look like.

I told her that we needed to get more fried chicken and a couple gallons of ice cream, assorted flavors of course. So we went shopping.

The supermarket was in the same lot that the fried-chicken restaurant occupied. Pam called it a strip mall.

After the war, only small individual stores and shops existed. There wasn't a large enough population base to support a mall or even a strip mall.

When we arrived, she told me to go get the ice cream and she would get the chicken. I gave her more money, and told her to get five meals like we just had, and we would meet at her car.

I got the ice cream. While standing in line, an older woman said I could go in front of her.

She said, "You wouldn't want it to melt, would you?" She was of course referring to the ice cream.

"Your friends would be mad at you."

I thanked her and said, "You don't know my friends. They would drink it if it were completely melted."

I paid, thanked her again, and went straight to the car.

Pam hadn't finished when I got into the car. I saw her exit. She went to another car and got in it. A sudden dreadful realization came over me, I had gotten into the wrong car. They all looked pretty much the same to me.

I got out and walked toward her. When I opened the door, Pam was laughing. She put the car in reverse and looked at me with a sly smile and a slight laugh. I simply said, "They all look alike to me." She laughed even harder at that.

When we got back to the machine I asked if she really wanted to see the future. "There might be aspects of it that you may find very disturbing."

"Are you kidding?" she came back. "I'm more than ready, this is as close to becoming an astronaut as I will ever come to. I can handle disturbing. I may react to whatever it is you're talking about, but I will be able to keep it together."

"Okay, but you have been forewarned." I liked the thought that she compared time travel to space travel as I once had.

"Yes sir Captain Kirk," she said, again using the same mocking tone and salute she had used when she had earlier used the name Mr. Spock. I was ready for her this time though. I had used the internet to find out about Mr. Spock, and in turn I discovered who Captain Kirk was.

I blindsided her with my knowledge of the whole franchise. Not just the original series, but all the other series that sprang from the original, and movies that filtered down from them.

After about ten minutes, she interrupted me and said in a stunned voice, "We need to go before the ice cream melts."

When we arrived at the machine I said, "I'll set the timer for the time we leave, plus five minutes. It's necessary to go back to a time that we didn't exist."

Pam asked why that was important.

I explained if we go back to a time before we left and we have physical contact with ourselves, there will be a massive explosion because the same matter, cannot occupy the same space simultaneously, and when I say massive, I mean nuclear.

I said, "Okay, we've got chicken, ice cream, and a woman that will be about 495 years old when we arrive," Pam said. "I bet I'll be the best-looking five-hundred-year-old woman."

"True, true, now are you ready to boldly go where only one man has gone before?"

She had a variety of looks that were meant to let me know how she felt. I would get to know them each in time, as we would end up spending quite a bit of time together in the years to come, but I'm getting ahead of myself.

This time however, she just nodded. I believe she was still a little stunned at my newfound knowledge of *Star Trek*.

I had already briefed her on what to expect when we arrived. I looked at Pam and asked once more if she was ready.

She replied, *"Let's boldly go where no man has gone."*

I said with a smile, "I've been there, remember?"

She gave me an unamused look, and asked if she could push the Enter button.

I said, "By all means."

She pushed it. The machine began to perform as it had before, and in a moment, we were whisked away to the future.

18

When we materialized, we gathered the things we had brought with us and made our way to the house. They saw Pam and started asking so many questions that, as usual, it sounded like a garbled gaggle of geese.

Then Jason said excitedly, "You brought food back with you." You could have heard a pin drop for about half a second after they realized there was food from the twenty-first century. Their eyes sort of glazed over. "Is it chicken? It smells like chicken, fried chicken. Who is this lovely lady?" He said, as if it were an afterthought.

I said, "Gentlemen, may I introduce you to Pam Brown. She is a librarian from the year 2010. Pam, may I introduce you to Dr. Mike Kinsey, theoretical physicist, Dr. Jason Simmons, theoretical astrophysicist, Dr. Kim Osaka, theoretical engineer, and Dr. Ali Asana, alternative theoretical energy physicist, and this is Donna Jackson. She is my housekeeper and so much more."

Everyone said hello nearly in unison.

Then I said, "Don't you think we could accomplish more by eating dinner first?"

"Absolutely, yes, certainly," the gang chimed. Pam handed a few buckets to Donna and the trimmings and pop to the other members of the gang.

I told them how lucky I had been to find the only library in town, and it also being where Pam works. I told them about how she originally thought I was an alien. Everyone laughed.

Pam quipped, "You haven't found aliens yet, have you?"

Ali said, "Oh yes, we have met aliens. They're only about four feet tall, and they're green."

Once again everyone laughed. Pam caught on and said, "I can drop this chicken on the floor and—"

She didn't get to finish before the gang in frantic unison said, "No, don't, please." Then they apologized.

Donna had set the table before I went back in time, anticipating I might be back soon.

Having just eaten, Pam and I sat down and observed. However before we started I said, "I was able to find not just one Bible, but many, they're everywhere. I even have my own Bible.

One of the things that I have learned is the custom of saying grace." I explained it was one of the many ways of paying homage to God. Then I said, "After dinner, I'll explain much more."

I told everyone to hold hands, bow their heads, and close their eyes. They looked a little bewildered, but followed my instructions anyway.

"Dear Holy Father, thank you for allowing us to travel through time without incident. We thank you for this meal that you have made possible. Thank you Heavenly Father, for the gift of faith and the love for you that knows no bounds. Amen." Everyone still had their heads bowed. I said, "Gentlemen, amen is like saying I'm through with the prayer."

Pam said, "Actually, amen expresses a solemn ratification, or hearty approval."

Kim said, "Can we eat now? I'm starving, and the food smells divine."

I told her to load her plate and start saying yum!

For a moment it seemed as if we were transported back to a simpler time. While eating, our conversation became more and more subdued, but still engaging. After dinner, we went to the drawing room. We talked until very late. I finally had to tell them it was late, and they all excused themselves.

Donna showed Pam to her room, and we all said good night.

19

I awoke to the smell of coffee brewing. I dressed and went downstairs. To my surprise, Pam was cooking. We greeted each other, and she poured me a cup of the coffee she had brewed. I nearly gagged as I took my first taste. It had only taken a few days to become accustomed to the coffee available in the past.

Pam heard my unfavorable, and unintentional reaction to the coffee. She said with a smile, "Is something wrong?"

I replied, "No, no I'm used to coffee like this."

"That's what I meant," she said, smiling. "I must admit, I'm disappointed that people still have to cook their own meals and clean their house by hand. I would have thought machines would have been invented by now to replace people at those tasks."

Donna was walking down the stairs at that moment and said, "If it hadn't been for the war Ms. Brown, perhaps those things would have been invented. That wouldn't be the end though. People would still want more. The problem with the world is, I want something new, and I want it now! The sooner I can make something newer, the faster I can put someone else out of business, or possibly make their job obsolete. Mankind has always had an uncanny ability to make trash out of something that is still of use, including people. The planet still has many natural resources. However, we have learned that everything is recyclable.

Pam and Donna did most of the talking that morning. It had been some time since Donna had another female to talk with, and had never been able to talk about my time travel to another. Another thing that she and Pam shared. It didn't matter that there was a five-hundred year difference in their lives, their conversation transcended time. I guess some things never change.

It was about three o'clock in the afternoon, and the gang had arrived. The conversation turned from everyday chitchat, to that of a scientifically structured conversation.

After my debriefing of my trip, I asked Pam to explain to the others what religion was about since I was new to it. Pam cheerfully agreed. "There are actual two books that are combined to make the Bible. The Old Testament tells the story of man from the beginning of time to the birth of Jesus."

That's all it took, and we got into a scientific-evolutionary, versus religion-creationism argument.

This exchange continued for some time with Pam just sitting there smiling. I think she knew exactly what would happen.

After some time, Pam was finally able to speak. "Everyone, you will need to keep an open mind in order to understand what is about to be put forth to you. That should be easy for men of science such as yourself. Now if you will give me your attention, I will tell you all about the beginning of everything. Before I start though, I am going to purpose something that will be impossible to understand using your scientific minds."

Ali asked, "Then what mind do you purpose we use?"

"Your open mind, the mind that God gave you to believe in whatever you wish, and believe me ladies and gentlemen, you will have to believe."

"What will we have to believe?" Jason asked.

Pam asked him, "Jason, can you tell me how old the Earth is?"

"Around four and a half billion years old," he answered.

"You're thinking with your scientific mind. I want you to think openly."

"I'm sorry, but I can't be more open than the truth!"

"It's only the truth because you don't have faith, and have not read the Bible."

"Then tell us Ms. Brown, how old is the Earth?"

"For those of us who believe in the Lord, the popular belief is about five to six thousand years old."

Of course there was an outcry of radiocarbon dating, fossilization and such.

Pam said, "Listen, there's a lot you'll find hard to accept until you use your open and accepting mind. Here is an example of a true story that can make you understand things differently.

Early in the twentieth century, in New Mexico, a poor soul fell off a cliff. He landed feet first. That was evident because his boots were at the bottom of the cliff, with the lower portion of the legs crushed inside them. Wild animals had carted off the majority of the body. However, the pair of boots, and what remained of the person were found fossilized. The boots were fairly new, and still had the manufacturer's stamp on the bottom. After they were traced to the maker, it was determined the boots at the time they were found, were only about forty-two years old. Therefore, fossilization is not an accurate barometer for testing something's age."

On the other hand, dinosaur bones that are scientifically believed to be some sixty-five-million years old, have been found with tendons intact. Tell me how something organic like that survived all those years without being fossilized or being consumed by microbes?

It was a good point, but the gang still was not swayed.

"Are you discounting radiocarbon dating?" Ali asked.

Pam's simple answer was, "Has carbon dating ever been wrong?"

Ali answered, "Yes."

"Then as people of science, how can you wholly believe a machine which has been proven to be wrong before? How can you put one-hundred percent faith into something that is not right one-hundred percent of the time? As scientist, do you accept answers that are ninety-five percent right? Have lie detectors been improved enough that the results are allowed in the court system yet?"

I told her that they are still not admissible.

Her logic stunned me. She was scientifically correct.

Then she said, "Satan is always trying to tear God down and put false thoughts in people's minds."

"Who is Satan," I asked?

"He was God's right-hand man. He became vain though, and betrayed God. His punishment was to be cast into the bowels of the earth, what we Christians call Hades or hell. It is a nasty place to be, but Lucifer, who had been an angel, made it his home and took the name Satan.

"If you don't give yourself over to the Lord completely, when you die, your eternal soul is cast into the fiery pit known to the religious community as Hell, to burn for all of eternity. Satan's main aim is to cast each and everyone of us into this pit. He thrives off your aguish."

"You make it sound so horrible, but as a scientist I need to have more proof than a pair of boots," Jason said.

"I am sorry to tell you this, but you'll have to accept everything on faith. That is Christianity. Everything is faith based. When something bad happens to you, and you get that feeling that everything is going wrong, that is Satan. His main goal is your negativity. Satan thrives off of it. People remember negativity much more than when things go right. Let me ask you this Dr. Kim. Radio waves have been traveling away from the planet for some 575 years at light speed. We have been able to receive radio waves for the same amount of time. Yet in all those years, has there been any contact from aliens?"

"No," they all said.

"Now Jason, you may not be a gambling man, but you can figure the odds of something happening."

"Yes Pam, what is your point?"

"The point is Doctor, there is only one Earth. Is our planet the only earthlike planet?

How many galaxies are there? Tell me, how many planets are there, that are the correct distance from their sun to support life? How many of those planets have a moon the correct distance from them to create proper tides? In all these years that people have searched the skies, why has there been no contact, or evidence of other life supporting worlds? Dr. Simmons, can you tell me what the odds are that we're alone?"

"Scientifically, and statistically speaking, I would think with the uncountable billions of galaxies there are, we should have bumped into others by now, statistically speaking that is. Only if they are as advanced, or even more advanced than we are though."

"There are thousands of earthlike planets that have been discovered," Jason said.

"Still we have not had first contact yet," Pam asked?

"That is correct Ms. Brown, but you're dealing with a lot of unknowns," Jason continued.

"In the scheme of geological time and the time man has inhabited this planet, the 575 years of radio is an insignificant amount of time, astronomically speaking."

"I realize that light speed for that long, is certainly a very far distance to comprehend, but think about how many light years the universe is across!" Jason said. Our galaxy alone is over one thousand light years across, and there are billions of galaxies.

"That's a scientist for you," Pam said, "always looking for something to be a naysayer about. You're thinking that we are the most advanced simian-based species in the universe, that is thinking with a closed mind. As scientist, shouldn't you have an open mind that there may be a civilization somewhere, that is much older, and much more advanced than ours?"

"Ms. Brown, you have given us nothing tangible," Ali said. "You say that we must take it on faith. We are men of science."

"Yes, I am asking you to take it on faith, only because that radical gang, the ORC, destroyed all reference to Christianity. Come back to my time, and I'll show you stories about real people in history that you have heard of, speak about Jesus Christ. For example, Pontius Pilate condemned Jesus to death.

"The reason there is no religion now is, there is nothing left about God for you to read. From what I gather, if not for Caleb putting the few remaining clues together, you might never have found out about God.

You must remember. Jesus did live. He was real. The fact that you knew nothing about him, is because no one was left to carry the Word forward. What the ORC did was exactly like the Spanish Inquisitions, only in reverse."

"The Spanish Inquisitions?" Ali questioned.

Pam explained what that was to everyone's shock. "God wants you to become a Christian on your own accord. He wants your love for him to be unconditional.

Instead of trying to bring people to religion by any means necessary, the ORC did the opposite. They murdered people, and burned all religious books, symbols, or artifacts. What the ORC did was tantamount to genocide. I consider it no small miracle that we're all sitting here discussing Christianity at all with all the ORC did to wipe it from existence.

Therefore Doctors, the world could be so different if not for the barbaric acts of the ORC."

"We discussed the pros and cons of stopping the war from happening, and we all agreed that the war was an appalling necessity," Ali said.

Pam said, "We're not discussing preventing the war. We're talking about stopping the genocide of whole cultures, of all religions. Most of the people that died in the war were killed before the ORC came into power, weren't they?"

I said, "I did some research after finding out about the organization, and I discovered a few things about their kill rate. Obviously, after the war ended in 2185, the ORC was responsible for the vast majority of deaths every year after that, until they were disbanded around 2200. Here is one disturbing fact though, in 2183, the ORC was responsible for more deaths than the war was."

Pam said, "These were peace-loving people that the ORC killed. All they wanted was to believe in what they chose to believe in. That is what this country was founded on."

I said, "I discovered that even though they were religious people, they were nonetheless, heroic patriots. I found entries of people who had been awarded the Silver Star, the Bronze Star, even a Medal of Honor winner, all were put to death for their beliefs."

"Religious beliefs are what this country was founded on," Pam said.

"Caleb, did you find any census records from 2185?"

"Yes I did Pam, and by that time, the population had dropped to about three billion people."

She asked Donna if that would be a manageable-sized population. She agreed that the war was a terrible thing, but that would be a manageable population.

She asked, "Why didn't they oppose the ORC? Why didn't they fight back?"

Pam said, "In my time, there were conscientious objectors to some wars. These were people that refused to go to war for one reason or another. Some were hippies. Some were religious, and they objected on that basis. I can imagine, after not having a war of any kind for so long, perhaps the Christians that the ORC dealt with went to their deaths thinking physical violence wasn't right, so neither was fighting in the war.

"That's Christianity, it's giving, not taking. All Christians from all different faiths since the inception of religion, have battled in wars to protect their faith. The reason that they always fought, was to protect their right to be free, free to choose the faith they believed in. That was the cornerstone for the foundation of our country. The Christians the ORC dealt with, were right to not want to fight, but when it's thrust upon you, you must respond.

"When America was a young country, we fought a couple of wars against Britain. They believed since the settlers in America were mainly British, it was British land. After all, British money built the country. They felt they deserved to claim eminent domain. The founding fathers did not take their claims well, and after fighting for a few years, they beat the British back to England.

"Those Americans were mostly Christians, but they fought to protect their right to choose their religion, and subvert British tyranny. I believe that a Christian from my time would not hesitate to do battle with the ORC. Will someone please tell me why if these people were in good-enough shape to kill Christians, why couldn't they fight in the regular war? Were there no jobs they could do other than kill our own?"

Donna asked, "What is a hippy?"

Pam laughed for a moment and said, "They were another group of peace-loving people from my time. Some were Christians, some were just free-spirited people that practiced nonviolence, but that's a story for another conversation."

"Now can someone tell me why members of the ORC were allowed to do what they did?"

No one knew how to answer Pam. She looked at the blank stare from all of us. Finally she spoke in a very sad tone, "I guess humanity had lost its compassion." I could see how much it hurt her to see that could have happened.

Having had a glimpse of her world, I could see how if you lived your whole life by one set of standards, and then got a glimpse of what man had descended into, well, that would be a great disappointment. I think it's a normal reaction to want better for your descendants.

Then to see what was in store for them in the future would have to be very disheartening.

It was getting late, and Pam and I needed to get back to her time. We all said our good-byes as they walked us to the machine. I looked at the gang from the deck of the machine.

"You all know that I'm no good at speeches, so you won't get one. I brought these Bibles, and reading guides for all of you to read and learn; to see if this is the kind of life you would like to lead. In addition, I will come back on Saturday next week at three o'clock. Since starting to time travel, I have aged seven days, while you have aged only two days. I don't wish to die before any of you, so from now on, I will try to time my trips day for day, so I can age with all of you."

With that, they left the cave. I pushed the Enter button, and once more we were whisked away to the year 2010.

20

Once again the whirring noise ceased, and the black veil dropped away. Pam and I were home, or at least what I would call home for the foreseeable future.

I walked her to the car, said good night, and we went our separate ways home.

I stayed at the machine that night to finish my forged documents, for my appointment with President Johnson at the university the next day. I had forgone Pam's advice to get a room for the night, it was late, and I had much to do.

The next day, I arrived at the university a few minutes early. I told the secretary who I was. She said, "Dr, Bronson, President Johnson is waiting for Dr. Baker, the head of the department." I said, "Thank you," and took a seat. No sooner had I sat down when Dr. Baker arrived. The secretary stood up as he entered and introduced us.

President Johnson emerged from her office. She greeted us together, asking if we would like coffee or another beverage. We both declined and went into her office. It was quite a stately office.

After we sat down, I held my portfolio up and said, "Who wants to look at my credentials?"

President Johnson said she would take them. Dr. Baker asked what aspect of theoretical physics I was working on. I didn't want to look too advanced for the job, neither did I wish to look too dumb.

I said, "I'm dabbling a little with string theory, black holes, and, I'm sure you might think it a little silly, time travel."

"Now what kind of theoretical physicist would I be if I didn't accept your theories until proven right or wrong?" said Dr. Baker.

This echoed what Pam had said about the gang and I, when trying to explain things in the Bible.

He asked if I would care to share any of my hypotheses.

I said, "Okay, what is the fastest thing known to man?"

Dr. Baker replied, "Light." Then he said questionably, "Isn't it?"

"Right now it is, but I have been doing some very promising calculations."

"That's why you're looking at time travel also, isn't it?" Dr. Baker asked.

"Yes, you got me on that one. Now if you want to know more you'll have to hire me," I said jokingly.

Dr. Baker said, "I think he's serious Mary. You had better give him the job." He then leaned over, shook my hand and said, "Welcome."

I was a little stunned. I said, "That's it? I'm hired?"

Dr. Baker said, "Ever since I won that silly little Nobel Prize five years back, Mary can't say no to me, or is it the millions of dollars donated every year because I'm here Mary?" He didn't wait for her answer. "Nevertheless, I get my way a lot. I see promise in you, and I want to hear more about how slow the speed of light is. I'm looking forward to working with you, may I call you Caleb?"

"Yes, please do."

Dr. Baker jokingly said, "You may call me God."

"No, I can't do that. It would be blasphemy. I would hate to get struck by lightning right after getting a new job, especially in the president's office."

"Oh!" Dr. Baker said. "A religious one. Where did you find this one, Mary, at church?"

"As a matter of fact I did, and watch the blasphemy around me too. I don't want the lightning to bounce off you and kill me."

"In that case, you may call me Joe." He said to me.

I shook his hand and said, "Thank you."

He said, "If we can only prove one aspect of the theories you have, I would get a big fat raise for sharing a second Nobel

Prize. Of course for you, it would mean you could write your own ticket at any college with its own physics department. A college might even create a physics program just for you. If we build a time machine, are you going to destroy our work because it's ungodly?"

I replied, "I only do God's work. If we discover something groundbreaking, it will only be because God has made it so."

Dr. Baker replied, "What about free will?"

"Free will," I said, "is only for things I can control. God guides my hands and mind. God is in control of discovery. What one does with it, is free will."

"God wants us to follow his path. If we make a big discovery, it will only be because God wishes it so."

Joe studied me for a distrusting moment, he then asked if I would be talking about religion while we worked.

I told him he had nothing to worry about, but if he wanted to discuss the subject I would always be willing to assist him in his search for the truth.

He then asked if I would like to see my office.

I said, "Thank you. Yes, I would."

President Johnson said, "Joe, will you also show Dr. Bronson where administration is so he can get squared away with them?"

"Yes, I'll take care of it, even though it's not in my job description," he said sarcastically.

President Johnson said, "Go on, get out of here you two eggheads."

As we walked down the hall, Joe asked if I was a little bit dazed.

I said I had expected the interview to be a little bit more rigorous.

He said, "I'll bet you're curious as to why it was so quick."

"Well, you already told me that the president can't say no to you," I said.

"Yes, but what was the reason I picked you so quickly?"

I admitted that I was stuck for an answer on that.

Joe asked, "What about the black hole? Is that tied to your time travel theory?"

I said, "Joe, we all know that it would be death to pass the event horizon of a black hole."

Joe lost that "little boy at the moment of discovery" look in his eyes when I said that. I added, "There has to be some way around that problem."

I then asked him where the nearest Hadron Collider was.

He looked at me and said, "They can't get enough speed out of one. You can't make it work."

I smiled and said, "Not the way they build them now."

He said, "Now? What do you mean by now?"

I had almost let the cat out of the bag. It was bad enough that Pam knew the truth, to let Joe in on it would be a disaster.

When someone experiences a peak moment, such as a Nobel Prize at such an early age, the longer past the said peak moment, the more one would crave repeating that feeling. I could see Joe was drooling for another peak moment.

After I left the college, Pam told me to go to an address she had written on a piece of paper, and the woman there would rent me an apartment. Pam had called ahead for me, so the woman knew I was coming. After that was done, I went back to the machine, gathered some things, and waited for her to get off work.

When she got there she asked, "What's going and what's staying?"

We both grabbed a few boxes of items and loaded her car. On the way to the apartment she asked how the interview went. I told her how simple it was, and that I had expected to get the job, but not that easily.

"It seems Dr. Baker and I have been working on the same things. The interview lasted all of fifteen minutes, and Dr. Baker welcomed me to the college without talking it over with President Johnson. It seems that Dr. Baker won a Nobel Prize a few years ago, and he thinks I am the key to him getting another one."

Pam asked if I divulged any secrets. I told her that I had not, and I didn't have time to anyway. "Dr. Baker was almost giddy. He was acting like a child at the beginning of the Renew Celebration."

She asked what that was. I looked at her in bewilderment and said, "You don't celebrate Renew yet?"

She said she had never heard of it.

"Renew is a week-long celebration of the New Year that starts on the twenty-fourth of December, and ends on January first. December 25, being Gifting Day, a day where family and friends get together, exchange gifts, and have a feast. Then on December 31, the village has a wonderful dance that ends at midnight, the start of the New Year. There are fireworks and much more. It's the biggest event of the year. The next day, January 1, people get together again for another feast, and we watch soccer all day."

She sat there in stunned silence while she digested what I had just told her. Finally she said, "Some things never change."

I asked what she meant by that.

She told me about the book of Luke, chapter 2 the birth of the baby Jesus. She told me that Christmas, which we call Gifting Day, was actually the birthday of Jesus Christ. The ORC could not erase all knowledge of Christ, and they could not outlaw Christmas. It was too popular, so they bastardized Christmas to hide it.

She looked at me and said, "Caleb, you have been celebrating the birth of Jesus Christ all your life. The ORC never got rid of religion. They just covered it up and rearranged things. Caleb, you are a Christian, and have been all your life."

I sat there in stunned silence for a moment and said, "Are you sure that is enough to make me a Christian?"

"You were doing the best you could with the information you had," she said. "God knows your true heart. I believe you have been sent here by him just as Pastor Lind said. Why remains to be seen."

Then I told her that I had been mulling over something for some time now, and that I had decided to dive into the

Bible with all my heart. "I am going to revive Christianity in the future. God told me to do so in one of my dreams."

Pam said, "There is a seminary college in town. You could take classes while you teach."

I asked what a seminary college was. She said that it was where I could learn more about Christ, Christianity, and become a pastor.

I said, "It's as if God knew I would come here, and have these opportunities laid at my feet."

Pam said in a matter-of-fact way, "I'm sure he did."

Pam was getting ready to leave, and I asked if she would pick me up for church Sunday. She said she would, just before she left she sat across from me.

She began, "Caleb, I cannot tell you how impressed I am, that a man with such a logical scientific mind such as yourself, would be as open-minded to something as hard to comprehend as Christianity is."

I told her, "On the contrary, as a man of science I must keep an open mind in order to accept new theories, at least until they are either proven to be right, or proven wrong. We've talked about that already."

She stood up and said, "I wonder what God has in store for you."

I asked what she meant by that.

She said, "Life is preordained by God."

I asked, "What about our abilities to change our mind?"

As she walked through the door, she said, "You don't understand. The Bible is not just the story of the creation of man, or the life of Jesus Christ. God would be pleased if we gave ourselves over to this guide. In that way, life is preordained. It's only lost for those who choose to sin. Read Daniel 4:19 to the end of chapter 4.

"God lets us choose for ourselves in many aspects of our life. For example, what I will have for dinner. It's the big things in life like believing in him, that if we choose wrong, we would be in peril of losing our eternal soul."

That night I thought about attending the seminary college, and when I finished, I would go forward to the future, to that terrible time when man lost faith. I decided I would go to the year 2230—about forty-five years after the end of the war, and about thirty years after the disbandment of the ORC.

I would go to that time and revive Christianity once the ORC, and the atrocities they committed had been largely forgotten. I would see to it that Christianity survived. I would do this or die trying!

I must have had a look of determination, because Pam looked at me oddly and said, "Go to bed. You look tired." We said good night, and I prepared myself for bed.

I picked up the Bible. It didn't seem to be a lot of reading, so I decided to read the whole book.

It seems King Nebuchadnezzar had a disturbing dream one night. He summoned all the wise men from Babylon, but none of them were able to interpret the meaning of the dream. Finally, Daniel came. They called him Belshazzar.

The king told Belshazzar the dream. He described a marvelous tree that fed all kinds of animals, beasts, and birds. They ate its fruit, and received shelter from within its branches.

A messenger from heaven came to him and commanded him to cut the tree down. He told the king to strip all the vegetation from it. He said to leave the stump in the ground though. Then he was given the mind of an animal, and was commanded to join the other animals. He was to live among the plants until seven times, or years passed by him.

Belshazzar told the king that, in the dream, the tree was the king himself. He said that the king was mighty and had grown tall, and that he could see the world.

Belshazzar told the king that cutting the tree down, meant that he would lose everything, but all will be restored to him when he acknowledged that heaven rules. He asked the king to renounce his sins without a reply.

The prophecy was then fulfilled twelve months latter. The king was driven from Babylon and made to join the beasts in the wild. At the end of seven times, Nebuchadnezzar praised the Most High.

After that, his sanity, honor, and kingdom were restored. He then praised the King of heaven, giving him all the praise and glory.

I wasn't tired when I started my reading, but when I finished, I was so tired that I had to put the Bible down, and fell into a deep sleep.

21

That night I had an amazing dream. I have had nightmares about falling before, and every time I would wake up in sheer terror moments from impact. That night instead of falling, I found myself gliding. I could flap my arms similar to that of a bird's wings. I could maneuver as smoothly as any bird I had ever seen.

I flew through the clouds for a while, and then I came upon a structure unlike any I had seen. The closer I came to the building, a feeling unlike anything I had ever felt started to come over me. I was starting to feel unworthy, insignificant, and humbled. I also felt a calming sensation, and I felt loved. I began to feel the presence of another, one who is greater than I could ever imagine.

I began to see details of the structure. It appeared to be about 75 by 150 feet, without a roof. I saw an entryway through one end of the structure, which appeared to be about 30 feet wide. I softly landed by the entrance of what I would find later to be a tabernacle.

Brilliantly colored curtains covered the entry. They were blue, purple, and scarlet. All the curtains appeared to be of the same dimensions, about forty by five feet. The curtains were adorned with embroidered parameters.

The four beams that held up the header of the entryway, were adorned at the base with silver bands and brass bases.

I entered the courtyard and began to turn in a circle. From beginning to end, the bright curtains and their posts were the same as the entry.

All the curtains had gold rings tied to them, and were hung from the post with gold hooks.

The first item I came upon was an altar of bronze. It was for burnt offerings. It appeared to be made of wood and overlaid with bronze. On each corner a ring hung, and a horn was attached to it. All of this was made of bronze. The altar was accompanied by wood poles covered in brass for carrying purposes.

After that, I came upon a brass basin filled with water. A figure in a hooded robe approached me. I saw no face, in fact where the face should have been, there was nothing but a black void. The figure had me sit on a bench next to the basin without speaking a word. It then knelt down in front of me and removed my shoes and socks. It then turned to the basin and scooped some of the water with its hands. When it turned around, instead of a dark void, a brilliant light shone from where its face should be, and it began to wash my feet.

When it was through, it gave me a pair of sandals made from some sort of straw. Then it handed me a robe to wear. I changed into the robe, and the figure led me inside the central tent and left.

I could clearly see the main component of the whole complex. It was about fifteen by forty-five feet. The structure was built in a tent fashion. The fabric that covered the columns was comprised of the same-colored cloth that lined the outer walls. The material was adorned with angelic cherubim woven throughout.

There were columns similar to the ones around the perimeter, however these columns were covered in gold, and all the decorations were made of gold. There were eight crossbars with two silver disks under each crossbar.

Inside, there was a bread table, a lampstand, and an incense table—all made of gold.

Past that was a smaller room. It contained the Ark of the Covenant entirely made of gold. When I entered the room, I felt as if every worry I had ever had vanished, I was completely at peace.

I heard a voice. It seemed to come from nowhere and everywhere at once. It was the softest voice, and the loudest voice that I had ever heard at the same time.

I dropped to my knees screaming in agony, grasping my ears in a futile attempt to muffle the sound, but it was coming from inside my head also. I understood nothing that I had heard.

I looked around and saw no one. Then the voice spoke again, "Caleb, this is your Lord God Almighty." I kept my eyes looking at the floor for fear of what would happen if I were to gaze upon his likeness. "You pose an interesting situation for me. In the future, there will be a great persecution of my people. They will be persecuted for believing, and worshiping me. What do you think of that?"

God was asking me for my opinion? "Father, I have thought about those days often as of late. They were very dark days. If I knew how to change what will happen, I would."

The Lord said, "You have invented a vessel that transcends time. You are the only one who could have a chance to right things. You are my representative."

"What should I do my Lord?" I inquired.

He replied, "You shall know what to do, and when to do what I require."

"I must tell you, I am a little apprehensive."

"Stop," the Lord commanded in a loud voice. "Don't you know that you your-self are Gods temple, and that Gods spirit lives in you. If anyone destroys Gods temple, God will destroy him; For Gods' temple is sacred, and you are that temple" (Corinthians 3:16–17, NIV).

"If someone destroys you, then they will be destroyed. Is God's temple not sacred?"

"Yes, yes it is."

"You are that temple. 'The son is the radiance of Gods glory, and the exact representation of his being, sustaining all things by his powerful word. You will become, as much superior to the Angles as the name he has inherited is superior to theirs' (Hebrews 1:3–4, NIV).

"When your time comes, you will have a seat by my side. You will succeed Caleb. You must succeed, or my children will not survive."

At that moment I heard a muffled banging noise. I felt like there was a rope around my waist tugging me away from the temple. I went faster and faster until everything became a blur. I heard the knock again, and I came around enough to answer the door.

Pam took one look at me and said, "What happened to you?"

"I don't know. I had a dream last night, it was so vivid."

She said, "Well looking at you, I'd say you were in a fight." Then she grabbed part of my hair and said, "You have a white shock of hair overnight, and look at you, you're all sweaty." She walked over to the bed and felt it. "My goodness, you must have lost ten pounds in sweat."

Pam told me to take a shower, and she would cook us some breakfast.

I was exhausted, and she swayed me with no argument. She got busy in the kitchen, and I took a shower. I had sweated an awful lot.

I didn't take a very long shower, because I felt I would pass out from the heat if I stayed any longer. I came out looking not much better than when I woke up.

Pam commented on that fact. "Maybe once you eat you'll come back a little."

I told her I was hungry, and thanked her for cooking. She said she didn't think I would have made it to church if she hadn't done so.

I was very hungry. When I finished the first plate, Pam had hardly eaten half of her meal. She asked if I wanted more.

I said yes, thanking her for her help. She cooked me another breakfast, and I ate it in such a short time that she still hadn't finished hers. She jokingly commented that I devoured the meal faster than I did the Bible.

Then she said, "What happened to you last night? Is this because of time travel?"

I started to talk, but I stumbled with my words, I didn't exactly know where to start.

Pam said, "Why don't you start from the beginning?"

I told her how I had not felt tired when I went to bed, but after reading the Bible for a short time, I dozed off.

I began to dream. It was so vivid, I was sure it had been real. I was up in the clouds flying like a bird. I told her how I had came upon a structure that was adorned with very colorful sheets lining the inside walls, and how they were adorned with gold, silver, and bronze. I described the layout of the interior floor, and what items I found there.

I then described the tent-like structure, and that it had several cherubim woven into it. I stopped at that moment, looked at Pam quizzically and asked, "What are cherubim? I don't know that word."

Pam only said, "Continue with your story, I'll tell you later." She seemed very excited.

"Inside the tent-like structure were two rooms. One held some biblical artifacts. I went into the next room. There in front of me lay the Ark of the Covenant. Then a voice spoke. It was unlike any other voice I had heard in my life. At first I thought I would go deaf. Then the voice spoke in a manner that was understandable and soft. We talked for some time about the future of the world, and my part in it.

Pam, one time you mused at what God had in store for me, what kind of tool for him I would be. I think I now know what my purposes will be."

Pam sat there in stunned silence for a moment. She said, "Do you remember reading about the Holy of Holies?"

I replied I had not.

"But it was one of the first stories you read about. What about your eidetic memory?"

"I don't remember it," I said very confused.

"You spoke directly to God, did you see him?"

"No, I was afraid to look upon his face. We did have a short discussion about the future however."

"What did he say? What does God want of you?"

"He spoke about the future of religion and man. I need to enroll in the seminary today."

"God has chosen you to be his personal representative," she said.

Just then she rose from her chair, walked over to me and knelt on the floor. She held my hand and began to pray. "Holy Father, I thank you for sending your emissary to us. I know Caleb has much to learn before he is ready to do your bidding. I will, as your humble servant do everything I can to help prepare Caleb for the task you have presented to him. In your name I pray, amen."

I put my hand under her chin and lifted her head. She had tears in her eyes. "Rise little angel, I am not a holy man, I am just a man and nothing more. We are all God's servants, and anyone that puts himself above another is being a blasphemer. There is a lot for me to learn, and I would appreciate it if you would help me as much as you can."

She wiped the tears from her eyes and said she would be honored to help me.

Then she said, "It's hard not to be in awe of you. You have spoken to him."

"Perhaps, then it may have just been a dream, but I am still just a man and nothing more. If cut, I bleed just as you."

I looked at the clock and said we should go or we would be late. I didn't want to be late. I had a new agenda, and I fully intended to be what God wanted me to be.

The next day, I entered the seminary. I had an interview with President Chapman. He read my application for a moment and then said, "You put on your application that you work at the college."

I answered that I would be starting next week.

"You also wrote that you're a theoretical physicist."

"Yes sir, I am."

"Do you see any conflict of interest between your job and joining the seminary? Frankly, I am a little apprehensive about you joining our ranks. With your IQ, your career, and your ability to soak up knowledge, you could be a distraction for the rest of the students attending our institution."

"Then sir, may I suggest we not share this information with the student body?"

"This is something that we will not be able to keep secret for too long."

"Then may I suggest you announce my arrival. Use me as an example, God can change the life of anyone. That sort of thing!"

He thought for a moment and then said, "Perhaps, it's smart."

"Sir, I feel like I'm at a crossroad in my life, and I want to make sure that I don't make a big mistake, and then find out too late that I had. Just because scientists may dispute the word of the Bible, it doesn't mean the Word of God is wrong. Man wrote the Bible, Perhaps they interpreted the Word incorrectly."

"That is borderline blasphemy, and shows how dangerously smart you are."

"I have lived a life away from the light for too long, and I long to be a new person in Christ, a new Christian."

"A very commendable attitude," he said. "You understand that most everything you believe in now, you will have to disavow. You can't serve two masters."

"Yes, sir, I'm ready to start my life anew. I am ready to begin serving the one, and only true master, our Lord God Almighty."

He thought for a moment then reached his hand across the desk, and we shook hands. Then the president said, "I will keep a close eye on you Caleb, welcome to the seminary. I hope you know what you're doing."

"Yes sir, I also hope I know what I'm doing. I feel if I make a mistake, the repercussions will be enormous."

He looked at me oddly and said, "I feel like you have an objective beyond this seminary, would you like to share more with me?"

"I would sir, but I prayed about it last night, and I believe God is not ready for me to share this with anyone. Let me just say that my main goal is to spread the word of God to every corner of the Earth." I couldn't tell him the truth of course.

He looked at me even more strangely, hesitated for a moment and said, "I'll accept that explanation for now, but you must understand. You can't keep secrets from God."

I had to contain myself to keep from laughing. If he only knew.

22

After breakfast, I went to the office supply store, and bought items from a list I had made the day after I was hired at the college. I had bought so much that there was no way I could carry it all.

I expressed my problem to the clerk, who responded by telling me she could call a cab for me. I asked if she thought it would cost very much. She asked where I was going. I gave her the address, and she said it shouldn't be too much, then made the call.

Shortly after she called, the cab pulled up outside the store. I thanked her.

She said, "No sweat."

This caught me off guard for a moment, and then I remembered the little girl at the library using that slang term. This twenty-first-century jargon would take some time to get used to.

The cab driver helped me carry my things to the cab, and put them in the trunk. This was my first cab ride, and I didn't know the rules. I tried to get in the front seat without knowing the proper etiquette.

The driver told me to get in the back and added, "We're not friends."

I thought the response was a little harsh, and it put me off a bit, but I didn't let that show.

He asked, "Where to?" I gave him the address, and in a few minutes we were in front of the apartment building.

He opened the trunk and helped me put my things on the sidewalk.

Then he held out his hand and said, "That will be $10.30."

I gave him $10.30 exactly. He didn't look too happy without a tip. Then I said, "as you told me at the store, we're not friends."

I wasn't going to give money to someone who wasn't at least trying to be friendly. I would find later that, while he didn't necessarily deserve a tip, my justification was off.

I put my things inside the hallway, and made the two trips up the stairs with all I had bought. I had to negotiate three flights of stairs, and the packages, while not heavy, were awkward to carry. They were somewhat of a strain to handle; but I made it, having to rest a bit once I finished.

Once I caught my breath I began sorting the items out: one pile I would keep at the apartmen, and one I would take to the college, another I would take to the seminary.

After I sorted things out, I got online and started collecting string theory information that was up to date. I added some things that made it look like I was heading in a different, yet promising direction. It wasn't too difficult. The real problem was dumbing it down enough, to make it look like I still had work to do on it.

This would keep Dr. Baker and I busy for months before we would be able to disprove the direction we were heading, and have to abandon the theory altogether.

The same would be true with time travel, folding space, and any other theory I might propose in the future. All of the theories would start with great promise and end in great disappointment, for Dr. Baker that is.

Dr. Baker was, for the time, a brilliant man. I'm sure if I told him everything I knew, he would not just be amazed, he would probably understand all of it.

There was part of me that wanted to tell him all I knew. I knew I couldn't, but to see the look on his face when I explained physics from my time, would have been priceless.

Pam was coming over after work to help me with some of the more often quoted parts of the Bible. Not that some parts of the Bible aren't important, but some stories were told more often than others. This was to help me blend in.

She would be here soon. I decided to take a break from what I was doing, and straighten the place up a bit before she arrived. I was just finishing when she knocked on the door.

Pam had brought Chinese food, and I was hungry. We sat down, said grace, and we ate right away. Pam debriefed me on my day, while I quizzed her on our forthcoming evening.

When we finished, we washed dishes together and didn't say much, but it felt a little familiar. It took a little while, but I finally figured it out; she reminded me of my housekeeper, Donna. This was a comfort to me. She was someone I could trust, and feel at ease with. I wasn't sure, but could I be developing feelings for Pam?

I had too much to learn, too much to do, and not enough time to get everything done. Romance was not what I was here for.

I cleared off what was left on the coffee table, so we would have room to do Bible study.

She told me the first person I would need to learn about was the first person, Adam. We talked about Adam and Eve, the serpent, and the tree of knowledge.

We would talk about the first murder of a man by another, Cain killing his brother Abel, and about Noah, the ark, and the flood. It amazed me that not one person thought, "Hey, maybe I'll look the fool, but if he's right. I'll get the last laugh."

Then Exodus, and the story of Moses and his people, and the many miracles that God performed through him.

I had already read about Mosses in the book of Exodus. The book told the entire life of Moses, from birth to death. It told about his lifelong struggle to free his oppressed people. The legendary words he used when he first requested of Pharaoh, "Let my people go" (Genesis 5:1, NIV).

As God released each plague, Moses became more and more demanding of Pharaoh that he let his people go.

Pharaoh could finally take no more, and he released Moses and his people. Pharaoh had one final betrayal though. He chased the tribe to the banks of the Red Sea, where Pharaoh planned to trap and kill all of the faithful.

Then through the power given to him by God, Moses raised his staff and parted the Red Sea.

His people ran across the sea floor, as Pharaoh and his men gave chase. When the faithful reached the far shore of the Red Sea, Moses lowered his staff; and the waters returned, drowning Pharaoh and all his troops. Moses and his people were finally free.

It told about Moses, and his followers building a tabernacle for God. As I read the description, I thought about my dream. The book was describing the same building I had seen in my dream. The walls, the drapes with the cherubim, the Ark of the Convent overlaid with gold. It was described exactly as I had seen in my dream.

I had dreamed about this, and the dream had been so vivid I believed it to be real. Had I just dreamed the whole sequence, or was it real? I had read about it just a few days before. That might explain why I would have a dream about the subject, but not my physical reaction to the dream. However, it was by far, the most vivid dream I had ever had.

I have an eidetic mind though. Why didn't I remember reading the passage? It's such an important passage. Did God wipe it from my memory to make it seem new? There have been things that I have had to think about for a moment before I could recall them, but never anything that was as important as this, and this was the first time I could ever remember forgetting something completely. It was as if I still thought of my first memory of the tabernacle coming to me in the dream, it was quite unsettling to me.

Then there was the white shock of hair I had developed overnight. Later that night, I tried to dye it to match the rest of my hair, but the dye just ran off it. It wasn't oily, it felt like the rest of my hair, but the dye would not take. It seemed like this was to be my badge of honor so to speak. Pam said we would tell everyone that the hair resulted from a nightmare.

Then she said it was the only thing she could think of, short of spray painting it.

I said no to that right away.

She laughed and said, "I was only kidding."

I said, "Of course it's easy for you to laugh, you don't have to explain yourself."

She laughed even more at this and said, "No one will question you when you tell them a dream caused it, especially if you tell them you dreamed about a personal audience with the Lord."

I replied, "I can't tell them what I discussed with God."

She said it would be okay if I left out the part about going to the future to reinstate religion.

"You seem to be sure of this," I said.

She told me people would think it odd, but they wouldn't question it.

I asked how she knew this.

With a look of wonderment, she said, "I don't know, they just won't, I'm sure of it."

I thought back to Pastor Lind's comment, "The Lord works in mysterious ways." Maybe making everyone think the white shock was no big thing, was one of those ways."

Pam laid out what she thought would be pertinent to learn for the night and excused herself, saying she had been neglecting things since we had met, and needed to get some things done, like clean her house. She said, "Reading Leviticus should keep you busy enough for the night."

Pam stood up, and I helped her put her coat on. She told me that she would drop by the next night to give me another assignment to read, and to test me on my reading of Leviticus.

I told her I would be ready. As she left I noticed a sparkle in her eye as she smiled and said her good night. It was like looking at a star on a clear crisp night. Then she was gone, and I was alone again.

Alone—the word meant something much different than it had. At least I had Pam to confide in, but I was finding that not being able to confide in anyone else was a hard thing to do. I had my first moment of doubt just then. Why did I have to be God's emissary? Why couldn't one of my colleagues do God's bidding?

The answer came to me though. God had spoken to me, and had chosen me to do his bidding. In my mind, that was the end of the discussion. I sat at the table, opened the Bible and began reading. "The Lord called to Moses and spoke to him from the Tent of Meeting." (Leviticus 1:1, NIV).

23

It didn't seem to take me very long to finish reading Leviticus. It was an interesting story, and when I completed the book I reviewed what I had just read. I was sure I had it committed to memory. I was confident I would do well on a test.

I put the Bible down, stretched and yawned. It was almost two o'clock in the morning. I wandered to my bedroom and crawled into bed. In seconds I was fast asleep.

That night in my sleep, I was flying as I had in my previous dream. This time I flew over a country setting, as I cleared a forest, there was an open field that met a lake. It was a very serene setting, and I felt compelled to land there.

As I stood by the lake's edge, I saw another man walk up alongside of me in the reflection of the water. He addressed me, "Hello Caleb, it's so nice to meet you."

I turned but there was no one there. Stunned, I looked back at the lake and there he was. He explained that I could not yet look upon him with my eyes, thus the reflection was all I could gaze of him for now.

I wondered if what I was seeing was a true representation of him. He laughed, and as he did, his face morphed into a several different faces—some were women, some children, some men.

"What should I look like?" he said. "Should I be young or old, man or woman, and what color? Black, yellow, red, or white?"

I got on my knees and bowed my head. "Please, Father, forgive me. I am new to your life, and need to learn very much."

"Rise up faithful servant, you have nothing to be sorry for. You are changing everything about your life to do the good work of carrying the Word forward. You have been bestowed with the heavy burden of seeing that it is done. Do not worry, you yourself will grow stronger and stronger in my word as time passes.

"There are those who know the word and don't live by it. They have doomed themselves to an eternity of continuous pain and anguish, in the bowels of the earth. You only started living the word one week ago. There is room for you to misstep. However, you have always lived by a code, and that code is fairly close to the way you should live. This will only mean a slight adjustment for you Caleb."

"I fear that I am just a man. Can I do what you ask of me?"

"Fear not Caleb, you shall persevere. You must persevere."

"You have that much faith in me Lord," I asked?

"*No, that's not the reason,*" he replied. "*It's because you have that much faith in me!*"

I was taken aback, bewildered, and humbled. He believed in me!

He then said, "It's time for you to go Caleb."

With that, I was whisked away before I could even say good-bye.

The next thing I knew I was waking up in my bed, soaked again. When I started to regain my faculties, I got up and went to the bathroom. I wanted to see if I had acquired any more white hair.

After a quick check in the mirror, I breathed a sigh of relief. I had no additional white hair for which I had no excuse.

I took a shower and went to the Pancake House. Again, I ate two breakfasts that morning. It seems a talk with the Lord must be a draining event.

As I walked back to my apartment, I wondered how many times I would experience one of these *visitations,* over the years to come.

Then I did something I would never have done before the Lord came into my life. I dropped to my knees on the public sidewalk and began to pray by myself. It really wasn't a conscious act; it was more of an automatic thing, like I had done it my whole life, and it was proper.

"Dear Lord, this is your humble servant Caleb. I am honored that you have chosen me as your conduit to save your word, and man's love of you. I pray that your strong hand will guide me down your righteous path, on this journey for which you have chosen for me. I will do everything in my power to be your righteous emissary. Lord, help me understand. I have no doubt in you. My concerns lies within myself. However, I turn myself over to you wholly. Your wisdom is infinitely superior to mine. You have a plan, and I am not one to question your decision. Thank you Lord, for hearing my words. I will talk to you often my Lord, now that I understand better, Amen."

I opened my eyes. I noticed that people were walking around me and giving me odd looks. I couldn't blame them. I was just like them only a few days before.

I stood up and felt an instant spurt of rejuvenation, I felt revived. Seconds before I prayed, I felt like taking a nap; now, I felt energetic enough to go all day, and I did.

24

That night Pam grilled me some more about the book of Exodus, and about Moses, and the miracles he performed through the power of God.

She talked about Moses going up Mt. Sinai and seeing the burning bush, his conversation with the Lord, and the presentation of the Ten Commandments.

She talked about how God commanded Moses to go throughout the land and destroy all the pagan idols, and commanded him not to worship any other gods, because they were false gods. The only God to worship is the Lord God Almighty. Then the Lord commanded Moses to build a tabernacle, and told him how it should be constructed, and what should go inside and adorn the structure.

After discussing Exodus and Moses for sometime, we began to talk about the book of Leviticus, and the Day of Atonement. Because of Israel's sins, to avoid God's wrath, they had to atone for their sins.

To atone is to cover up, or in other words, to pay. So they had to pay for these sins through ritual sacrifice.

The blood from the sacrificed animal covered their sins, and they were forgiven.

Pam's questioning period lasted about two hours, until she was satisfied I had memorized the book in its entirety, and I was getting very tired. I was committed to learning the whole Bible though, front to back.

I told Pam about my dream, She said, "You spoke with God again?"

"I don't know if it's God, or just a vivid dream. I want it to be the Lord, and I believe it is the Lord, but why does he only contact me in my sleep?"

Pam could only speculate that in sleep, our minds are clear of all that clouds them when we are awake. Other than that, she didn't have an answer for that question.

"I am glad God has chosen me as his emissary, but I hope he lets me sleep tonight, I'm really tired."

Pam ran her fingers through my hair and told me, "If God talks to you, I'm sure he'll give you enough rest."

As she ran her fingers through my hair, I felt odd for a moment. The way she looked at me when she did it—well, I never was a ladies' man, but it felt like it was more than admiration—it felt like a touch of wanting to be closer to me personally. Was Pam starting to have feelings for me? I cleared those thoughts from my mind and got back to the task at hand. This would not be the end of my pondering the subject though.

I was in fair physical condition, but I decided that what God had in store for me would be a challenge for anyone, no matter what their physical shape may be. I wasn't sure, but I had the feeling he may be preparing me for the struggles I was to face in the future. It's kind of odd to think of where I was going to go in the future, when in reality, I would be visiting the past, a past that I had never seen, or been a part of. The future, the present, and the past—they all seemed to be melting into the blur that my life was quickly becoming.

Everything was going so fast, and needed to be doing so, or I wouldn't be able to accomplish the goals in the time limit I had set for myself; after all, I would not live forever. "This year to come would be a very busy year for me," I thought.

I had no idea how busy it would be though.

I told Pam I didn't want to study any more that night, I was pretty tired. Pam suggested she read the Bible to me to pass the time, and I could just rest and listen.

I agreed to this. I could rest and still attain some knowledge. I made myself comfortable, and Pam began reading from Daniel 5.

Since it's such a long book, instead of writing it all down, I just summarized it.

King Belshazzar held a lavish feast for one thousand of his nobles. He ordered gold and silver goblets that his father had confiscated from the temple in Jerusalem be brought so his nobles, wives, and concubines could drink from them.

As they drank from them, they praised the false gods of gold, silver, bronze, iron, wood, and stone.

Then a hand appeared and began writing on the plaster.

As the king watched, he became pale and his knees weakened, and finally gave way. The king sent for a variety of wise men to decipher the writings. He promised gifts of wealth to the one how could decipher the writings; none could though, which worried the king even more.

The queen heard the commotion in the banquet hall, and told the king to relax. There is one who can read the writings on the wall.

Daniel was summoned. The king offered him the same riches as he had offered to the other wise men, but Daniel refused the gifts and translated the words.

It told of the king's father Nebuchadnezzar, and how the Lord had bestowed greatness and glory upon him. God gave him all the nations and peoples to be his subjects.

He was greatly feared because by his word alone, he could have you put to death, or spare you, promote you, or humble you. People were afraid because this could happen on a whim. He became arrogant, hardened with pride, and was deposed from his throne. He was driven from his people and was given the mind of an animal. He lived with donkeys, and ate grass like cattle. He was made to do this until he acknowledged the Most High God.

Daniel told Belshazzar that he had become prideful and set himself against the Lord and instead worshiped gold, silver, bronze, iron, wood, and stone. He did not honor his God, who held his life in his hands.

Basically, the writings on the wall said, "Your days of reign are numbered. You have been judged, and found wanting." God divided his country between the Medea and the Persians.

Belshazzar commanded Daniel be adorned with purple cloth, and a gold necklace around his neck, and Belshazzar proclaimed Daniel the third highest ruler in the land.

That night, Belshazzar was slain, and Darius and Medea took over the kingdom.

That is where the book ended.

It took sometime before Pam had finished reading Daniel 5, she said she was tired. I said I was too, so we said our good-nights, and she went home. I immediately went to bed and fell asleep as soon as my head hit the pillow. I felt totally rejuvenated the next morning.

25

I started to do equations on wormholes, so I would have something to show Dr. Baker when I started my research that next Monday. I took the spiral notebooks I had, and scribbled some equations out.

When finished with my equations, I spilled some coffee on a few pages, and milk on others. I wanted it to look like I had been working on these problems for some time.

I took the notebooks and some towels, and went to the laundry room. I placed them in a dryer, and turned it on for five minutes. The result was I had notebooks that looked like they had been handled for some time.

That chore being done, I set my sight on the next task at hand—buying groceries. There was a supermarket a few blocks from my apartment. Pam had chosen an apartment that was located close to the library, the college, the seminary, and of course the supermarket.

This would be my first venture to a supermarket. When I bought the ice cream, I shopped at a small store like the ones in my time. They are only little stores. The very name Supermarket, made me a little nervous.

My mind began constructing the store. I saw aisle after aisle, of shelves piled high with various products. I thought, "If that is true, I may never emerge." I finally got control of myself and went inside.

It was of course, much larger than the stores from my time, but I soon realized I would not become lost forever, and I began to fill the basket with items from a list I had compiled at the apartment.

When I emerged I had four bags of food, and cleaning supplies. It was quite a struggle to handle all those bags myself. I was sure that before I got home, I would certainly drop everything, scattering and breaking all I had purchased. Why did I have a third-floor apartment?

Just then I heard a familiar voice say, "Hey, do you need a lift?"

I turned to see Mary, the college president.

I said I would appreciate it if it wouldn't be too much of a burden.

She laughed and said, "The only one of us that looks like they're having a burden, is you and those bags."

I thanked her, put my things in the backseat, and climbed into the front seat with her.

She started to ask where we were going when she saw my shock of white hair. She then asked what had happened to my hair.

I stumbled for a moment, and cursed myself silently for not thinking up a story prior to having to explain it. Then the voice inside my head, not my voice, God's voice said, "Tell her you had a very frightening dream, and woke up like that." So that's what I told Mary. She said, "Don't tell me what the dream was about, I hate horror stories."

That was the way it went when I had to explain the patch of hair. I knew God must have something to do with this, because the explanation was a little thin I had thought, for everyone to except it on face value.

I told her that my apartment was a few blocks away, and I pointed down the street where it was located.

When we arrived she got out and picked up a couple of bags from the backseat. I told her that I lived on the third floor, and that I would make the two trips it would take to get the bags to my apartment. She scoffed at that and said a few flights of stairs wouldn't kill her, then she added, "I'm a senior citizen, not dead. Don't write my obituary quite yet."

I laughed and said I was just trying to do the gentlemanly thing.

She replied, "I haven't seen anyone do a gentlemanly thing since the Victorian days, and no, I'm not that old."

Once we were in the apartment, she helped me put things away. When we were done she said that she had run into President Chapman earlier, and he told her I had joined the seminary.

"Caleb," she said, "don't you think that's a little drastic?"

I agreed that it was a large step to take, but assured her that there would be no conflict with my work at the college. She said that the two occupations were like trying to mix oil and water, that they don't go together.

I said, "You attend church."

She said, "Yes, I believe in God, but my field of study is philosophy, not theoretical physics. You're supposed to have concrete proof before you believe in something. Do you have that proof?"

I answered I did not, but I couldn't get the proof by only working in the lab either, nor could I disprove it, so I had to keep an open mind until it could be disproved.

All she said was, "Touché."

I said, "Why not look at this as a hobby?"

"A hobby," she said with skepticism. "just as your job needs you to believe in your work, the seminary will want your undivided attention. Do you know what they will expect from you?"

I said, "Not exactly, but I'm ready to take on this challenge."

"Well remember, I expect results from your work, big result."

I said that remembering should be no problem. "I didn't tell you yet, but I have an eidetic memory."

"You do," she said with great surprise. "how is it then I have never heard of you before?"

I told her that I didn't normally tell anyone because people always want me to say something that would be earth-shattering. "Sometimes, I have been made to feel like a circus sideshow, a freak. So it's not something I normally share with people, and I would appreciate it if you would keep my secret."

She apologized for prying and said my secret was safe with her. Then she said, "What did you have for dinner on June 1, 2004?"

I said, "See, now I'm the circus freak."

She said, "Relax, I was just kidding."

There was a moment of awkward silence, and then I said, "A Cornish hen, stuffed with rice pilaf and blanched carrots. For dessert, I had a slice of apple pie and coffee."

She asked if I was pulling her leg. Again slang, but I knew what she meant.

I said, "You wanted to know if I was telling the truth."

All she could muster was, "Simply amazing."

26

When Pam got off work, she came over to help, as she would for what would become many months.

That night, Pam and I went over the book of Joshua. This book starts with the death of Moses, and the commissioning of Joshua by God as the successor of Moses.

Pam began telling me that at that time, the Lord also told Joshua that, just as he had promised Moses all the land that he put his foot on, Joshua would also receive the lands he trod upon.

It tells of the Israelites' preparations to enter Canaan by crossing the Jordan River. Through the Lord's mighty power, the waters of the Jordan were piled up on the north, and the waters flowing to the Sea of Arabah, or the Salt Sea, were also stopped. The entire Israel nation crossed the river, directly across from Jordan. Not one man's sandals became wet.

The Lord commanded Joshua to select twelve men, and to pick up twelve stones from the Ark of the Covenant. Then the Lord said that these stones were to serve as a memorial to the twelve tribes of Israel forever.

The twelve tribes surrounded the heavily fortified walls of Canaan. Then Joshua circumcised those who had not yet been circumcised.

On the fourteenth day of camping at the place they named Gilgal, they held Passover. They had a great feast, and by morning there was no manna left. They would be eating Canaan's food the next year.

I stopped Pam when she got to this part of the story and said, "They seem like such violent people, what happened to love, compassion, and peace?"

"You must understand Caleb, the Israelites were God's chosen people, and this was the land that the Lord had promised them."

"I'm sorry Pam, I don't get it. If God had decreed this land for the Israelites, why did he make them wander the desert for forty years, and then make them battle to take it over?"

Pam simply said, "Anything worth having is worth waiting for, and if you have things handed to you on a silver platter, you'll be less appreciative of whatever it is, even if it's a country."

"Okay, I understand. It kept them from becoming complacent, and gave them a sense of accomplishment."

"Yes, it's human nature to value something that you earn, rather than something that falls into your lap, and for them, the land was sacred."

Pam was right. Things that you earn or create with your own two hands, are held special by that person. These things remind you of your achievements. Then Pam asked if we could continue, I said, "Yes, I understand."

Pam continued the story. Joshua had ordered his troops to march around the fortified Canaan walls while seven priests blew seven trumpets. They did this once each day for six days in a row. On the seventh day, they did this march seven times. At the end of the seventh time around the structure, Joshua commanded the priests to blow their trumpets, and his troops to shout, for the Lord had given them the city.

They faithfully carried out Joshua's order, and the walls of the mighty fortress gave way. The Israelites ran through the opening and killed all, including animals, except the prostitute Rahab and those in her house, fore she had hid their spies.

Joshua's men laid waste to the entire town, and seized all the precious metals for they were sacred to the Lord, and would go into the treasury. When they had finished all this, they burned what was left of the city.

"Wait," I interjected. "They wandered the desert for forty years, then they conquered this vast city and demolish it? Why?" I asked. "The city was, how shall I say this, contaminated by paganism. Joshua pronounced the land where the city had stood to be cursed for the one who tried to build there again."

I protested, "They took all the precious metals. Some of that must have been images of pagan gods, don't you think?"

"No, I don't think that, I *know* there had to be a lot of false idols, but they would be melted and turned into currency without the idolatry."

I said, "That cleansed the metal of its stigma of once being a false idol?"

"The best I can tell you is the idols were destroyed."

"Now, may I continue," Pam asked.

"Please do," I said.

Some of Joshua's men had kept some of the plunder, and this angered the Lord. Then word came that the Ai were coming. Joshua sent troops to confront them, and they were beaten badly. Joshua was very distraught and threw himself to the ground.

Then the Lord told him of the betrayal, and that through a process he would have Joshua ferret out the guilty party, and they would burn in a fire with all their possessions. After that, Joshua divided the land between the twelve tribes.

Then Joshua sent the twelve tribes to their lands and he died.

"That's it," Pam said, "that's the end of the book of Joshua."

I said, "That's it, he just died? It seems a bit of an anticlimactic ending don't you think?"

"You have to keep in prospective that quite a bit of the Bible was written several centuries after the event; from stories passed down through the ages."

I responded that a scientific mind wouldn't respect that type of depiction.

She asked, "What about your scientific mind?"

"Well, it's a little hard to swallow I must admit, but there is too much hard evidence to just disregard the whole book. No, I believe that it took place as the good book says. After all, I have to keep an open mind and accept things on faith."

Pam smiled at me and said, "Maybe there is hope for you after all."

We were finished for the night. I asked Pam if she would like a bowl of ice cream. She said that would be nice.

As I was dishing it up, I asked Pam, "With all the help your giving me, I feel I should be paying you. You know I have no spare time, which must mean that you don't either." I turned around with the ice cream to see a big smile on Pam's face.

She said, "You dope, I'm not doing this for you per se. First, this is God's work, and I'm a servant of our Lord. Besides that, I couldn't live with myself if I didn't do everything to prevent the total loss of religion."

"So I'm running a close third?" I joked.

She laughed and said, "Since God has made you his emissary, my main mission is to prepare you for your journey through life with the Lord. Keeping the word alive is something I take very seriously. It's not all about you." She laughed.

As we sat there and ate our ice cream, I thought how much Pam was beginning to feel comfortable to be around. What was I thinking though? Pam was like my teacher. Without her, it would take me a longer time to learn what needed to be learned, to complete God's plan.

We talked about the little things in life for the rest of the night.

About midnight, Pam said, "I have to go home. It's late, and if people see me leaving your apartment night after night, they might get the wrong idea."

I said, "What would those dirty-minded people be thinking?" She chuckled and gave me a little kiss on the cheek, then she was out the door, and once again, I was alone with my thoughts.

After she was gone, I couldn't think of anything else. I was becoming attracted to Pam, about that I was certain. What was I going to do? If we formed a real relationship, I couldn't take her with me to the future; it might be too dangerous. No, I had to keep my feelings to myself.

Again, sleep did not come easy to me. I couldn't get Pam off my mind. Not only did we have a lot in common, she was dedicated to the mission that God had put before me. Pam was a good woman, a godly woman.

I would have to put those thoughts out of my mind though; I already had college and the seminary to contend with. When you add those two engagements with the time I would spend with Pam at night, well, there wasn't enough time for a fourth engagement.

I prepared myself for bed. I knelt next to my bed and prayed. "Holy Father, I call upon your vast wisdom tonight. I am confused about my relationship with Pam. I do understand her desire to help me with the task you have laid upon my heart, but I am torn. I can't see how I could do all I need to do, and have time to give Pam the attention she deserves in a relationship.

I am changing my life so much, that my head is spinning. I am not unsure of the task you have put forth to me. It's just these feelings for Pam are very hard to ignore. Lord, I am still on point for my impending future, but if you could give me some kind of sign, I would appreciate it. I feel selfish for asking something about my personal life, but if this wasn't on my mind, I think I could increase my comprehension of your word. All the glories of the world are for you Lord. In your name, amen."

I laid my head on the pillow, but tossed and turned for what seemed a long time. At some point I started to doze off, but was startled awake by the voice in my head. It said simply, "Things take time." I said aloud, "Lord, is that you?" I waited a moment, but no answer came. I wondered if this was a reference to Pam. Although it didn't seem to answer my prayer, at least it was something.

27

The rest of the week was fairly uneventful, and it was finally Sunday morning. Pam picked me up early and we went to, where else, the Pancake House. We gave praise for the food, then ate and had lively conversation. Pam picked me up a little earlier than she had in the past. It gave us enough time to have an extra cup of coffee and chat. We didn't talk about my work, or hers; it was like it was a normal conversation for a change.

We finished and headed to the church. When we got out of the car, we walked next to each other. Suddenly she put her arm around mine as if we were a couple. I thought, "Is this what the voice meant?" I looked at her arm when she did this. She noticed me looking, and asked if it was all right for her to hold my arm. I patted her hand and replied, "Perfectly all right." We smiled at each other, it was as if we had been doing so forever.

Inside, we greeted people as we went. We came to the same row of pews that we sat in, the previous week. Pam said, "I like to sit here."

Pointing to some other pews, and said, "I was hoping we could sit over here."

Pam looked a little disappointed but said, "If that's what you want, okay."

I chuckled and said, "Got you."

She said, "Fine, you sit over there, and I'll sit where I want." It was cute, she said it with her nose in the air a little.

Then we both laughed and sat where Pam wanted. Once we were seated we both laughed for a while. We both had big smiles the rest of the service.

Yes there was a spark between us, but neither of us mentioned it. I think we both knew we needed to focus on our mission for the Lord.

The praise group finished their songs, and Pastor Lind went to the podium.

"Good morning," he said. The congregation reflected the welcome. Pastor Lind said, "Today, we're going to talk about unyielding faith. We are going to talk about Noah and the great flood. Please turn to Genesis 7:1."

I was fairly excited because I had read this material; for once I wouldn't feel lost. We all opened our Bibles to the chapter and verse that Pastor Lind had directed us to, and he began.

He talked of how Noah was a righteous man, and lived his life in accordance with God's laws.

———

However, the Lord was unhappy with man on the whole. He found them to be corrupt and violent.

He told Noah that he was going to destroy man, and the earth. He commanded Noah to build an ark. God told Noah the dimensions, the interior layout for the ark, what animals would be placed where, and on what level to house them.

The Lord said he would spare Noah, his family, and a male and female of every animal to repopulate the earth, after he had cleansed it with the floodwaters.

Noah built the ark as God had commanded, all the while the sinful people made fun of him. Upon completion of the ark, God put it on the minds of the animals he had chosen, and they peacefully entered the ark side by side, the lamb as well as the lion, without incident. There were to be two of every kind of unclean animals, male and female, and seven pair of every kind of clean animal, as well as seven pair of every kind of bird, also male and female, so when the earth was cleansed it could be repopulated.

God then commanded Noah and his family to gather every kind of food there was to feed Noah, his family, and also all the beast on the ark.

When this was done God spoke to Noah.

"Seven days from now I will send rain on the earth for forty days and forty nights, and I will wipe from the face of the earth every living creature I have made. And Noah did everything the Lord commanded him" (Genesis 7:4–5, NIV). On the seventh day when the rains came, Noah's family and all the animals were shut in the ark. All the sinners who had scoffed at Noah for building the ark, were now banging, clawing, and pleading to be let in, but God would not yield.

After the floodwaters receded, God made the ark to rest on solid ground, and the door opened. The animals peacefully left the ark. Noah, through unyielding faith, had completed what the Lord had commanded.

"To be scoffed at all the time while building the ark," Pastor Lind said, "to be constantly ridiculed and still follow the righteous path—that takes faith. That takes commitment. Are you committed? Are you following the righteous path? Is your faith unwavering?"

I got caught up in the moment and said aloud, "Yes!" The pastor said. "Well amen Brother Caleb. We need more enthusiasm like that." The whole congregation laughed a little. I looked at Pam and she was smiling, not the embarrassed type of smile, but a smile of approval.

Then the pastor said, "Let's pray." With that the sermon was over.

As we started to leave, I was once again mugged by several people, this time though, they were telling me they wished they had the conviction to shout out like that. I simply asked why they didn't, and was answered with several, "I don't knows," accompanied by blank looks of wonderment.

Pastor Lind caught up to me. He had a big smile on his face. "I heard your answers to their questions. Did they come from your scientific, logical brain, or did God put it on your heart to say that?"

"I really don't know, it was a rather impulsive thing for me to do. I'd like to think it came from our Lord."

Then Mary appeared and I became a little nervous. She addressed Pastor Lind first. "Well, Pastor, that was quite an arousing service you gave today."

As she said it, she slowly turned her head toward me. I felt I was becoming a little flush.

Just then, Pam was able to break away from the people she was talking to, and as she had when we walked into church, she put her arm around mine and said, "Mary, wasn't it refreshing to hear Caleb commit to the Lord aloud, and in front of the whole congregation?"

She smiled and said, "I only hope he's half that enthusiastic with his job."

I assured Mary that I would be jumping into the job with both feet.

She replied that she wouldn't have hired me if she didn't think I was right for the job.

I thought if she was going to make me feel uncomfortable, all be it in good fun, I would take the chance to give her a little taste of her own medicine. I said, "I thought Dr. Baker hired me?"

All Mary said was, "Ouch!"

Then she said, "I'm going to get some lunch with the Saunders. Would you two like to join us?"

I looked at Pam. She had a smile on her face, which I took for a yes, and how could I say no to my new boss? We went to the Pancake House. The conversation was lively, and sometimes the subject would be about current events, which I knew next to nothing about, so I said nothing; I only chuckled when everyone else did.

Then a near disaster, Mary said to Bill Saunders, "Bill, you went to MIT too, didn't you?"

He said, "Only for one year, then I transferred to Stanford. It cost so much to go to MIT. I didn't have a full-ride scholarship."

I said, "Yes, I was lucky to get a full-ride scholarship. Still, I had to flip burgers for a little extra money." I felt I had covered myself pretty well.

When we said our good-byes, we walked to our cars. As Pam was driving away she said, "Flipping burgers, where did that come from?"

"You, you gave the list of slang sayings, and their meaning. Well, I did a good job there didn't I?"

"Yes you did."

"I was able to glean much from that source. I was worried when Mary said Bill had gone to MIT. I thought I would be found out."

Pam said she was a little worried too.

I said, "At some point, I expect you'll want me to meet your parents."

Pam said nothing, she had tears welling up in her eyes, and then she said her parents had been killed in a car wreck three years ago.

I immediately apologized, and she said there was no need to, adding I didn't know. We sat in silence for a second, then I told her that I would never hurt her on purpose. She took hold of my hand, and through the tears managed a smile, then she said, "I know, you have too much class to do something like that."

We arrived at my apartment and she was still holding my hand. I asked her if she would like to have some coffee.

She smiled and said, "Of course, I have to fix my face though." She didn't wear very much makeup. She had no need to; she was very attractive without it.

We walked the three flights of stairs to my apartment. We talked about all sorts of things for so long, that we drank a pot of coffee.

Finally she said, "I should go home, it's getting late."

I said, "Yes, tomorrow will be a busy day."

She threw her arms around my neck and said, "I'm glad you time traveled to our time, Caleb."

Then she gave me a peck on the cheek, and she was gone.

28

That Monday, Pam came over to the apartment after she got off work. It had been such a hectic week, I was still trying to catch my breath so to speak. Between attending the seminary, and my duties at the college, I was becoming somewhat ragged. This was the first time in my life that I felt as if I were actually burning the candle at both ends.

When I had worked long hours in the past, I was the one in charge. If I thought it's enough, I would say to myself, "Time to get some sleep." When I would awake the following morning, I didn't use an alarm clock, I slept as long as I wished. Now I had to be up by six o'clock, Monday through Friday, no matter how I felt, and I felt tired that morning.

When Pam arrived that night I expressed how I felt, her response was to grab my cheeks with her hands and squish my face, shaking it a little while saying mockingly, "Oh, you poor little baby. Do you need a nap?" When she let go of my face I tried to be funny, sucking my cheeks in to make my face look as if she had made it look permanently squished. She laughed at this and threw her arms around my neck, and I also began to laugh.

As our laughter began to subside, I unconsciously found myself putting my arms around her waist.

As I have said, I have never been a ladies' man before, but that didn't mean I was without any feelings. At that moment, I felt as if I were in some sort of trance. We just stared at each other for a moment. It felt so right, it felt natural, it felt in a way somewhat innocent.

We were staring at each other for what seemed like an eternity, and then I did something that for me was quite impetuous. I leaned in and kissed her, not a friendly little peck on the cheek either. This was a kiss of passion; she didn't resist either. The kiss lasted but a moment.

When I released her, I began to apologize for my overt action, but barely got a word out before she said, "Shut up." Then she threw her arms around my neck and began kissing me in return. We kissed for a moment—or was it an eternity?—Then I finally found the strength to break away from her.

She asked why I had pushed her back.

I told her that there was only so much I could take. I added an apology for being so forward.

She said, "Are you that obtuse?"

I asked her what she was getting at.

She replied, "Caleb, what type of person would take everything you have told me since we have met, and not run away thinking you are crazy?"

I replied, "I thought you were interested in the whole concept of traveling through time to save religion."

She said, "Of course that is something I am looking forward to, but I won't know about that until I get to know you a little better." She continued, reminding me about the odd behavior I had exhibited when we had first met, before she knew the whole story.

I acknowledged that I had believed she was just being nice, "Helping a nerd," I said cautiously, not knowing if I had used the slang right. Then I asked why she had listed it as the first slang term, on the paper of slang terms she had given me?

She said that it was because, "You are a nerd." then added, as she put her arms around my neck, "You're lucky though, I like nerds." Then she said, "One nerd in particular."

I joked, asking her who that would be. She laughingly told me that for a nerd, I was at least fast at catching on and had a sense of humor, and then we kissed again.

Once more, I pushed her back, telling her that I needed some moderation, because although I am a nerd, I'm still a man, and I respected her too much to push boundaries.

She said she understood, and that she wouldn't bother me anymore. Then she turned, and took two steps toward the couch before I grabbed her arm, spun her around, and said "Forget that," and kissed her again.

When we stopped this time, we looked into each others' eyes, and she told me she had been waiting for this moment since we had first met.

She then said, "Why don't we blow off learning about anything, or writing anything tonight? Let's go see a movie. Let's have a you-and-me night."

"Blowing of" was a new term for me, but I needed no explanation for it. I told her I would like nothing better, but that I would prefer to work, saying I had too much to get done, and so little time to accomplish all that would be needed, to do the work of I Am.

She said, "If you need to have a little break, why don't we go home?"

I replied that I was home. She said she had meant my home in the future, the one I had come from. She added that we could take a couple of days off and rest up.

I agreed, it would be nice to rest for a day or two. I looked at her and said with affirmation, that I did feel a need to be pampered for a day or two.

She slouched her shoulders, and simply let me know she was flabbergasted.

I let her go on for a moment, then said, "Gotcha."

She gave me a soft punch in the arm, and I began to laugh. Then she joined in, and we both laughed for a short while.

Then she said, "Well, let's go to your time."

I agreed and told her, "You know what we have to do before we go?" She was stumped.

I said, "To the grocery store for supplies."

She said, "Of course, what shall we get for everyone to eat?"

I said, "My strawberries should be ripe by now. For breakfast, we should have pancakes, bacon, and coffee, as big a can of coffee as we can find, and a can opener."

I explained to Pam that in my time, every thing was packaged in irradiated-vacuum-packed plastic, that there were no can openers. "It's a little strange having to remember something so little, that can make such a vast difference."

"For dinner, let's get some big juicy steaks, potatoes, and a green salad."

Pam said her mouth was beginning to water already. We got in her car, and off to the supermarket.

While there, we separated to make shopping faster, and played a little game of hide and seek while we shopped.

True love can turn even the most mature man into a little boy.

I had clothes to change into in my time, but Pam needed to get a few changes for the trip. Once we arrived at her house, she told me that she had a little surprise for Donna. She told me to wait in the car, and that she would be faster by herself.

She returned with a paper sack filled with cloths, and we drove to the cave. Once there, we stowed what we had brought with us, and I set the controls so we would arrive at three o'clock. Since we were not expected, we wanted to arrive before Donna started to cook dinner.

I looked at Pam and asked if she was ready? She nodded affirmatively, and I pushed the Enter button. We heard the whirring noise once more, and the black veil enveloped us again, and we were whisked away to the future.

29

When we emerged from the cave, it was a warm sunny day. We had thought ahead and bought cloth grocery bags. The last time we had brought food back, we made the mistake of using paper sacks, and by the time we reached the house, the condensation from the frozen and refrigerated foods had nearly disintegrated the sacks.

When we arrived at the house, I asked Pam to help me play a little joke on Donna. I said we would knock on the door, and hide behind a bush next to it. I explained we were not expected, so she wouldn't know it's us. I realized afterward that this was a bit sophomoric, but after Pam and I had revealed our true feelings about ourselves to each other, I felt, well, a little giddy.

Pam was more than willing to go along with the prank though. We put the groceries on the ground behind the bush, and I told Pam to crouch down and hide. I knocked on the door, then ran back to hide with her.

A moment later the door opened, but Donna said nothing. We played out our role though, and waited. Donna didn't say, "Who's there?" or even stick her head out the door to look around. The door was just left open. This of course confused Pam and I until we heard Donna say from inside the house, "It is a nice day to let some fresh air in, but Dr. Bronson and Pam, aren't you two more mature than to play a children's game of hide and seek in the bushes?"

For a moment we looked at each other in disbelief, then shyly stood up and carried our bags into the house. Donna was just inside the house, holding the door open with a sly smile on her face.

I was stumped, I needed to know how she knew, so I asked.

She replied, "Doctor, no one comes to visit except the other doctors, and they are all at work this time of day. Also, they would have remained at the door, like the grownups they are."

I said, "My dear woman, you know that Pam and I are mature people."

"Yes," she said sarcastically, "I could tell by the way that you two hid behind the bushes."

I said, "How did you know we were hiding behind the bush? You never stuck your head out the door."

She simple pointed to the door, or so I thought at first. Then I saw it, there was a security viewing screen mounted on the wall behind the door.

Pam laughed at me and said, "Well Doctor, you may have an eidetic memory, but your powers of observation could use a little improvement."

Now Donna was laughing as well, and their laughter became more and more uncontrollable. Eventually, I became infected by their joy, and I began to laugh also. This was not my usual demeanor, however once I started, I found it, well, intoxicating.

I realized at that moment that I suddenly felt a sort of relief, like the daunting tasks that God had put before me had vanished—not that they were gone, but as if they didn't matter at that moment.

When I realized that it was all right, that I could have this release, I broke down and began to weep.

When Pam and Donna noticed that I was sobbing, they stopped laughing to find out why I was crying.

"What's wrong Caleb?" Pam inquired.

"Nothing," I replied. "I feel as if I have just been under so much pressure as of late, and only realized it when I began to laugh. You need not concern yourselves with this outburst. I really needed a release. Thank you Donna for the prank. I may have burst had you not done that."

She said, "Your welcome Doctor." Then she added, "You see Pam, I told you I could make him cry."

We all broke down laughing and hugging, until Donna said, "Dinner wouldn't cook itself."

So we composed ourselves, and while Pam and Donna began putting groceries away, I excused myself for a much needed nap. I asked Pam to wake me when the gang arrived, and went to my room. I think I fell asleep before my head hit the pillow.

It was a little after six o'clock before Pam knocked on my door. She opened it, came in, then sat beside me on the bed. She ran her fingers through my hair, bent over, kissed me on my forehead, then asked, "How do you feel? Did you get enough sleep?"

Even though I was still quite groggy, I managed to respond that I still felt tired, but better than I had when we arrived.

Pam asked if I wanted to sleep some more, or if I wanted to get up?

I said if I didn't get up now, I would miss out on the steaks that she and Donna cooked. I added that they smelled delicious, and I wasn't about to miss out on this meal.

This would be our modus operandi on all our trips forward, to my time. Bring a large amount of groceries, and have a feast with our friends from my time. I think Pam enjoyed seeing the smiles on their faces when they dug into the feast. That would be our trademark for the future.

After dinner, while Pam and Donna cleaned the dishes, the gang and I sat around the table. I began to tell them about the last week in the past.

I began by telling them about the vivid dreams I had. They set there in stunned silence as I spun the tale. I told them of how I flew like a bird. How I landing on the entryway to the tabernacle, of having my feet washed by the ghostly figure, and of my audience with the Lord in the Holy of Holies.

I told them of how in the morning when Pam woke me from my trance, how exhausted and drenched I was.

Then I told them of the second dream. I told them how this time, I had landed beside a lake. Then I told them of Jesus walking up to me, and how I could not look upon him directly, but could only gaze upon his reflection. When I described how he had morphed into several different faces and races, they were astonished.

Jason asked if I was sure I was experiencing these visitations, or if I was just having a vivid dream?

I assured them that as far as I was concerned, they were very real, and asked how they could explain how I forgot that I had read the book of Genesis, and how in the world I got this shock of white hair?

They agreed that it was odd that I forgot something. They could not think of a time when this had happened to me. They were sure they would have remembered such a thing. Everyone was also at a loss to explain my hair irregularity.

Then I postulated a theory that God made me forget, as a way of letting me know that it was real, and not a dream, and of course, that the hair was a physical reminder. Everything we came up with was just a theory though.

I also told them about my outburst in the middle of the sermon, shouting out the word *yes* to his rhetorical question, and the ensuing barrage of people that mobbed me as I left the church. Then I told of the lunch with Bill Saunders, which was nearly a disaster in front of President Johnson.

When I told them that Bill had also gone to MIT, they all gasped, knowing how easily it could have gone bad. I told them, "Fortunately, he only went there one year, so I was able to talk my way around the situation."

The rest of the time we were there was spent having Bible study, eating, talking about people we knew, and our interaction with them. We talked about my assimilation into the day's society. We also drank pot after pot of coffee.

30

Our vacation was over, it was time for Pam and I to go back to the twenty-first century. I was not only able to catch up on the work that I needed to; I was also able to get some much needed rest.

Time travel was becoming mundane, even for Pam. Nevertheless, we made our weekly visits to inform the gang on how things were going.

Nothing of much to report on happened for some time. Pam and I made our weekly trips back, or should I say forward, to the time I came from. It really was like having a vacation every week. We always had a feast for the gang when we returned.

I would always report on how Dr. Baker was coming with his work. He was having some difficulty though, with a breakthrough in a theory of a mechanism that would contribute to our understanding of the origins of mass of subatomic particles.

His dilemma was somewhat ironic though. To prove his theory, he needed to use a Large Hadron Collider (LHC).

I so wanted to say, "Let's just go to the cave and do the experiment. I've got a collider hidden there." Of course I couldn't, Dr. Baker would have been so dumbfounded by my collider he probably wouldn't have been able to carry out his experiment.

Dr. Baker had one big problem though. He had made a critical math error. He had inserted a less than sign where a more than sign was needed. The mistake was near the end of the equation, and poor Dr. Baker couldn't see it. I walked by that board an untold amount of times. I so wanted to show Dr. Baker the mistake he had made. However, I couldn't do that. It would be ethically wrong for me to do so.

I had told the gang of the mistake, and they all agreed that I needed to stay out of it, but said that they did have the greatest empathy for the doctor.

A few weeks after I told them about Dr. Baker's mistake, we were visiting the gang when Dr. Kinsey showed me the paper that would eventually be written by François Englert from the Universite Libre de Bruxelles, Brussels Belgium, and Peter Higgs from the University of Edinburgh, Edinburgh,

United Kingdom, and proven in 2013. Dr. Kinsey said, "They received the Nobel Prize that year for their theory. They did note a contribution from a Dr. Joe Baker."

I asked the gang, "Well, what do you think about me steering Dr. Baker in the right direction now?"

"What do you mean?" Mike asked.

"I'll just drop their names around Dr. Baker and tell him I believe they might be able to help him."

When Pam and I got back, I did just that. In about two weeks they got back to Dr. Baker and told him they had found his mistake. He was heartbroken when they told him how simple his mistake was. They both assured him that these things happen, and that he would get mentioned in their paper.

This did little to comfort Joe though. He wanted the Nobel for himself. He had worked a long time for basically a footnote. I understood how he felt, but there was nothing that could be done.

I tried to pump him up, as the slang term goes, but to be that close and lose was heart wrenching.

I said, "Well at least you have one Nobel and a contribution to another, I have neither."

When I got home that night, Pam was already there. I had long ago given her a key to the apartment, and people had also long ago figured out, that Pam and I were a couple. We tried to hide our feelings toward each other, but it was too obvious to everyone else.

One day after the church service was over, and Pam and I were in the lobby talking to people, Pastor Lind came over to us and just blurted out, "Well Caleb, when are you going to make an honest woman out of Pam?"

I was caught off guard by the comment because of the slang. I said, "Why would you think Pam isn't an honest woman?"

Before he could answer, Pam stepped in and said, "We've been talking about getting married, but Caleb is dragging his feet."

I believe that my face at that moment, must have turned a very deep shade of red. I could only stammer.

Pastor Lind said, "You better get busy Caleb, Pam might lose interest in you, and some other guy may come around and sweep her right off her feet." He put his arm around Pam's shoulder and said, "You know, I'm single Pam, what do you say?"

She laughed and said, "Well Pastor, that's a very tempting offer, but I think I'll give Caleb one more chance."

They both were laughing at my expenses. I felt like I was being squeezed, and it was very uncomfortable.

Pam laughed so hard once we got in the car, I finally asked if she would like me to drive. She laughed even harder at this, pointing out that I couldn't drive, and adding that I just wanted to drive so I could have an accident and shut her up.

I tried to keep a straight face, but her laughter was so intoxicating that I became infected with it, and it soon took me over.

Since meeting Pam, my sense of humor seemed to have grown. I wasn't sure if it was because people from her time had a better sense of humor or was it because she made me so happy. I voted for the latter.

The laughter had died down by the time we arrived at my apartment. Once inside, Pam heated some milk and made hot chocolate. We relaxed while we watched a football game. Football didn't exist in my time. It wasn't soccer, but it would have to do.

That Sunday we did nothing all day except talk, watch a little television, and play Scrabble. Pam wouldn't allow me to use words that had come into use after 2010. I missed out on several words because of this, but it was just a game, and it did seem fair.

It was getting late, and Pam said she was tired. I walked her to her car, gave her a kiss, and she drove off.

We never talked about marriage the entire evening, but I had thought about it from time to time that night.

After she left, I couldn't get the thought off my mind. I lay on my bed for some time thinking about the subject. I finally came to the conclusion that Pastor Lind was right. It was time to make an honest woman out of Pam.

The next day after college and the seminary let out, I walked to a jewelry store that I passed every day on my way home. I don't think I had ever even looked through the window. That day though, I went inside.

I looked at several different rings, and I could afford most of them. I don't know if it was me thinking to myself, or if God was planting the thought in my head, but it came to me to just buy a simple band of gold for the both of us. After all, the never-ending circle of life is what the ring symbolizes, and I never wanted the circle to be broken.

It was winter, December 15 to be exact. The college and the seminary would soon be going on Renew, or Christmas holiday as this time period called it.

Pam had saved all her vacation time since meeting me. She had four weeks coming, and unbeknownst to me, she had requested all four weeks off during the holiday.

This would have been an imposition for a lot of businesses, considering the time of year, but the library is not a very busy place during the holidays.

Her boss inquired as to why she wanted so much time off at once. She simply replied that she was getting married.

He said, "Congratulations! It's about time, and when are you and Caleb going to tie the knot?"

Her reply stunned her boss a little. She said with a smile, "As soon as I tell him." Then she turned and said, "Happy holidays!" over her shoulder as she left.

That evening, as Pam and I sat in my kitchen, we discussed the fact that I had learned enough about the Bible that, while I could not be properly ordained, I knew enough to spread the word.

Pam said, "We should go after the holidays are over."

I asked, "Where do you think you're going?"

She said, "To the future with you, to reinstate religion. What do you think I meant?"

I said, "That is out of the question. The future could be fraught with unknown dangers. Besides, if we were to go away together, it would be awkward since we're not married."

Pam came back with, "Well let's get married then."

I asked, "Are you proposing to me?"

She said, "Well I can't wait for you to propose to me. I don't think that will ever happen. So yes, I'm proposing to you."

I said, "I can't accept your proposal." Then I got on one knee, reached into my pocket, pulled out the box of rings and opened it.

I then said, "Pam Brown, you have trusted me when you had no reason to do so. You know my biggest secrets. You have been faithful to me and the Lord. When I look in your eyes, I see a gentleness I have never known, a love that is true. I have loved you for a long time, but have only allowed those feelings to surface as of late. I love you Pam, and cannot imagine a life without you. You have been my center, my rock. Life without you would just be an existence. Pam, will you do me the honor of marrying me?"

I took the ring in one hand, and her left hand in the other, and then I slipped the ring on her finger.

I started to apologize for the ring being so frugal, but she stopped me in midsentence, telling me it was perfect, and all she would ever want. Then she said, "Yes, I would be proud to be Mrs. Dr. Caleb Bronson."

Then she told me about the conversation she had with her boss earlier in the day. I have to admit I was floored. How did we come to the same conclusion on the same day? The Lord does work in mysterious ways.

I said, "Now, even more than before, I can't allow you to come with me."

The ensuing discussion lasted for some time. I tried to tell her that she would be just like I was when I arrived in this time. She countered that, although it was awkward for me in the beginning, I was able to adapt.

I countered, "Besides that, in the future, communications won't be very good." I continued trying to reason with her, telling her there were raiders in that time. She knew what they were, but said that this was a Holy mission, ordained by God himself, if misfortune was to befall her, then it would also be God s' will, and who were we to go against the will of God?

She asked, "Who will minister to the women, you? You, by your own admission don't do well with them. What if one comes to you with a female problem, what will you do? Will you just sit them down and explain how their bodies function? No, you will need me for those situations."

Then she dropped the big bomb, she said if she didn't go, there wasn't going to be any wedding.

I started to protest, but she cut me short, saying, "If I stay, how often will I get to see you? My guess is not very often. If you die, how will I bury you? You'll be two-hundred years in the future. I won't have a time machine to go to the future to bury you." Then she added, "Why do you think I was the first person you met when you arrived here? I think it was God's plan all along."

We had been giving each other reason after reason, for her staying or going. When she gave her last rebuttal, I could argue no more.

That was that, it was settled. We would get married, and we would both carry the word forward. Instead of one emissary for God, there would be two.

31

Only a few people had found out about Pam and my engagement. We wanted to keep it quiet until we went to church.

That Sunday at church, we told Pastor Lind and Mary about the engagement before the service started.

During the service, I noticed that there was a buzz going around the church. I mentioned this to Pam, and she said she believed they were talking about our engagement.

When the praise group finished their set, Pastor Lind got up, but before he started his sermon he said, "Well, for those of you who have heard the rumor, and for the few who have not, I'd like to let you all know that Miss Pam Brown, has consented to become Mrs. Dr. Caleb Bronson." He then said, "Why don't you two stand up and be recognized."

A raucous applause came from the congregation.

I resisted at first, but Pam pulled on my arm when she stood up so I followed her. As we stood there, everyone applauded, those who were close shook our hands and gave Pam congratulatory hugs.

This went on for a few minutes when Pastor Lind had to wrest control of the congregation as I had done with the gang in my time.

We sat down and Pastor Lind began. "I had something else to speak about today, but this is a special day. Today, two from our congregation have promised themselves to each other. This union is not to be taken lightly.

This union is a promise that they both will enter into, with full knowledge of its commitment to each other. A commitment they will enter into for life."

He looked over at us and said, "Are you scared yet Caleb?" Everyone laughed; Pam and I just sat there and smiled.

He continued to tell about how marriage is a covenant not to be entered lightly. "The bond between a man and a woman is something that should never be broken. The woman should be obedient to the man. However, the man should discus decisions with the woman. They should make decisions together. A marriage is not meant to be a one-sided thing. It should be viewed as a business partnership.

"If you had a business partner, you wouldn't make a decision without first discussing it with your partner. If you did, you probably wouldn't have a partner for long would you?

"That's the best advice I can give a couple, don't lie, don't hide, and be faithful to each other. Respect each other, be open and honest with each other. These are qualities that constitute a lasting union"

After the service was over, I knew we would be besieged by well-wishers, and others wanting to know about our impending nuptials. Not being a fan of crowds, I tried to persuade Pam to leave immediately, but she would have none of that. She said, "You don't understand tradition. From the proposal to the wedding, it's all about the bride. In case you have forgotten, that's me, and these people only want to wish us well."

So we received congratulations, and best-of-luck wishes from everyone that came by. The Saunders, Dr. Johnson, and Pastor Lind waited until the crowed thinned out a little before they approached us.

Dr. Johnson spoke first, "Well Caleb, I wondered how long you were going to string this poor girl along."

Pam said, "I know, I was just about ready to throw in the towel."

I said, "Almost to the finish line and running out of gas. I thought I could get more mileage out of you than that." Everyone laughed.

Pastor Lind said, "I could see it in your eyes that first time you and Pam walked through the door."

Pam said, "You could see love in his eyes?"

"No," the Pastor said, "Fear." Again everyone laughed.

Pam told me later that she thought Pastor Lind was right about that, and he was.

At this point, Joy Saunders and President Johnson separated Pam from me. Then Pastor Lind and Bill Saunders had me to themselves.

Each group had their own, and separate questions about our plans for the future. We had both agreed that we would tell everyone, for now at least, things would stay as they were. Pam would work at the library, and I would stay at the college.

The women were giggling quite a bit, and then I heard Pam say in a raised voice, "Hawaii."

Then she said aloud again, "Caleb doesn't know it yet, but Hawaii is where we are going for our honeymoon."

Bill said, "Well, it looks as if you've been told."

Pastor Lind asked, "Have you set a date yet?"

I must have looked stunned. Bill and Pastor Lind both started laughing. Then Bill said, "Earth to Caleb, is anyone home? Pastor, I think Caleb just got his first taste of married life."

Pastor Lind said, "You have no idea what you've gotten yourself into, do you son?"

I answered with bewilderment that I suppose I didn't.

Bill patted me on the back, and with a smile said, "Nothing to worry about, it only get's worse from here on."

Kay said, "I heard that." Everyone laughed. Why was I the only one not in on the joke?

Bill said, "I'm hungry, let's go get some lunch, my treat."

Pastor Lind said, "Never look a gift horse in the mouth. Besides, that will give Bill and I time to make you feel more uncomfortable about you're impending nuptials."

Pam said, "I heard that Pastor, don't start stirring things up; stop making trouble."

"Now Pam," he said, "we're just trying to get Caleb ready for the road ahead."

She came back with, "It sounds like you're putting a lot of potholes in the road."

Pastor Lind said, "Not to worry Pam, we'll pave them over before we're done."

We all piled into our cars and went to the café that Pam, the others, and I, had went to the first time we had gone to church together.

When we got there, other people from the church were setting at several tables pulled together, making one big table. We sat with them, and the questions began to fly.

It was a surreal time. While we ate, Pam was controlling the conversation between herself and the women at the table. It was her day after all. I sat there and basically got bombarded with a montage of how life as I knew it was over. "Let the bad times roll," I said at one point. This led to an outburst of laughter that lasted for a good minute.

When Pastor Lind asked when he would be marrying us, Pam and I stared at each other in a moment of uncomfortable silence. Then at the same time, I said, "We haven't set a date," while Pam said, "Next Saturday."

There was another uncomfortable moment of awkward silence, and then Pastor Lind said, "Well, at least you have time before Saturday to come to some kind of compromise. I am going to marry you two though, right?"

On that we did agree, which made Pastor Lind smile, if only slightly. He then said somewhat shyly, "Just to let you know, I have Saturday open." With this said, everyone laughed.

Pam said, "Well, we really didn't discuss the date. I thought we could spend Christmas together in Hawaii."

Bill Saunders said, "How will you get tickets, Christmas is only ten days away?"

Pam reached into her purse and pulled out two tickets. "I bought them two months ago."

There was a moment of stunned silence, then Pam told me with a tear in her eye, "I told you Caleb, I knew from the moment we met."

Now the silence was even more deafening. No one spoke until, while still having my eyes locked on Pam's eyes, I said, "Pastor Lind, you are now booked for Saturday." With that, everyone at the table cheered.

While everyone congratulated us, our eyes didn't divert from each other's for a second. I knew at that moment that we had something more than love. What we had was ordained by God himself, and I think Pam knew it.

The women were all worried that we wouldn't be able to put a proper ceremony together in time.

Once again, Pam surprised everyone, including me. "Well, I may have bought the tickets two months ago, but I bought my dress four months ago. We can rent a tuxedo for you any time. I put invitations in the mail Thursday, and I swore the baker, the florist, the caterer, and the photographer to secrecy, under penalty of death of course."

Again there was stunned silence. I finally said, "You are simply amazing. You did all this by yourself. How much did it cost?"

She said, "I charged it all to you." With that, the most uproarious laughter of the whole lunch erupted, lasting for a long time, while I sat with my mouth open in disbelief.

Pastor Lind looked at me and joked, "Caleb, you've been married since you met Pam, and you're just now finding out?"

I said, "I guess so, it's been a wonderful year." Tears began to run down Pam's cheeks, and the rest of the women also began to cry.

Joy Sanders said, "That was one of the loveliest exchanges I've ever heard."

After everyone calmed down, the women started talking about plans for the impending nuptials. While the men and I just talked, Pam had everything under control, which was evident.

Pastor Lind leaned over to me and said, "Normally, I would insist that you two have couple's counseling for a while. However, Pam seems to be set on marrying you, and I've known her most of her life. She only makes good choices, and from what I know about you, I believe you two will do fine."

He then stood up, clanked his glass with his fork a few times, and said as he raised his glass, "A toast to Pam and Caleb. May your union be long and fruitful. May your children be strong and healthy, and may your love be as strong when you are old and gray as it is today. To Pam and Caleb and to love, may you both know happiness all your days."

When lunch was over, and everyone had said their good-byes, Pam and I got in her car and started to go to my apartment. When we got to the supermarket, I told Pam we needed to shop. She asked why. I told her we needed to invite the gang also. It was time to go to my time for a real feast.

32

We arrived back in my time and made our way to the house. Although in our time we weren't scheduled to return until Wednesday, but we wanted to give the gang the news.

Normally when we arrived, Donna was the only one there. However, when we walked through the door this time, Donna was not present. I thought this was odd and told my feelings to Pam. What if something happened to Donna?

I frantically started to search the house calling out for Donna. With Pam close behind, I opened the study door and had quite a scare when everyone shouted, "Surprise!"

I was really caught off guard. The gang surrounded Pam and I, congratulating us.

Pam had bought a bottle of champagne from 2010 and hid it in the cave the week before. She had told Jason where to locate the bottle. It had aged just over 450 years, and she had bought a very expensive and very highly ranked year.

The cave had been the perfect place to hide the champagne. It kept the bottle at a constant temperature and in the dark, as light destroys the flavor, and the bouquet.

Jason said he looked online for a similar bottle and found one for two and a-half pounds of gold. That was a very high amount.

My head was still spinning when Donna said, "Pam told me about your impending engagement, and she asked if I would arrange this little surprise for you two."

So I said, "I am the last to know that I would be getting married?"

Kim said, "I had it figured out that this would be the outcome months ago. At least I knew Pam was going to marry you, but you Caleb, I don't think you knew you were a hooked fish until you were landed."

That elicited a rousing round of laughter from everyone. I had to laugh also. It was true, I could not have been more oblivious.

As was usual, we ate our feast of the week, and the gang and I withdrew to the study to talk about what I had learned the week before. While Pam and Donna cleaned the dishes. When they were done, they came into the study, and we suspended our discussion. We opened the bottle of champagne' everyone was very impressed with the taste, and why not, it was well aged?

That night we talked mainly about the wedding plans and the honeymoon. I was as interested as the gang was, because this was also my first time hearing about them.

From everything she said, we were going to have a wonderful time. I was quite impressed at everything she was able to accomplish without me finding anything out.

The next day when we woke up I smelled the wonderful aroma of breakfast cooking. When I went downstairs I discovered Donna had made bacon, and a sort of pancake, cake. She had made this huge stack of pancakes and decorated them like they were an actual cake. She had wrote with icing, "Pam and Caleb, may your life be filled with joy and children."

I thanked her, but told her that my plans did not include a large number of children.

She said, "Did you let Pam know about your feelings, because I believe she feels different about the subject."

I dropped my head a little to avoid eye contact with her and said, "We only got engaged yesterday. We really hadn't discussed having children yet, much less how many to have."

Then Donna told me about the discussion Pam and she had the night before while fixing dinner. "Pam told me that she wanted to start a family right away, and that she wanted a large number of children also."

I was a little afraid to do so, but still I asked, "Did she give you a number?" I could feel the blood drain from my face as I asked her, but I wanted to hear the answer anyway.

Donna noticed my physical reaction to this information and asked if I was all right?

I told her I would be all right as I sat in a chair. She brought me a cup of coffee, and as she set it in front of me, Pam walked down the stairs and asked what we were talking about.

Before I could say anything, she saw the writing on the pancakes, and thanked Donna for such a marvelous surprise.

She then turned to me and asked, "Well Caleb, we have a lot to talk about before we get married. Have you thought about how many children to have yet?"

I took a sip of my coffee and told Donna how good it tasted, in a futile, childlike attempt to forestall the inevitable. I felt like I was in a bad dream and could not wakeup. Yes I did want children, but just not right away. However, I knew that Pam and I were already in our early thirties, so I knew that we needed to get started before we were too old to have them. Pam didn't have too many childbearing years left, and I had no desire to be raising children into my sixties.

I hadn't asked Pam her age as of yet, but I thought she was about thirty-two, which was also my age. Then it dawned on me, I had known Pam for a little over a year now, and she had not told me her birthday as yet. I had to have missed out on it. This made me a little upset, but Pam brought me back to reality.

She woke me from my trance saying, "Earth to Caleb, is anyone home?"

I came back around as if I were being fired from a slingshot. Pam and Donna were laughing at me a little. Then Donna said, "I have two things to say, One, I don't think the doctor has even thought about children as yet. Two, I don't think I have ever seen the doctor at a complete loss for words."

They both laughed a little more before Pam said, "I think he's shell-shocked."

I was spared by a knock at the door, or so I thought. It was Jason. Donna had invited the gang over for breakfast. It was still a little early, but the others arrived one by one, and greeted me with congratulatory hugs, still reveling in last night's announcement of the impending nuptials.

Within a few moments after the last of the gang had arrived, we were seated at the table. We were conversing and eating when Kim asked, "Caleb, have you figured out how many children you and Pam are going to have?"

I was to say the least, a little disconcerted that the subject was brought up again, but I knew that it would have to be discussed sooner or later.

Pam said that we hadn't discussed it as yet, and it was something we needed to do in private. Everyone understood this, and the subject was thankfully dropped, but not forgotten.

The conversation turned from children, to the women talking about wedding plans, then to we men talking about the honeymoon in Hawaii.

When Jason returned to his home the night before, he had gone online to find things to do and places to go in Hawaii. He had printed pictures of famous attractions to see while there.

As these were passed around, Jason gave a narrative of the historical importance of each picture, or the beautiful panoramic view that was in the picture. After all the pictures were passed around, Pam thanked him for the preview of our honeymoon.

After we had all eaten, as usual, the gang and I withdrew to the study to discuss the last week, and to do Bible study. They were all becoming quite knowledgeable about the good book, and had begun to take over as leaders of the assemblage.

They were really becoming very capable students of the Bible and Christian practices. This was a real comfort to me, as I no longer had the responsibility to teach them about the gospel. They had relinquished their souls to the Lord, and had begun to enlist others into God's arms.

This struck me as to be in conflict with what would happen in the past, when we would go to the postwar time and begin our mission that God had put forth to Pam and I. What would happen to the gang when their descendants began practicing the Word? Would they become Christians on their own, or would they choose the path of becoming scientists as the members of the gang had? Only time, and

God knew the answers to these questions, and I knew neither would reveal to me what was to be.

I thought about taking a trip a few years into the future, but I didn't want to know anymore about that subject. I had determined that, what was to be, would be. To try to influence the future with prior knowledge would be unfair to the ones whose life would be influenced.

The day went on, Pam and Donna prepared our evening meal. As we all sat around the table, and held hands for the blessing of the meal, I said, "Before we begin I'd like to make an announcement. Pam and I would like all of you to attend our wedding. I will come back in two days to pick you up. By that time I will have arranged a place for you to stay, and will be able to tell certain people cover stories about all of you. This was one aspect of the wedding I had taken charge of. I had already made their cover stories up.

I then said, "Jason, you and I have known each other for such a long time, I would like you to stand up for me."

"It would be my honor, Caleb." He said.

Then Pam said, "Donna, will you be my maid of honor?"

She answered that she would be delighted to have the privilege.

I said, "Excellent! Now let's eat before the food gets cold."

I started to say grace, but to my surprise Donna asked if she could have the honor. This was the first time anyone besides Pam or myself had performed the consecration of the meal God had provided.

"Most Holy Father, we thank you for this fine meal you have provided for us today. We also would like to thank you for the union of Pam and Caleb that you have seen fit to sanction. We are all very excited that they will be joined in marriage. May their union be a long and fruitful one, with many children to bless you and carry your word forward."

Neither Pam nor myself ever said the blessing again when we visited the gang.

33

Pam and I decided to come back to the same Sunday night that we had left.

When we got back to the apartment we sat on the couch and began to discuss our future. Of course, Pam wanted to discuss our raising a family. Although it wasn't my preferred topic of conversation, I still had to yield to it. After all, we were going to have children. We needed to be prepared for this inevitability.

Pam asked, "How many children shall we have Caleb?"

"To be honest darling, I haven't thought about it yet. I have known that we would have children someday. It's just, it's just I never thought about it when we decided to get married. I was thinking we could discuss this sometime in the future."

"I thought we could discuss the subject before our marriage." She said.

"Well we have a whole week to discuss how many children to have. I'm tired, and I really would like to just talk about little things."

"Good," she said "children are little things. Let's talk about those little things."

It seemed I was trapped. "Oh well, if not now, it would have to be sometime soon," I thought. "I might as well do it now. Besides, I do want children at some point. I just hadn't thought when that might be." I gave in, "Pam, I don't know, I haven't been around children since I was one."

She said, "You didn't know a thing about the Bible, and now you have personal audiences with God. I think you'll do just fine with children. You know, they require less from you than he does." She laughed, leaned in to me, kissed me, and then said, "You'll do fine. You'll learn as you go. That's the way it goes with most couples and their first child anyway."

"Wonderful, I'll just wing it."

"That's the spirit Caleb, just relax and enjoy the ride. Besides, I'll be handling most of their care anyway. That will free more of your time up to teach people God's Word."

I knew Pam was only trying to appease me, but I still had reservations that raising children would be a two person job. Still, if I was going to go through with this, I knew that children would be part of the equation.

I finally broke down and said, "I would like to have two children."

Upon hearing this Pam said, "That's it, two children?"

I felt a certain dread come over me because I knew that one child wasn't the right answer either. I fearfully answered, "How many were you looking to have?"

She said she knew it was kind of late in life for both of us to even start a family, but she was thinking of a number closer to five.

I was stunned, how would we ever get the Lord's work done if we were changing diapers all day? We would be doing nothing but chasing them around, keeping them out of things that they didn't belong in, and in general, spending most of our day tending to their welfare.

I thought about protesting, but even though I knew little about women, I knew that they were biologically geared for children. I knew in order to keep Pam from being upset, I needed to let her have her way on this subject. So I yielded to her on this issue. I would find myself bending to her will quite a bit for the rest of the time that we would have together.

I tried one more time, "Pam my darling, you know the path we have chosen will be fraught with unknowns. What will we do if we have five small children, and we run into a band of raiders?"

Pam smiled and said, "The Lord will not only provide food and shelter for us; through his power he will guide us around any type of harm that may befall us. As long as we believe in him, he will provide. Remember, you told me in one of your audience with him, that he would not let harm befall you."

"Actually, he said that if anyone tries to harm *me*, then they shall be dealt with harshly. He didn't actually say that harm could not befall me."

Pam explained that I needed to see the underlying meaning of those words. She said that, "God meant that he would protect you from harm because you are his direct representative."

"Yes," I said, "but he didn't say anything about you, or our children."

Pam said, "If something were to happen to me, or one of our children, would you not feel harmed?"

I replied that I would.

She then said, "Well then your family falls under that umbrella. We are covered under your covenant with the Lord."

So there was nothing left to say about the subject. Pam and I, per her desire, would parent five children.

34

It was Saturday, I think the gang was more excited than Pam or I were.

We had planned a small subdued ceremony with just the gang, the Saunders, President Johnson, Dr. Baker, and a few others Pam and I knew.

Pam however, had unbeknownst to me, put a blanket invitation in the church bulletin. When I came out of the room I was getting prepared in, it appeared that there were as many people in the pews, as there would be on any given Sunday service, and maybe even more.

Instead of being upset, as I was not a fan of big crowds, or being the center of attention. I was somewhat elated tough, that so many well-wishers would take the time to share this day of love with us.

Mike said with some excitement, "There must be about three-hundred people here."

I said, "Pam has been coming here all her life. These people helped raise her. They are her extended family."

Mike said, "That's some family."

The time had come for me to take my place at the altar and for the wedding procession music to start.

As Pam rounded the corner and I got my first glimpse of her, I was in awe. I believe I had never seen such a radiant vision in my entire life. She outdid the Pillars of Creation, one of the most spectacular celestial bodies in the universe. I believe I had never seen anything as beautiful before, or since.

Bill Saunders gave the bride away, and as he turned to sit, he said to me in a hushed voice, "This is a match that God would approve of if he were here."

I replied, "He is, he is."

Pastor Lind began the ceremony. "Today we are gathered to celebrate the union of two of God's children, Pam Brown, and Dr. Caleb Bronson.

They have written their own vows, but before they start, I would like to say a few words.

"Most of you know Pam. She has been part of our congregation her whole life. I baptized Pam when she was six months old. Then again at the age of five, when she told me she had a true understanding of God and could make the choice for herself. She has been a faithful servant to our Lord for all of her years, and I'm sure that you all know that.

"She has chosen to give her love to this man, Dr. Caleb Bronson. When I first met Caleb about one year ago, I must tell you that I liked him before he said one word. Furthermore, I see love and compassion in him for Pam. I believe they will have, and I wish them, a long and lasting love for each other, and for our Lord. That being said, I have given my full sanction for this union. Caleb, you may begin."

"I love you Pam, and I know that God has ordained this love. Because of this, I desire to be your husband. Together, we will be vessels for his service in accordance with his plan, so that in all areas of our life, Christ will have the preeminence. Through the pressures of the present and the uncertainties of the future, I promise to be faithful to you. I promise to love, guide, and protect you as Christ does his church, and as long as we are both alive. According to Ephesians 5 and with his enabling power, I promise to endeavor to show to you the same kind of love as Christ showed the church when he died for her and to love you as a part of myself because in his sight, we shall be one."

Pastor Lind turned to Pam and said, "Go ahead, Pam."

"I love you Caleb, and I know that you love me. Because of this, I desire to be your wife. Since we met, I have prayed that God would lead me to his choice, and I am confident that his will is being fulfilled tonight. Through the pressure of the present and the uncertainties of the future, I promise to be faithful to you. I will love, serve, and obey you as long as we are both are alive. Christ told us that the wife must submit herself unto her husband as unto the Lord. For as Christ is head of his church, so is the husband head of his wife. Caleb, I submit myself to you."

Then it was Pastor Lind's turn. "I hold up a ring"—he held it high for all to see—"a circle with no beginning and no ending. It is the symbol of life and of love. It is to be worn on the finger as a constant reminder of your pledge to each other and God. Caleb, repeat after me. With this ring, I thee wed."

I repeated the vow and placed the ring on her finger. Then Pam repeated the vow to me and placed the ring on my finger.

Pastor Lind said, "Today, all of you have been witness to a sacred union between these two. What God has ordained today, let no man put asunder. Caleb, you may kiss the bride." We gazed into each-others' eyes for a moment, then our lips met in a kiss that stayed in my mind until my last breath.

Everyone applauded as Pam and I kissed as man and wife for the first time.

Then Pastor Lind said, "Ladies and gentlemen, may I present to you Mr. and Mrs. Bronson."

Then we turned, and Pam and Donna hugged, while Jason congratulated me with a handshake, saying, "Honestly Caleb, I never thought I would see this day. I'm so happy for you and Pam, I can hardly contain myself."

I thanked him for his kind words, and then Pam and I switched. Donna was beaming a big smile and said, "You two are the perfect couple. I just know you will have a very long and fruitful life ahead of you."

Then Pam and I turned to each other and kissed once more, and we walked down the aisle hand in hand, never to be separated until death.

We held the reception in the church assembly downstairs. It lasted for about three hours, then Pam and I thanked everyone and left.

Pam had arranged our flight to take place after the Sunday morning service. We awoke that morning and picked the gang up for their first real service. They already knew the order of the service, so they were ready for the day's events. They were also ready for the questions that they would be asked after the service was over.

Pam had borrowed the church van so we would have room for the gang. We had woke-up early, to allow time to pick the gang up and eat. When we were all in the van, Pam asked where everyone wanted to eat breakfast. In unison they all said, "Pancake House."

Pam jokingly said, "Are you sure?" For which she received a resounding, "Yes!"

We ate and talked about what we would do on our honeymoon, as far as sightseeing and such. Pam had made arrangements for us to stay at a hotel called the Hilton, on the island named Oahu.

The church service went off without a hitch. Pastor Lind had Pam and I stand up and introduced us as man and wife. Then after the service ended, we were mobbed in the foray, similar to what happened the first day I attended a service.

We told everyone that we were pressed for time, and needed to get to the airport, so we excused ourselves. The gang said that they wanted to stay and experience the culture and food from this time. I told them I understood, but they could not stay. I explained that it was difficult for me to keep my secret. With the five of them, it could blow up in their faces.

They were of course, disappointed, but understood my concerns. Kim said dryly, "You get to have all the fun." I couldn't disagree with her observation, but had to stand my ground.

We took the gang back to the cave, and swept them back to the future. Then we got back to Pam's time and returned the van to the church.

Bill and Pam Saunders took us to the airport, and would pick us up on our return.

It was a very magical week in Hawaii. The food, the views, the ocean, and of course there was Pam. It was magical waking up to Pam in the morning. As I have said before, she was a natural beauty. I had been told by others that waking up to a women could change the way one might view her beauty, but Pam was different. She looked as lovely in the morning as she did any other time of the day.

Unfortunately, our week was over too soon, and we were on our way home. When we got back, I told Pam what I had been dreading to tell her all along. "We have to disappear."

"What do you mean disappear?"

"If we go to the future and stay, we will need to have an excuse as to where we moved, and why would we leave when I have such a good job, and you are such a fixture in the community. Then, if we made up a story as to why we moved, we might be found out that our story is a fake. No, I'm sorry Pam, but we have to leave this place behind and never come back."

I could see the sadness in her eyes. She was tied to the community through her entire life. This would be one of the hardest things she would ever have to endure; unfortunately though, not the hardest. That was yet to come.

Pam sadly asked, "Do you have a plan?"

"I thought if we had a boating accident we could fake our drownings. Our bodies would never be found. It would be the easiest way that we could disappear with no trace. It would be believable."

She numbly replied, "Okay, When do you want to do it?"

I said, "We shouldn't wait too long. I think we should do it this weekend."

"Where will we get a boat? Do you have that figured out already? How long have you been planning this," she inquired?

She was, and rightly so, very upset. "I have been planning this since last week. I thought about it while we were in Hawaii and I saw a small catamaran for rent on the beach. I decided that our honeymoon should be a happy time all the way. That's why I waited until now to say anything."

That next Saturday, we first picked a spot to hide clean clothes on the shore of Lake Washington, and rented a boat. The spot was only about one mile from the boat dock, so I first dropped Pam off, and then I took the boat about one hundred yards off shore, then I turned the boat over to make it appear as if we had an accident.

I swam the hundred yards in the icy water to the shore. It was so cold I feared I would not make it.

I knew it would be cold, but it was still a shock to my system. When I reached the shore, Pam had a towel that she wrapped me in, and hugged me to help warm me up. I told her that we needed to get into the sand dunes to keep from being spotted.

It was about five miles from the shore to the cave. We had to walk the entire way. We might be remembered if we took a cab or public transportation, and I didn't want to chance that.

I felt very bad about lying to everyone, and knew there would be a lot of tears shed over our loss, but it was necessary if we were to be successful in our deception.

It was about three in the afternoon when we arrived at the cave. We set the controls and left 2010, never to journey to this time again.

35

We went to my time and rested up from our strenuous day. I had already told the gang my plans, and they were all waiting for us at the house. They were very solemn when we arrived, almost as if we had actually died.

Donna took Pam into the kitchen telling me, "There is fresh coffee, would you gentlemen retire to the study, I'll bring it in as soon as I get Pam comfortable."

I kissed Pam, and we went our separate ways. In a few moments, Donna came to the study with the coffee. I asked her how Pam was doing.

She replied, "Well, she has just given up everything she has ever known and had to make the decision on the spot, how do you think she's doing?"

Donna had never spoken to me in this brusque manner before. I was taken aback. I then reminded her that I was doing the Lord's work, which is more important than personal feelings. I wasn't too happy about it either. I had met good people, and I would miss them also.

Then Donna said, "You could have given her some time to absorb what she was going to do, or were you unsure if you told her the truth she would still marry you? All I'm saying is yes, if she was going to make the decision, you should have given her time to absorb what was going to happen."

"You're absolutely right," I said, "I was very insensitive. I should have thought about it more. I should have at least consulted you about this. I should go talk to her."

Donna stopped me, saying that she would take care of it, and that I might make things worse if I intervened. She told me not to worry, that it would be all right.

I told Donna that I could see her point, and I would let her handle the situation. "Would you express how sorry I am for the way I handled this situation?"

"As I said doctor, I will take care of it. Now let me get back to Pam so I can comfort her, and smooth this fiasco over."

I must admit Donna made me feel like I was about six inches tall.

After about a half-hour, Pam and Donna came into the study. We all stopped talking, and our eyes were on Pam. You could tell just by looking at Pam she had been crying. In a way, she had actually died. I stood up and embraced her. I asked, "Are you all right? I'm sorry I sprung this on you at such a late date. I thought that keeping you happy, at least until after the honeymoon, would be more important than having your mind focused on the end of your friendships.

I know I was wrong. A man and his wife should be in congress with each other. This is entirely my fault. I feel as if I have failed you as a husband in my first attempt at a major decision."

Pam said, "I must tell you Caleb, I have been in shock since you told me what your plan was. I also must admit though, I hadn't thought how we would transition from my time to the future. You were right. We did have to die. How would we keep in contact with the ones we left behind? What if they tried to communicate with companies we would tell them we're working for?

If President Johnson called a place you said you were working and asked for you, they would say they don't have anyone by that name working there. Then the police would be involved. No Caleb, as much as I don't like it, it was the only thing to do."

I held her in my arms and comforted her as she wept. The gang decided that we needed some alone time and excused themselves. Pam gave them all a hug as they exited, and thanked them for being such good friends.

After they were gone Pam said, "At least I can keep my friends from this time, and they are good friends, so I didn't lose everything." With that she said she was tired and wanted to take a nap.

So we walked up the stairs and went to bed. "How long will we stay here before we start our mission?" she asked.

I said I thought that we needed to discuss a plan as to how to proceed. She said that she agreed, and figured we should take two or three days to make an initial plan, and after that we could plan our days one day at a time.

I agreed that her plan sounded good, and we would probably make adjustments as time passed.

Then I changed the subject, "When do you want to start trying to have a child?"

She said with a smile, "We could start right now." I agreed with a smile and turned off the light.

The next few days we worked with the gang to finalize our plans as to how we would proceed to spread the word. Pam came up with the idea of starting a school. It couldn't be called a college; we would be too small of an operation for that.

She also said that medical doctors were often religious in her time. So we decided that we would attempt to try befriend doctors.

We knew it would be a trickle-down effect, and it might take a long time to convince people that we were not a branch of the ORC.

With so many obstacles and dangers to overcome, you may ask, "Why do this?" Ask the everyday citizens why when they pass a burning building with people screaming for help inside. Why do they not hesitate to run inside and help? Most would say they don't know. Some might say it was the right thing to do. Me, I would do it without thinking about it. Why you ask? Because I'm a coward! A coward—that doesn't make sense. My answer is I would be more afraid of a lifetime of nightmares, hearing the screams of the dying inside. I'm not a hero. I'm a coward.

In the same sense, if I didn't do what God had commanded, I would hear the cries of tortured souls in purgatory.

So our plans were set. It was getting time to go, and we loaded up Bibles that we had the gang print for us. The gang walked us to the cave, we said our good-byes. I set the controls, the gang waved good-bye, and left the cave.

When we arrived in the year 2228, we just walked out of the cave with a backpack each. We didn't want to look like we had too much; this was so we would look unattractive to raiders.

We reached the town and it looked much different from Pam's time. However, the streets were still in place, so we were able to find our way around fairly well.

36

As Pam and I entered what used to be the center of town, we were shocked to see the devastation that we found. Pam asked, "Is this what the war caused?"

I told her, "I believe that this was a product of the postwar destruction caused by raiders. Stay close to me, we don't know what or who we might run into."

She asked, "Why would they do such damage to structures that were still viable?"

I said, "As you know, in your time there were people who committed this same kind of devastation. At times, even in the face of highly organized law officials, people still took part in activities that caused similar damage to structures as we saw. Among the lawless, this kind of practice was viewed as civil disobedience, although there seems to be nothing civilized about what we were seeing right then."

We walked cautiously down the edge of the street so we could duck into the bushes if we needed to hide. Pam began to feel very nervous because of the destruction we were passing, coupled with the uneasy feeling that someone was watching us.

I also felt as if there were hidden eyes on us. I had brought a stun gun for protection. These were not like the stun guns from Pam's time; they had no wires or darts coming from them. Instead, they shot a beam of ultrasonic sound that, unlike the stun guns of Pam's time, would cripple anyone. The ones from Pam's time were sometimes ineffective on the subject. I had seen video clips where a man became more enraged and actually seemed to become stronger from the voltage.

My stun gun worked without wires or darts. Instead, it projected a sonic wave that incapacitated the assailant through their auditory senses. It was effective from a distance of about three hundred yards, and unlike a rifle or a pistol, you could shoot from the hip.

As long as you pointed it in the general direction of your assailant, it would be effective because the beam spread out without losing its efficiency, the further you were from your target.

Even with a rifle accompanied by a high-power scope, you still had to take time to aim carefully to be effective. A rifle would also cause irreparable damage to the victim, which neither of us wanted. Whereas I could be off by as much as forty feet and still hit my target. Also, I could use it like a person might use a machine gun. The term "spray and pray" meant if you took a machine gun and fired it from left to right, you might hit people or miss everything altogether. There was no missing with my stun gun though.

A momentary blast would leave the assailant disabled for about fifteen seconds. I know this doesn't sound like much, but very few people would challenge it a second time, and no one would try a third time. It wasn't harmful, but for the few seconds it lasted, the pain was excruciating.

It also had a DNA sensor on the handle. If someone was somehow able to overpower me, they couldn't use the weapon. The DNA sensor rendered the weapon useless to anyone but Pam or I.

Pam was quite relieved to know that it was not only nonlethal, but that it also caused no permanent damage.

We continued down the street a little further and came across my old apartment building. It was in great disrepair, but we agreed to investigate the inside of it. We warily opened the door and called, but we got no reply. Again, we called out. "Hello, we mean no harm."

I looked the place over and thought it to be in good physical condition, even though the outside was not looking all that good.

I told Pam to stay right behind me, and to keep an eye on our back. We ascended the stairs. I would test each stair with a little bounce as I ascended them slowly. It was an eerie feeling, somewhat like the feeling one might get if they feared a ghost were present.

I don't believe in ghosts; I was just using that as an analogy. It was just a feeling of trepidation.

The stairs were solid all the way up to the third floor where my old apartment was.

We had brought freeze-dried, irradiated food with us. It wasn't like eating at the Pancake House, but we knew that our lifestyle would be altered drastically in this time. We had brought water with us, but we're saving it for drinking, not knowing if we would be able to find potable water here.

Fortunately, we were in the Pacific Northwest, so water was not a concern. But we needed to boil it to kill microbes.

I told Pam to unpack what food and sleeping gear we would need for the night. We had packed our backpacks with forethought. We only needed to unpack what we would need for the moment. This way, if we found it necessary to leave hastily, we could just grab the backpacks and leave.

As Pam went about her duties, I investigated the other rooms to ensure we were alone, or better still, find our first convert.

After a sweep of the entire building I found no one. I went outside and found a plastic barrel that someone had set under the roof's gutter to catch water. It was full and had a layer of slimy alga growing on top of the water. It's harmless and actually nutritious, but I knew Pam wouldn't care for it, so I found a can next to the barrel and scooped out the slime, then scooped some water out and put it through a filter we had brought for such a situation.

We only needed a half gallon for dinner and breakfast. After this chore was done, I went back inside. As I walked down the aisle toward the stairs, I rounded a corner to find a man pointing a shotgun at me.

"Don't you move a muscle mister, or I'll blow your head clear off."

I immediately thought about Pam, had he already discovered her?

To warn Pam I yelled, "Don't shoot, mister. I'm unarmed."

Pam heard my warning and desperately looked for something to use as a weapon. She located an old clothes iron that a previous tenant had left behind. Fortunately, Pam could see all the way to the bottom floor, where the man was standing. As she dropped the iron, a floorboard creaked and the man made a dive for cover. This gave me a chance to pull my stun gun, and I had him in my sight. He still had a hold of his gun; he didn't know what I was holding and asked what I thought I was going to do with it.

I answered if he wanted to find out, I could show him, then I said, "But I'd rather invite you to dinner."

He looked at me oddly and replied, "Really?"

I said, "We would enjoy the company."

He said, "Well, I've got my wife and boy here too."

I put the stun gun away and said, "We have enough for them too. Go ahead, get them and bring them inside."

I told him I would need to get more water, and I told him, "I'll meet you here when I come back."

I came back to find the man and his family waiting inside. He still had the gun, but had it at rest by his side.

As I approached him, he apologized for his actions saying one can't be too careful these days. I told him I understood, and that had our positions been reversed I probably would have reacted the same way. There were no hard feelings I assured him.

We climbed the stairs to the apartment. When we entered, Pam, being a little fearful, walked to stand beside me.

I started the introductions saying, "I'm Dr. Caleb Bronson, and this is my wife, Pam."

The man said, "Really, you're a doctor? My name is Dr. Martin Bartlett. This is my wife, Kay, and our boy, Aaron. What's your specialty Dr. Bronson?"

"I'm a theoretical physicist, not a medical doctor. Are you a medical doctor Martin?"

"Yes, I'm a general practitioner. At least that's what I try to do. Supplies are rare as I'm sure you know."

I agreed with him, not wanting to be perceived as unknowing. I couldn't believe the luck. A medical doctor—just what we thought would be a good conduit to ingratiate ourselves into the community.

We had gained his confidence. Of course, we had gained it by not killing him when we had the upper hand. Nonetheless, we achieved our goal—proving to him we were civilized.

Pam and Kay talked about things like daily chores, and tending to the community garden, livestock herds, and flocks of fowl.

Kay was very curious as to how we came into possession of the freeze-dried meals. Pam was up to the task of a cover story though. She calmly said, "We had gone through a small town, just over the old Canadian border, and had stumbled upon an old underground bunker that the raiders had missed. No one was left in the town, so we took what we could carry, and of course food was high on our list."

Kay said, "Of course, we aren't that bad off though."

Martin cut her short, "Kay, that's enough." There was a tense moment, then Martin apologized, saying shyly with his head bent down, "You can't be too careful these days. I forget my manners sometimes. This whole mess has turned me from someone who used to listen, to someone who reacts. I'm sorry Kay."

She smiled and rubbed his hand a little. "You've kept us safe this far. I know you're only doing what you think will keep us that way."

I tried to change the direction of the conversation from a tense atmosphere to a positive one. "Tell me Martin, do you have a school in your community?"

He said, "I teach as much as I can, but with very few textbooks, it's slow and tedious."

I said, "Is there a print-shop in town?"

"Well yes, but no one knows how to operate it," he said.

"I might be able to do it," I said.

Martin looked at me amazed and said, "Really?"

I nodded my head and added, "I could also teach. I have long ago lost my credentials, but that's just paper. I have a very good memory and can teach not just primary but also secondary school. Pam was a librarian at one time. She's very smart also, after all, she did marry me." Everyone laughed, and the mood in the air changed. We had met our first friends in this godless world. With the print-shop, I would have to read some manuals to get the machines to work, but I could do it. I would print text-books, and more importantly, Bibles.

Pam served dinner, and when she finished, the Bartlett's started to eat. I said, "Excuse me, my wife and I have a little custom we practice before we eat, can we all join hands?"

Martin gave me a sideway look. I could see it in his eyes. He knew what was coming next. I looked at his wife. She had her head bent and was nervously rocking back and forth; she also knew.

That voice I herd in my head every once in a while said, "It's o.k., just say it to yourself."

I listened to the voice and began to silently pray. "Heavenly Father, bless this food you have placed in front of us, and thank you for leading Dr. Bartlett and his family to us. You have given me a destiny, and your mighty hand is guiding me to that destiny. I think I should keep this short. In your name, amen." I said aloud, "Let's eat!"

Martin smiled at me and gave a slight, hushed laughed. He then said, "Kay and I have that same little practice."

Kay jerked her head up as if to scold him for letting the secret out, while knowing at the same time that their secret was ours also.

I had carved a cross from wood and had a cord running through it, making a necklace. I pulled it out of my shirt and said, "The ORC is gone Kay. The war is over. We can do this. This is still America!"

Martin said, "Listen, I don't know why I believe you, but I do. You just can't throw this kind of thing around though."

I said, "Who's going to hear us? We haven't said anything. Who would anyone tell? This cross that I wear around my neck is a death sentence. I ask you though, who will tell who?"

I held his hand as we all sat in silence for a moment. My eyes and Martin's locked. He said, "We are believers. It's good to have someone to trust in," he swallowed hard and said, "the Lord" as if it were like saying something horrible, instead of the wonderful thing he knew in his heart it was.

I smiled, and Pam started to laugh, and before long we were all caught up in her laughter. In a short time, we were hugging each other.

When we finally stopped laughing it was dark, and the Bartlett's wanted to get back to their house.

He gave us directions to his house and said they would repay the meal. He also said he knew of a nicer house that was closer to the school and print-shop, and that we could have it. He said it would take a little work, but we would be neighbors.

I shook his hand and said that I was looking forward to being his neighbor.

Kay looked at Pam and burst into tears. The stress of the uncertainty of the night had finally caught up to her, and this was just the release of tension.

Pam leaned over and wrapped her arms around her. She held her for a very long time as Kay said repeatedly while crying, "I have a friend, I have a friend." The relief of finally having someone to talk to about the Lord, must have been like a dam bursting. The poor women was emotionally spent. She lay in Pam's arms, a limp mess for some time.

Dr. Bartlett and I just sat there and watched as Pam told her, "It's time for a new beginning. You don't have to be afraid anymore. We are your friends, and we love you. *God loves you.*"

I looked at Martin as a tear began rolling down his cheek too. I didn't know if it was for the same reason as Kay's or if he was just overcome by her emotions. Whatever the reason, we looked at each other with that knowing look that said we had developed a special bond, that we would be close for the rest of our lives.

It was getting late, and the Bartlett's decided it was time they got home. They thanked us for the meal and everything else. It was still hard for him to say God's name aloud. I just nodded knowingly, and they left us.

37

Pam and I awoke the next morning. I believed the temperature was in the low forties. It was a typically cold Pacific Northwest winter day; but at least it wasn't raining.

Pam looked at me with a smile on her face and said, "Good morning husband, what a beautiful day it is."

I knew what she meant, but I still said, "Are you looking at the same sky as me?"

"Yes, we are," she said. "we're looking at God's sky."

I had to admit, it was a good morning.

We were startled by a knock at the first floor lobby door. A voice called out.

"Hello, Dr. Bronson, are you up there? My name is Mike James. Dr. Bartlett asked me to come over and help you and your wife move your things to your new house." Then he said, "Well, it's not new, but you know what I mean."

I called down, "Give us a minute, Mike. We just woke up."

He said, "Take your time Dr. Bronson, Dr. Bartlett told me to do whatever you asked. The doctor also said to tell you if you haven't eaten yet, they have a meal waiting for you."

I replied, "That's very nice, that will save us the bother." Mike said to call him up when we were ready.

In a few moments we had everything packed, and I asked Mike to come up. He was a short, stocky young man. I thought him to be about thirty-five years of age. I would find out later that he was only twenty-five. Life was hard in this world, and would take its toll on a young man.

He asked what I wanted him to carry. I asked if he would be so kind as to carry my wife's backpack for her. He said nothing. He put on Pam's pack and shook her hand saying, "Hello Mama, I'm Mike James, pleasure to meet you."

Pam said, "Hello Mike, it's a pleasure to meet you also, and please, call me Pam."

"Yes Mama, I mean, yes Pam." Then he shyly giggled.

I started to put my pack on when Mike said, "That's okay, Doc. I got it." He pulled my pack out of my hands and said, "Follow me." He started down the stairs with both our packs. It all happened so fast. I tried to protest him carrying both packs, but he would have none of it. They both had to weigh about 80 pounds, for a total of about 160 pounds, but Mike bounced down the stairs like he was carrying nothing at all!

I flashed back to Dr. Johnson's remark about my memory and muttered, "Amazing, simply amazing."

I found out Mike was orphaned when he was about twelve. Alone, he had walked into the town looking for refuge. The Bartlett's, being the good Christians they were, took him in and he had been with them ever since.

I asked him, "Where were you last night when the Bartletts happened upon us?"

He kicked a rock while looking at the ground and shyly said, "With my girlfriend."

Pam said, "What's your girlfriend's name?"

He said, "It's kind of funny, her name is Pam too." We chuckled for a moment, and then Pam said, "Well, just so we won't get mixed up, what's her last name?"

"Brown," he said. "Her name is Pam Brown."

We both stopped in our tracks and looked at each other. What were the odds? "Really," Pam said. "That was my last name before Caleb and I were married. Your Pam and I have the same name!"

This tickled Mike so much that he put my pack down and began to laugh uncontrollably. While laughing, he repeated, "No way, no way." Pam assured him she was telling the truth, and he laughed even more.

I would come to find Mike had a good heart, and would laugh at most anything that was the least bit funny; the Bartlett's would tell me that God had given Mike an extra large funny bone.

We arrived at our new home to find Kay cleaning it. There were a couple of men painting the outside. We were floored; the Bartlett's had left us the night before at about ten o'clock, and it wasn't even eight in the morning yet. I asked with amazement, "How did you get all of this done in such a short time?"

Kay said, "We're a tight-knit community. Martin put out the call last night after we got back, and we've been here for the last few hours getting the place ready for you. Have you eaten yet? I made some oatmeal, and toast with real butter and milk. Come over and I'll fix your plates. I need a break anyway."

We would soon find out that dairy products were a real treat, with the supply of hay they could harvest each summer, beef cows had more importance placed on them, so dairy cows were a little rare, and most of their products went to children.

We followed her to her home which was next door. She asked Mike to put our packs down and to go over and start painting the house. She gave him a kiss on the forehead, turned him around, gave him a loving swat on the behind and said, "I love you." He responded in kind, and dutifully did Kay's bidding.

Once Mike was gone, Kay closed the drapes in the kitchen, locked the back door, and shut the door that led from the kitchen to the rest of the house.

We thought this odd, but not being sure of the customs of the time, we said nothing. She then served us our meal and sat down with us. In a hushed voice, she said, "Please, Dr. Bronson, will you say grace *aloud*."

I knew when she said *aloud*, she meant at an audible level and not loud enough for others to hear. I said, "Of course. Dear Holy Father, we thank you for leading us to this place where godly people reside. We ask that in time, we will find more people to share your word with. We grow stronger in your faith with more people to fellowship with. Thank you for this wholesome meal, and Kay's hands and heart that prepared it. In your name we pray, amen."

Kay had a tear in her eye, but wiped it away and smiled. "Thank you, Doctor. It was good to hear your praise of him." Then she opened the drapes, and Pam and I ate what was given to us with great joy. We both knew we had found our mustard seeds.

When done with our meal, we thanked Kay. She offered us more. We thanked her for what she had given us, but declined more. Kay said, "I cleaned your bedroom first thing this morning. Why don't you go get settled in there, and I will get back to making your home a real home.

We agreed, and thanked her for the meal, and also for getting the house ready. As we walked over to the house, I looked over to see Mike painting away with the big smile that I would come to know as his trademark. Then I heard the voice in my head, which I had already decided had to be God's voice. It said, "He is the way."

"He is the way." I repeated silently to myself. What does that mean? It would be heartbreaking when I found the meaning. God works in mysterious, and yes sometimes, heartbreaking ways. Mike's name would forever be in our hearts. He was short in stature, but taller than anyone I would ever meet in courage. I'm getting ahead of myself though.

Pam and I walked up the stairs to our bedroom and found a real bed, already made up with clean sheets, blankets, and pillows. We had barely made it into the room when we heard Dr. Bartlett call out to us. I stuck my head out the door and said, "Good morning Martin, how are you today?"

"I'm great, how are you? Did Kay feed you yet?"

"Yes, great, thank you. What's on your mind, Martin?"

"I thought I would show you the print-shop. It would be nice if you could get things running over there. Maybe we could start a newspaper," he said.

"Well Martin, let it not be said you're lazy," I said with a smile.

He smiled back, saying that it was good to be ambitious. I agreed with him.

The print-shop was in total disarray to say the least. It would take a few days just to clean the mess enough to get around the shop. I soon found out though, that there was an abundance of free labor. Everyone wanted to pitch in and help. Some of it had to do with us being new, so there would be new stories to be listened to.

It didn't take long before we had three others helping us straighten up.

Martin said excitedly, "I found the machine manuals."

We cleaned off a big desk, which at one time someone had sat at and made their living. Martin told me that they would keep cleaning, and I should start reading the manuals and figure out how the machines worked. The others agreed that it was a top priority. So I sat, and began to learn how to run the presses.

About that time, Kay and Pam came over with soup and bread for our lunch. We all stopped working and ate. The other workers asked questions—where we were from and such—just trying to get to know us.

By the end of the day, the shop was looking like it had promise, and I had gotten an idea of how to run some of the machinery. Also, you could actually get around the place much better than when we started.

Finally Martin said, "I don't know about the rest of you, but I'm hungry. Let's go home get something to eat, and we'll meet back here tomorrow okay?"

Everyone agreed, and Martin and I walked to his house. He said Pam would be there with Kay and the boys waiting to eat.

When we walked inside, the aroma was wonderful. Kay said, "I hope you like venison roast with vegetables."

I said, "If it tastes half as good as it smells, it will be wonderful."

Mike said, "It tastes every bit as good as it smells." Then he laughed, I laughed too. His laughter could not be ignored.

Martin said, "Mike, Aaron, boys we are going to do something that we have never done before. This is a secret for now, so you can't tell anyone." He looked at Mike and said, "Mike, son, you can't even tell Pam about what we're going to do tonight. Do you understand?"

"Yes Father, I understand."

"Aaron, do you understand?"

"Yes Father, I understand."

"This is very important."

"Yes Father," they both said.

"Caleb, will you do the honors?"

"I'd be delighted to. Heavenly Father, thank you for bringing us to this house of people that will become such fine friends. We pray that you bless this house and those that live in it. We thank you for Dr. Bartlett's courage to confide in us, and share his love for you. Lord, we thank you for Kay and Pam. I feel that they will have a friendship that will surpass any that has been before. We also would like to thank you for Mike. If everyone had his deportment, the world would be a much brighter place."

Aaron said, "What about me?"

Kay said, "Aaron, don't interrupt, not during grace."

"Most of all though, thank you for Aaron. His youth is something that I'm sure you will mold into one of your greatest tools. Amen."

Aaron said, "Hey, I'm not a tool!" Everyone laughed, and so did I. I didn't know why until Pam and I got home. She told me it was a slang word from her time, and that she had not put it on the list. She then explained that Aaron thought it meant someone who was not very bright.

I started to laugh, and had a hard time stopping. When I did stop, Pam took the opportunity to interject. "You see, children can be a lot of fun."

I said, "Well, we should get started making some don't you think?"

She only smiled.

38

There were no land taxes. There were no deeds of ownership. All there was in place was an agreed-upon amount of community service hours one would volunteer, to keep the city in operating condition. I marveled at how they had all agreed upon this method of maintenance. I doubt it would have worked at any other time in history.

Also, people would see something that needed tending, and take care of it without having to be asked. The people had a policy of not passing the buck. It was like they were mature.

The next morning, I woke early, and looked out the front window to find someone had brought us food during the night, and had left it on the wide railing that encompassed the porch.

I opened the door, my attention was on the care packages on the railing. I took one step and tripped over something in front of the door. At first, I thought someone had pulled a prank on me, but my irritation soon changed to fear. What I had tripped over was a wolf, a full-grown, 250-pound, full-blooded wolf! I found out later that the world record for a wolf killed was about 175 pounds. Then I thought, "They used to kill these animals just for sport." This realization saddened me deeply.

I was stunned for a moment, and then I realized that the wolf was standing between me, the open door, and Pam. I yelled at her to stay in the bedroom and keep the door closed. She came out though, not being able to hear me clearly, and began to come down the stairs.

The wolf started to walk into the house. I had to do something. I lunged at the beast, grabbing it around its neck, and tried to wrestle it to the floor. I could feel the muscles ripple as I struggled with it to no avail.

I yelled at Pam to get back in the bedroom, but she would have none of that, and joined in the struggle.

After about a minute of struggling with all my might, I realized that the wolf had bitten neither Pam, nor myself. In fact it was licking us and wagging its tail.

I told Pam to release the animal, and we both let go. There we were, lying on our backs with one of the fiercest animals God had ever put on earth, and now my greatest fear was getting licked to death.

When we realized we were not going to die, we started to laugh. The wolf continued to lick us for a little longer. As I'm sure you can understand, we both let out a sigh of relief realizing that we were not going to be eaten.

There was a throw rug in front of the door for people to wipe their feet on when they entered. The wolf gently bit on a corner of it and pulled it to the side of the door. It then curled up and laid down on it, proclaiming it as his.

I laughed. Pam said she didn't get what was so funny.

I said, "Who else can say they have a wolf as a pet?"

She said, "Who would want to?"

I asked her, "What shall we call him?

She had no answer. Just then the beast stood up looking at me, and then it hit me. "His name shall be Sampson." With that, Sampson let out a howl of approval, stood up on his hind legs, and put his forepaws on my shoulders. He was a magnificent beast. It was all I could do to keep from falling over.

Standing as he was, he towered over me by a good foot, if not more. I petted him while he licked me all over. I laughed, "We have a wolf, we have a wolf for a pet."

Then Pam said, "What will the neighbors think?"

Then it struck me. Everyone walked around with guns. I had to alert the community before someone tried to kill him out of a realistic fear. I had to let everyone know that there was nothing to fear.

With Sampson still standing on his hind legs, I commanded him to lie down on his rug. He got down, curled up on his rug, and laid there motionless.

We both looked at each other and I said matter-of-factly, "Well, at least he minds."

Pam said I did need to warn the community. She agreed that Sampson was in danger.

I went to the Bartlett's first. They had just woken up. Kay put on a pot of herb tea, as getting coffee was a rare commodity, and there was none. I began to lay out what the beginning of my morning was like.

As I spun my tale, I could see their eyes getting wider. Finally Martin said, "You mean you got a German Shepherd." Then he gave a nervous laugh, the kind of laugh you would laugh if you only hoped you were right, but still thought you were wrong.

So to make him understand, I told them about my eidetic memory and my IQ. "There is a wolf in my house, curled up on a rug, by my front door. I assure you that I didn't lose my mind overnight."

He said, "You have an eidetic memory."

I said, "Really, that's what you're taking away from this conversation? I have a wolf in my house!"

Martin said, "Right. I'll get my rifle."

"No, Martin," I said as I stepped in front of him. "There is no danger. What I need is for you to tell the rest of the town what has happened. This is the will of I Am."

"Who is I Am?" Martin questioned.

"That is another name for God."

"I've never heard that name." Then he said, "What can I tell the townspeople? What will I tell them?" he asked.

I told him, "There is nothing to tell but the truth. Why would you tell otherwise?"

He said, "Of course, if I told something else, I'd have to explain myself later."

I said, "And still have to tell them about the wolf."

I told him to breathe, and that this was going to be okay. He asked me if I had ever had anything like this happen to me before. I told him no, nothing like this.

It wasn't time to tell him about the miraculous things I had witnessed.

Martian told me to go home, and keep my wolf out of sight until he came over to the house. "Don't open the door for anyone but me, understand?"

I told him that I would follow his instructions, and I went home. I waited as Martin and Mike went around the town explaining what had transpired, and not being able to answer why. It had to have been frustrating for them.

It was about two hours later before Martin knocked on the door. I answered the door, and Martin cautiously peeked through, as I opened it just barely. I was enjoying his anxiety with the whole situation. It was funny at his expense.

Once again, at Martin's expense, I opened the door wide, and he walked in.

"Where's the wolf?" he asked.

Sampson yawned behind Martin, and Martin slowly turned around to see Sampson lying on his rug, panting.

To say I sensed Martin losing his composure, would be downplaying the situation. Martin was focused on Sampson. I closed the door. I seemed to be almost evil at that moment, but it was all meant in good fun.

Just then, Sampson as if on cue, leaped up on Martin's shoulders as he had mine, but knocked him down, pinned him to the floor, and began licking him unmercifully.

After Martin calmed down, I told Sampson to lie down, and he obeyed.

Martin picked himself up and sort of chuckled. "Well, that was, ah, weird. I'll, ah, just go home now, and, ah, I'm going home now." As if this was an everyday occurrence, Pam and I said, "Okay, see you later."

When Martin left the house, Pam and I laughed. We laughed so hard we didn't even realize that Mike had come into the house.

All of a sudden we heard Mike say in an innocent voice, "What's his name?"

I turned around to see Mike with his arm around Sampson's neck as if they had known each other since birth. While Sampson licked his face, Mike started laughing so hard he fell beside Sampson and they played for quite some time.

With the food that was left on the porch railing that morning, Pam had cooked a meal and we asked Mike if he would like to eat with us.

He said, "Really, that would be nice."

Pam jokingly said, "I would like to meet my twin, Pam Brown. Do you think you can get her to come over? We would both like to meet her."

Mike said, "Yes, that would be nice. I think Pam would like that."

He ran over to the Bartlett's and told them he was eating with us, then ran to his girlfriend's house.

Mike told Pam about our invitation, and Pam was excited to be meeting the newcomers. When they arrived, they were breathing heavily; they had ran all the way to get here.

Both Pams talked the day away, about what, I could only guess. Mike and I talked about Sampson for the most part. At times we would mix it up, and all four of us would be talking to each other at once. The constant for the evening was Sampson though.

Sampson was our special friend, but that day, he lay beside Mike while the four of us talked and laughed all day.

From that moment on, Sampson had a special relationship with Mike that would last their lifetime.

As the Bartlett's had done, we also adopted Mike and Pam.

I know they were happy to have the extra family, as we were also.

39

Sampson would mostly stay with Pam during the day while I was away. That comforted me. Believe it or not, I knew Sampson would protect her.

We were almost ready to try to print something by the end of our first week. It was time to travel back home once again.

Pam, Sampson, and I walked to the machine. On our way, I wondered how Sampson would handle the trip. As we got to the mouth of the cave I got my answer. He was apprehensive at first. He uttered a soft growl, and as we got deeper into the cave it became louder. Then I turned off the cloaking device, and he laid down and whimpered.

Pam chuckled and said, "Look at what the big bad wolf is afraid of."

I said, "I can't wait to see the gang's reaction to Sampson."

We first went to the year 2100. By this time, Pam and I would be forgotten, and we could still buy good food. We chained Sampson to the machine; actually, we did this for his own protection. I turned on the cloaking device, and the machine and Sampson vanished.

Food cost about twice as much as it did in Pam's time, and Pam commented it was less than what she thought it would be.

We then arrived in my time and walked to the house. As we got within sight of the house, Sampson broke away from us. We were expected, but no one knew about Sampson. I tried to run after him, but that was a joke. How would I ever be able to catch a wolf running at full speed.

It was a nice day, so Donna had the back door open for fresh air. We were about one hundred yards from the house when we heard Donna's screams, or was it a blood-curdling shriek? Either way, we called out for Sampson to come to us. When we arrived, he had Donna pinned to the floor, while Donna screamed and tried to fight off the attack.

Donna was still screaming. She hadn't realized yet that she was in no danger. I commanded Sampson to go lie down. He gave a little snort of divergence, but went to the door, pulled the rug to the side, and laid down. Sampson did this everywhere we took him. It was as if he was saying, "This is my spot!"

We picked Donna up, apologizing as we did so. The look on Donna's face as she slowly realized that Sampson was ours, and she was no danger, looked like the faces on the other people this had happened to. Sometimes he would break away from us, but what was I to do about it? He's a wolf!

Then she said, "That thing is yours?"

"Donna, this is Sampson. Sampson this is Donna, don't eat her. There Donna, now Sampson won't eat you," Pam said.

Donna excused herself, saying she needed to wash the dog slobber off her face. I corrected her, telling her it was wolf slobber. As she walked away, she mumbled "wolf" in disbelief. Then she told me to get him out of her kitchen.

I told Sampson to come, and I led him into the study and told him to stay. There were no throw rugs in the study, and Sampson seemed lost. I went to the kitchen and retrieved the rug from there. I threw the rug down, and Sampson pulled it into a corner and lay down. "What an odd animal," I thought.

The gang arrived soon after that. I told them to stay in the front room, and I told them to remain calm, and that they were in no danger. Then I said, "Come here, Sampson."

As he came around the corner, the gang pulled back with a gasp. They stood still as he went from one to the next, licking each hand as he passed them. "You see," I said. "nothing to fear. He is as tame as any household pet."

They were amazed. "How did you tame him? Have you been gone a long time?" Jason said.

"Well first, he found us." I then told them about the spill I took on the porch, when Sampson found us. "We have been gone just one week, and he came this way, tame. Plus, he obeys commands."

"What do you feed him?" Ali asked.

"We don't. He hunts. We haven't seen him hunt, but he leaves at times, and returns on his own," I said. "The only care we give him is a roof over his head and a bowl of water."

Mike asked how he got outside. I told them he doesn't scratch or whine; he butts his head against the door, and it makes quite a loud noise.

As I expected, the gang broke up laughing at that. I have to admit, the first time I witnessed Sampson doing this, I had to chuckle; it was an odd way to get our attention.

Then I told them about the Bartlett's, and how meeting them had nearly been a disaster. I told them about how we had cautiously opened up to the Bartlett's, and how they revealed that they were closet Christians. We also told them about Kay's breakdown, how the poor woman began to sob uncontrollably, saying over and over that she had a friend. She did have friends, but she had been afraid to confide in all but one of them, for fear of retribution.

Ali asked how they found the courage to confide in each other to begin with.

"Martin told me they had met during the religious purge many years after the war, when they were both five years old."

When relocating religious families during the war, the ORC always put families together in this manner. First, they would match a man and a woman together, then place children with them. They would be sure that none of the people in the made-up family had ever had any prior contact of any kind with each other.

So although Martin and Kay grew up as brother and sister, they were totally unrelated, and as such, there was nothing odd about it. In fact, it was something that happened often after the relocation process. When you're that young, and you trust and love someone for that long, the love can easily change from one of a brotherly/sisterly love to that of boyfriend-and-girlfriend love, and proceed to marriage.

"You must understand these were different times," I said.

Some saw this as a perversion, but as I said they were not brother and sister, in fact they weren't even step-siblings. The real problem that could arise, would be an accidental pairing of close relatives that had never met before, but the ORC made DNA testing mandatory, after being in existence for only a few months, so this problem never arose.

Another practice the ORC established was when they paired families together, they cautioned the families that any family member could be a spy for the ORC, and if caught practicing religion, they would be put to death on the informant's say alone.

So everyone was afraid to open up, but Martin and Kay had both been placed with a good, kindly couple after the purge.

While they didn't know the Bible, they did know about God, but rarely spoke of him.

One day, Martin coaxed Kay to walk deep into the woods. She was scared to go so far, but trusted Martin. They got far enough into the woods that Martin felt comfortable to talk openly, and he did.

After that, Martin and Kay would go to this spot when they could, and praise God as best as they could.

He told her of how his parents knew the ORC was coming and gave him instructions as to what to do after they were separated. Martin knew he had to keep the word alive. They didn't know very much about the word, but as the gang and I had done all our lives, they also lived by a certain code.

Kay also had been prompted by her parents to keep the word alive. They told her not to trust anyone, but when Martin opened up, she felt compelled to open up also.

I thought about how God told me that my conversion to Christianity would only require a slight adjustment. The Bartlett's had it comparatively rough. All we did was try to live right; Kay and Martin lived a secret, a deadly secret.

When we got back to 2228, I told Pam that we needed to visit the Bartlett's. Pam said, "Okay," she never questioned me about these decisions. She dutifully did what I asked, but I always discussed things of a large importance with her. I told her that I was going to take the next big step with them. She said, "Are we finally going to give them a Bible?"

I told her, "It is long overdue, even though it has only been a week. I have waited too long to give it to them."

It always amazed me how Pam seemed to know what I was thinking. I believe when you find your soul mate, often your so attuned to their thoughts, that you often know what they are thinking, and can finish sentences for each other, and things like that.

We got back and the Bartlett's weren't home, so Pam put on a pot of tea, and we waited while I read the Bible.

After about an hour, Sampson gave a low gurr noise, announcing the Bartlett's arrival. Then we heard the knock on the door. I answered it without looking. There I was, still holding the Bible with the door wide open. They had brought their friends, the Moore's. There was an awkward moment until Dr. Bartlett said, "Their okay, they believe."

Then he asked what I was reading. I told them to first come in and close the door. We had met Brent and his wife Mary, and saw them as being good-hearted people.

Then I told them what the book was; there was nothing but silence. Finally, Martin said, "May I look at it?"

I handed him the book. He put his hands on the book very gently, and didn't pull it from my hands; rather, he waited until I let go of it.

At first he just held it, studying the cover. Then he held it to his chest, over his heart. I believe he was praying silently, holding the book that you could die for, as countless numbers of people had in the past.

He was in a sort of trance. When he came around, he handed the book back to me, apologizing as he did for holding it for so long.

He didn't see it, but I had another Bible sitting on the end table. He tried to hand the Bible back to me, but as I held up the other Bible, I said that the Bible he was holding was his to keep. Kay came alongside of Martin and asked where we got it.

I told her that when the purge started, my grandfather could see what would eventually happen, and he hid a few copies. "I can't think of anyone else I would rather see with it than you. I made a promise to Grandfather to carry the word forward." He then told me gruffly, "Don't promise me, promise God." He made me say it out loud. I did, and he said I would have to hide this from everyone, but the time would come when I should start planting the mustard seeds. "You are those mustard seeds. You are the beginning of the new age of God!"

They were stunned at first. Martin said that they would be killed. I replied, "Did God not give his only son to wash away our sins?"

They stood there silent. It dawned on me that they didn't know about the crucifixion when the purge came. They were too young, they hadn't learned, or had forgotten. I would come to find that they actually knew very little about religion. After all, they were only five when they had been removed from their parents.

Think about that for a moment. They knew so little about God, but they still risked their lives to keep the word alive.

I asked everyone to sit down, and I would read to them about the sacrifice that God made.

I started reading at Matthew 26:14. I told them of Judas and his betrayal. I read about the last supper and how, even though

Jesus knew Judas would betray him, Jesus still broke bread with him. This stupefied them, but I told them that Christianity is like that, you give because it's the right thing to do.

As I was going over that part of the Bible, Pam came from the kitchen with a tray. On the tray was a cup of wine and bread.

Then I read about the Holy Sacrament.

While they were eating, Jesus took bread. Gave thanks, and broke it, and gave it to his disciples. Saying, "Take and eat; this is my body" (Matthew 26:26, NIV).

Pam passed the tray around and told them to eat it once she had passed it to everyone. They waited until I put the bread in my mouth, and then followed my lead.

Then he took the cup, gave thanks, and offered it to them, saying, "Drink from it, all of you. This is my blood of the covenant, which is poured for many, for the forgiveness of sins." Matthew 26:27–28 (NIV)

Pam handed the cup to Martin first, and it was passed in a circle until it came back to her. After this was done, I continued to read to the end of Matthew 26.

When I finished, the Bartlett's and the Moore's were shocked. They asked me why the people didn't stop it. I told them that the Roman soldiers would have slain them, and that unfortunately it had to happen, in order to save all of us.

"You see, God sacrificed his only son to wash away our sins. As horrible as it was, nothing could, or should have been done. It was preordained."

I then explained how preordination worked. From there, question after question came to Pam and I, we answered all we could; some were a little off point, but we would steer them back on point, and did what we could to answer all they asked.

I gave Brent Moore my Bible. He was somewhat hesitant to except it, protesting that it was too valuable. I explained that I had an eidetic memory. I then had to explain what an eidetic memory was. The Moore's were stunned. Martin explained he remembered hearing about it once in medical school but to know a person with this ability was for him, a special event.

I said that I couldn't forget something if I tried; in fact, if I tried, that would only reinforce the memory.

They were flabbergasted; they had taken in a lot of information. Their first sacrament, first Bible, finding out that God sacrificed Jesus to absolve us of our sins. It was a lot to absorb in couple of hours. They left at about ten o'clock.

Pam and I picked things up, and went to bed. First though, I pulled a floorboard from the closet. I retrieved a Bible from my cache, then we got under the blankets, and I began to read from the Bible.

"Brothers, my heart's desire and prayer to God for the Israelites is that they may be saved. For I can testify about them that they are zealous for God, but their zeal is not based on knowledge.

Since they did not know the righteousness that comes from God and sought to establish their own, they did not submit to God's righteousness. Christ is the end of the law so that there may be righteousness for everyone who believes" (Romans 10:1–4, NIV).

The whole story of my life that I told the Bartlett's and the Moore's was, of course a lie, but I had to tell them something, and the truth wouldn't do. They were harmless lies, but necessary.

40

One summer morning, Mike and Aaron were walking down a trail by the river to pick some wild blackberries. Sampson and I were at the print-shop. We had gone there early, and I was getting hungry. I figured Pam would have breakfast made soon, so Sampson and I were walking across the road when Sampson stopped. I called for him, but he stood his ground and began to growl. He turned, took a couple of steps toward the river, and turned back to me and whined. He then turned back to the river and ran with all dispatch.

The voice in my head said "Go." I immediately turned and ran after Sampson with a feeling of foreboding. Sampson ran so fast that I nearly missed seeing him take the trail.

I put the rest of this narrative together from what I observed, the story Aaron told, and what Dr. Bartlett told me later.

Aaron was walking in front of Mike. He rounded a bend on the trail and froze. Mike was a few paces behind him. When he caught up to him, he immediately took Aaron by the shoulders, put him behind a tree, and told him not to move or make a sound.

He then bent over to pick up a tree branch to use as a club and began to recite Psalms 23.

Then without hesitation, he walked toward a four -hundred-pound black bear. He raised his hands and yelled loud to make himself look bigger and scarier.

It didn't work. The bear lunged at Mike. I believe this was when Sampson broke away from me to go to their aid.

Mike swung the branch, but the bear blocked it, knocking it from his hand, and Mike on the ground. Mike landed on his stomach. The bear then bit him on the shoulder and lifted him up, wrapping his arms around Mike's waist, and digging his claws deep into his chest, shaking him violently, and then changing his bite hold.

The bear shook Mike violently and released him. Mike crumbled to the ground.

That's about the time Sampson got there, and still running at full speed, leaped, and grabbed the bear by its snout, going over its head in a flipping motion.

This broke the bear's snout but not its fight. It grabbed Sampson in a bear hug, much as it had Mike, except Sampson was facing the bear. He was able to reach the bear's throat, and with one mighty jerk, he tore its throat out. The beast still had fight in him though.

That's when I arrived. I saw Aaron standing where Mike had told him to, and told him to go get his father. Aaron was frozen with fear though. I turned my attention to Mike, who was bleeding profusely. We were mere feet from Sampson and the bear as they struggled in their death throes.

Mike could hardly talk but managed to ask about Aaron. Injured as he was, he wanted to know if his brother was all right.

As I pulled off my sweatshirt to make a compress for Mike's wounds, I said, "You saved him. Aaron is fine."

By now, Sampson had killed the bear, and he came to check on Aaron. He sniffed at him, howled a mournful howl, and started to run back to town.

Grievously injured as he was, Sampson ran to the doctor's house. Again, without slowing down, he rammed his hard head into their door, knocking it down and began barking at the Bartlett's. Martin saw how tore up he was, grabbed his medical bag, and ran after him.

It took about three minutes before Martin got to the site.

Mike looked at me as I applied pressure to his wounds, he was only able to whisper, "Psalms…23."

I could tell he was fading. Tears welled up in my eyes as I relinquished my position to Martin and began what would be the last request of Mike's young life.

"The Lord is my shepherd,
I shall not want.
He makes me lie down in green pastures,
He leads me beside quiet waters,
He restores my soul.
He guides me in paths of righteousness for his name sake.
Even though I walk through the valley of the shadow of
  death, I will fear no evil,
for you are with me your rod and your staff they comfort me.
You prepare a table before me in the presence of my enemies.
You anoint my head with oil; my cup overflows.
Surely goodness and love will follow me all the days of
  my life,
and I will dwell in the house of the Lord forever.

Psalms 23 (NIV)

Martin had worked feverishly to save Mike, but the bear had done too much damage. As I finished the Psalms, Martin shut Mike's eyes and began to cry. Aaron and I got on our knees, then the three of us hugged and cried.

Sampson came over, smelled Mike, and let out a mournful howl the likes of which I had never heard before, nor since.

I was sure the bear was dead. Sampson was half mad though. Mike and he were very close.

He ran to the bear and began mauling it, tearing its fur from it. I could hear bones cracking.

Mike had been Sampson's good friend for just one year. This goes to show you the type of man Mike was. It took

Sampson a few hours, but when he was finished you couldn't tell it had been a bear anymore.

Kay and others arrived at the site. Kay began screaming, "No! No!" Martin grabbed her arms, his hands covered with Mike's blood, holding her back so she couldn't see him. A few men gently picked Mike up and took him to the clinic.

As I said, Sampson stayed with the bear for the next few hours. When he was done, he made his way to the clinic, he was in pretty bad shape. The front door to the clinic was propped open. Sampson walked in and, with what little strength remained, leaped up on a gurney and laid down.

Dr. Bartlett had always been a little bit apprehensive of Sampson, but he numbly turned to Sampson, and started to mend his wounds. I guess the need to keep busy and keep his mind off the tragedy outweighed his fear. Plus, he probably saved Aaron also. Whatever the reason, I was glad he was taking care of Sampson.

Dr. Bartlett told me that Sampson would stay in the clinic for two days and would need a few more days of rest after that.

In that moment of such great loss, Mike's last words were Psalms 23. With that, he had told me what, "He is the way." meant. We had found our mustard seed, and though we had grown in the number of the faithful, we were still not public. I began to think I might have failed God by not going public with what I knew sooner.

Mike was loved by everyone. The whole town came for his funeral two days after the tragedy.

For those two days, I played the events over and over in my head, wondering if I hadn't hesitated, Sampson wouldn't have turned back to make sure I was following. The few seconds he lost could they have made the difference. Should I have gotten Martin on my way, instead of following Sampson? Pam knew I was beating myself up over the whole mess and tried to console me, but it was asking more than I was ready give.

I prayed that night, asking God why he had let such a tragedy occur. The voice in my head never came though, even though I requested an answer several times. I asked Pam why God would not give me an answer. She told me that first, God didn't talk to everyone and would probably only talk to me on important issues. I said, "Mike is gone. How can there be a more important subject than why? I need to know why." Pam took my quivering body in her arms as I began to sob, and said, "God would not have taken someone as special as Mike without a good reason. He has already told you why, or the answer will come."

I lay in bed thinking, unable to sleep. Then it came to me. "He is the way, and we found our mustard seeds." I sat up in bed. "That's it! I know why now!" Pam mumbled, "Good," and said, "go back to sleep."

I fell asleep right after that. It's funny how getting one answer can make everything come together.

41

It was the day of Mike's funeral, and everyone in town was gathered at the grave site. There were over four thousand people in attendance. This was a fitting tribute to Mike; as I have said, he was loved by everyone.

Martin and Kay had asked me to preside over the ceremony. I thanked them, and said that I was going to ask if I could speak anyway. They were pleased that I was so willing to do this. I said that it was an honor to have known Mike, and an even bigger honor to speak on their behalf.

Although I confided in them, I had never told them that I, on occasion, talked with God. That might be just a little too much for them. So I didn't reveal my true relationship with our Lord.

We arrived at the cemetery that afternoon. The sky was a bright blue, not a cloud in the sky anywhere. It was a day that would have made Mike smile. On a day like this, I would catch Mike looking at the sun. He would do so for a few seconds, then bend over and rub his eyes for a moment, and laugh. He truly was one of God's innocents.

Someone had put together a little stage and a sound system. There were chairs for the Bartlett's, Pam and I, and a few others. Brent and Mary Moore were also among the few people sitting with us, and of course, Pam Brown, she was near catatonic, she never quite recovered from the incident, her love for Mike being deeper than anyone's.

Brent went to the podium first; he got the crowd to settle down and introduced me as the main speaker.

I got up and said how befitting it was to see such a large turnout for Mike. I pointed at the sky and said, "He's smiling at us right now." People believed I had meant the nice sunny day; the Bartlett's and the Moore's knew my meaning though.

I started, "Today, I'm supposed to stand up here and tell you things like what a good man Mike was and how he will be missed. All of that is true of course, but Mike was much more than that." I held up some notes. "I wanted to do justice to Mike on this day. He deserves it."

Then I threw the pieces of paper in the air and said, "A few pieces of paper. How can you put Mike's life on a few pieces of paper? How can you put any man's life on a few pieces of paper? The answer is you can't. Mike was a miracle. I know

317

what Mike would want today if his voice could be heard. How do I know? I heard his last wish. I know what he wanted. He wanted me to quit lying to all of you. That's right. I have been keeping a secret from all of you, just as Mike had."

I reached into the inside pocket of my overcoat and pulled out a Bible and held it up for everyone to see. There was a murmur in the crowd. I said, "Please quiet down. This is not what Mike would have wanted, and we're all here for him today. This day is Mike's day, so if his last request is for me to be honest, that's what I need to do."

The crowd quieted, and I started again. "I have been telling you that I am a theoretical physicist. That is true, but not the whole truth. I am also a Christian. More than that, I am a pastor, a man of God." There was a gasp across the crowed; it was not hushed.

I said, "There, all of you who gasped still believe. If you didn't, you would not have gasped." There was a moment of silence, then an older woman said, "He's right. Bless Mike. Down with the ORC, and praise the Lord."

After that, it was like an avalanche. The rumble became louder and louder. I finally heard an older man begin singing "Jesus Loves the Little Children." The chorus grew. It grew until it seemed the whole gathering was in chorus.

I looked over at the Bartlett's. They were holding hands, and through tears, I could hear them singing along.

The chorus went on for several minutes; they just repeated the chorus over and over. Finally, Brent got up and said,

"Pastor Bronson has more to say." This was the first time I had been referred to as a pastor. They quieted down very fast. To them, whatever I was going to say would be earth-shattering. For them, it would either be something new, or something they had not heard for many years.

Once they quieted, I said, "I talk to God. There are those out there that know what I mean. Others may say that they pray, but I have conversations with God. Other times, God just gives me a clue. One day, shortly after we had arrived here, God gave me one of those clues. All I heard as I walked past Mike while he was painting our house was, "He is the way." At that moment, our eyes locked, and Mike gave me one of his trademark smiles. What was that supposed to mean? I prayed for more information, but none came.

"When we first met the Bartletts, I heard God say, "You have your mustard seeds." I have to tell you, when you have to figure things like this out on your own, it can make you a little crazy. I didn't let it though, because if I did, I would lose sight of what it really meant.

"Well, I now know what they mean. I think you're not supposed to know the answers until the time comes to put them to use. That time is now for both messages. "He is the way." What did that mean? When this tragedy took place, I know all Mike was thinking about was, "Lord, grant me the strength to allow Aaron to get out of this mess."

Did you see how I said Aaron and not us?

I think Mike knew exactly what would happen to him. When I got to him, he could barely talk." At that moment, I held up the Bible and said, "Mike asked me to recite Psalms 23. I think it's only fitting that I do so now," and I did.

When finished, I looked out over the somber crowd and said, "Now I wish to tell you about mustard seeds. A young boy was possessed by a demon. Jesus came to drive the demon out.

Jesus rebuked the demon, and it came out of the boy, and he was healed from that moment.

The disciples came to Jesus in private and asked, "Why couldn't we drive it out?" He replied, "Because you haven't got the faith. I tell you the truth, if you have faith as small as a mustard seed, you can say to this mountain, move from here to there, and it will move. Nothing will be impossible for you." Matthew 17:18–21(NIV)

I closed the book and looked at the crowd. "Mike was everything that is good in man. Mike gave his life to save his brother. Don't mourn the loss of Mike. Rather, rejoice knowing that he is in heaven. His place is next to God. Mike is just waiting for us to join him.

"We have some work to do first though. I am announcing the beginning of a Sunday service that I will conduct to praise God. Pam and I will also start a seminary. There is a lot of work to be done. We have an obligation to save the Word of God. We have an obligation to Mike. It's what he wanted. We will print the first Bible that has been printed in several years, and we will ask for volunteers to go to surrounding communities to help spread the word."

So it began. Mike was the way. His death sadly, was what was needed in order to get the masses to open up and participate. I don't know if I could ever have opened up if Mike had not shown me the way. It was a loss that would haunt me the rest of my days. What God has ordained, though, let no man question.

So I did the best I could. I pushed it down. Mike was a diamond, I concealed my unhappiness for the rest of my days.

There was about ten minutes of the service left when I noticed the crowd began to make way for someone or something. I finally got a glimpse of what was causing the disturbance; it was Sampson. The doors of the clinic open inward. He had somehow made his way out of the clinic, and had made his way to Mike's grave site. He lay down next to the coffin.

After the service was over and most people had left, Sampson stayed. He stayed until the last person was gone, and the men who had volunteered to bury Mike had left. He stayed there until Sunday morning, when I was to hold the first service.

I checked on him every day, as others did. Every time I went to check on him, I would find bowls of food and water. It appeared that he had not touched any of it, but he had touched the community's heart. I don't think I had ever witnessed such a feeling of loss to that point, with the exception of how the Bartlett's felt.

I had always been, for the most part, in charge of things that happened around me. This was different though, I was helpless this time. With all I knew, I couldn't fix this. For the first time in my life, I came to understand that, no matter how smart I was, I was nothing in comparison to what is already written.

42

About eighteen months after we had moved to the year 2228, Pam and I traveled to my time in the future to give an update to the gang. As always, we brought a feast with us, and as always, Pam and Donna would put things away and begin to cook dinner. I would usually take a much-needed nap, do research, or study.

This was not a chauvinistic, "the kitchen is a woman's place thing." It was that they both knew that I had my work to do, and I was always short on time. Plus, they enjoyed each other's company, and would always talk nonstop while busy in there.

I went to the study this time and began reading the Bible as I had so many times before. Yes, I have an eidetic memory, and I have read the whole Bible twice and then some. However, I find it a comfort to read, and it is God's Word, so not doing so is a moot point.

The gang all lived close to each other, and they would meet at one or the other's house before they would come over.

I heard a knock on the door, and their conversation announcing the gang's arrival. Donna opened the door and greeted the gang as they entered the house.

When I came out of the study, I noticed my good friend Dr. Jason Simmons was missing right away, but thought he was talking to Pam or using the restroom. We began to catch up on our lives, and as usual, they began to quiz me on what I had accomplished since we had last met.

I said, "Gentlemen, not so eager. Shall we wait for Dr. Simmons?"

For a moment they just stood there looking at each other in stunned silence. Then Dr. Kinsey said, "Are you sure you're not thinking of someone you knew at the college you were working at?"

I started laughing. "Oh, that's rich." Then in a raised voice, I called for Jason. The others stood in embarrassed silence while I did so. Then Pam and Donna came in. Donna spoke first. "Who are you calling for sir?"

Pam chimed in, "He said Dr. Simmons."

Donna said, "Who is Dr. Simmons?"

The rest of the gang stated that they also didn't know who Dr. Simmons was. At this point, I knew this was no joke. Not that the gang was unaccustomed to pulling a prank on Pam and I, but they weren't that good at acting. I had to make sure though. If my assumption was correct, something had changed in the past. Something had changed in the life of Dr. Simmons or his family line.

Perhaps he had never became a physicist; perhaps he had become a Christian. After all, we had succeeded in spreading religion throughout our corner of America. Since we had reinstated religion, there would be changes along the way in the future.

It seemed obvious that Dr. Simmons and I had never crossed paths, but I still had the memories of our long friendship.

Then I thought if a union never took place somewhere in his ancestral past. What if through my changing the past, Jason was never born? I could live with the thought that because things changed, he never became a physicist, but the thought of Jason never having been at all tore me up inside. I was brokenhearted, totally devastated.

I explained to everyone what the possible scenarios were. When I finished, Dr. Asana asked if there was anything that could be done to correct this, adding that he would like to meet this Dr. Simmons.

I let out a sigh of frustration. Then I said, "This had to happen. It is God's will. To attempt to change things would be to challenge God, and as much as this sorrows me, it must be so. If you look at it differently, you can say that somewhere at some time, someone in his linage took a different path with their life. It's free will that Jason is not with us anymore."

Dr. Osaka said, "I don't remember him, but if he was as much a part of our gang as you say he was, well, I feel as if part of my life is missing too."

Then something awful dawned on me. "You all understand that, as my time passes in the past, there is a real risk the rest of you may be awaiting a similar fate."

Dr. Osaka said, "Including you, Caleb?"

I could hear Pam catch her breath. "I believe that would not happen. If something happened to change my life, I may never have invented time travel, and God's work would not get done. Also, I first traveled into the future and met Jackson, remember? He knew who I was, so I had to exist in this time and the future in order for me to be here both now and in the future."

They pondered this for a moment and agreed I must be right.

Then Dr. Asana asked, "I wonder how long it will be before another one of us vanishes?"

The three of them looked at each other for a moment. I knew they were trying to figure out which one of them would be next. When the time came, would they disappear? Would it be painful? Would they just slowly fade away? Or would they go to sleep one night and all that would be left in the morning would be an empty bed? I could understand their uneasiness about the situation.

I said, "This will not do. Dr. Simmons is gone, and the rest of you are thinking about your uncertain future. I want to have my same old team back."

Pam asked how I planned on that happening. I said, "Simple. We have to go back to the time machine. We will travel back to last week and have dinner as we did last week with all of us present."

Pam said, "What about the rest of the gang and their futures?"

Mike asked, "What then? Will we just be living the same day over and over again?"

"No, Pam and I will be living the same day over and over. For the rest of you, it will be as if every time we visit will be a new day for you."

Kim said, "You and Pam will start to age. We will notice that. What will you do about that?"

"When that happens, we will tell you all the truth, and we'll have to keep telling you every time we come back." I turned to Pam. "Pam, will you help Donna pack up the food we brought?"

Ali said, "Hey, we still have to eat."

I said, "No, you don't. When Pam and I go to last week, this week will not, for all intent and purpose, have happened as yet. Therefore, you will not have been hungry as of yet."

Sometimes, I hated being so concise. After I said my piece, no one else had much of anything to come back with.

As was the case this time, all Ali could muster was a weak, "Oh, I guess I'll enjoy this meal last week then."

So Pam and I made our way back to the time machine and went back one week in time.

We made our way to the house, lugging all the things back again. We got to the house and I told Pam that we needed to keep up a show about what the future might hold for them. She said that having Jason back would lift her spirits enough to hide her sadness.

I reminded her that loss leaves room for someone or something new to enter your life. It's like the circle of life, never ending, and always coming back to a new beginning, just as Pastor Lind had said at our wedding.

43

After Mike's death, Pam and I stayed in the Bartlett's time slot. We would now only periodically travel to the time I was from. We could never go back to her time though, as we were presumed lost at sea.

I would miss the people from her time also. I could only imagine how Pam felt. She had given up everything and everyone she had ever known.

Neither Pam, nor I enjoyed our visits to my time as much as we used to anymore. It became more of a chore each time having to tell them the same things every time. They would always ask how Mike was doing. This was the hardest thing to go through though, having to relive that terrible day over and over. It was very hard on both of us.

We discovered on one trip though, that if we controlled the conversation a certain way, they would not mention Mike at all. When I realized this, I wrote a script for Pam to memorize to avoid the unpleasant subject.

Now, instead of being visitors, we were becoming actors.

As we got older and they began questioning that, we had to explain that we were reliving the same day, over and over each time we came. It was extremely trying on both of us.

I felt sad for the gang too. Any one of them would have been able to build the machine; fame and fortune would have been theirs. They kept the secret though. They understood the importance of changing the past. All it would take, would be one fanatical or politician with their own agenda to change the world.

Four years after Mike's death, the Mike James Seminary had their first class of graduates. We had fourteen graduates in our first class; Brent Moore was among them.

I asked five of them to go north, to the Canadian provinces, and eight to go south, to the southern states and Old Mexico. That left me with Brent Moore. I told Brent that it was time for Pam and I to move on, and it was time for him to take the reins of the seminary.

"What will you do? Where will you go?" he asked.

"Pam and I will go east. There is still much of God's work to accomplish. Remember Brent, there is a reason you are taking over. You are a faithful man. If you have any doubts, pray. God will provide, or else it will be something you can handle on your own."

I gave him a hug and said good-bye to him and Mary. Pam followed me. When she hugged Mary, it seemed she didn't want to let go. They both said how much they would miss each other.

I finally got them to stop, saying that we still had to say good-bye to the Bartlett's. I expected it would be harder to leave them.

While we walked over to the Bartlett's, Pam started to talk about our six years here and what we had seen and accomplished. I was also sad to be leaving. We had become good friends with so many in the town.

When we arrived at the Bartlett's they had lunch ready for us. We blessed the food, and I thanked the Lord for letting us find them.

We talked about how things had changed in the last six years we had lived next door to them, how God was making a comeback, and how one day, the whole world would sing his praises. We were sure the day would come, and it would.

We said our good-byes to the Bartlett's, and left their house to find the streets lined with people, well-wishers, and others thanking us for being so brave as to bring the Word back. A homemade sign saying, "Thank you for pulling us from the dark ages. We are no longer godless."

As we passed the last few people at the edge of town, I wondered what adventures God would lay before us.

Our life after we left was like it had been since we started our journey. We would meet the faithful wherever we journeyed and set up seminaries every place we traveled to. We were making good progress.

Our life had real purpose. Religion was starting to flourish. There were of course, branches of religion that taught differently from my method. However, I felt it better to have God's word spread by any means, as long as it was spread without incorrectness or embellishment.

44

It was now 2251. Pam and I had tried to conceive children for some twenty-five years with no success. Pam wanted to try fertility drugs, but I told her if it was God's will, we would have children.

She knew once I had said that, the discussion was over. I had played the "If God deems it, it will be so" card. This was a card we had decided a long time ago could not be trumped. She knew I was right.

We never discussed the subject again. Then one night, a few days after the discussion, Pam went into a deep sleep. She had one of my dreams for the first time.

Later, she recounted the dream to me after she had recovered. She said it was like the first dream I had described.

She was flying through the clouds when she came upon the Holy of Holies. Inside, she described the same faceless figure who washed my feet, had also washed hers. Then the figure led her inside the inner chamber, where the Ark of the Covenant was placed.

She described the voice as I had, all those years ago. She told me that God had said she would have two children. She told the Lord she had been barren for some twenty years, she could no longer conceive.

The Lord then said, "Am I not your Lord God Almighty?"

She said, "Yes."

"Can I not do what mere man cannot?"

"Yes my Lord. You are all knowing, and all powerful."

"Then if I am as you say, there should be no more to discuss."

"Yes my Lord. Thank you for giving me children. I have waited so long."

"Yes, and you never complained. You prayed to me for help. Remember this, if you believe, and give homage to me, the things you want, shall come to you in time."

"Then I felt a tugging on my midsection, and I woke up soaked."

That was the only time Pam talked to God. It was the conversation she had always wanted though.

As God had promised, Pam became pregnant about two months after she had her conversation with him. When she found out, she was so excited, she told everyone she met.

We felt fortunate to be in Miami when the pregnancy occurred. It was a large community, and there were several doctors and a good hospital.

The pregnancy went perfect however, and the babies, fraternal twins, were both born healthy, and with a good set of lungs. I never knew such a loud beautiful noise could come from such small lovely children.

We decided to name them Cain and Abel. We knew that their lives would be much different than their namesakes.

That first night the children came home, Sampson took his rug and dragged it to the boys' room, and from that day on, he slept in their room. I have to tell you it was a comfort to know they were protected.

We had made our way to Miami, traveling east through Chicago, New York, Washington DC, and then to Miami, where the children were conceived and born.

We stayed in Miami for about four year's altogether. Once we thought the boys could handle traveling, we moved to Kansas City, Missouri, and stayed there for three years. The people of the Midwest were only too glad to see us open up about the Lord.

I had seen many faithful people since Pam and I started our journey, but the people from that area were so much more ready for the Lord; well, it was so invigorating to see people, though still afraid, willing to come out for the Lord. God was making a comeback and would be here to stay.

Pam had told me that in her time, the Midwest was known as the Bible Belt, because they were known for their unwavering faith. That's not to diminish the faithful from other places we had been, but just the same. They gave me a different feeling than I had felt elsewhere.

45

For the next twenty years, we zigzagged our way across the country, from north to south, and then back again.

We had made our way to Salt Lake City, and Pam told me that there was a religion based there in her time. She said that it was one of the religions that God did not want revived.

She said it was a made-up religion, with a self-proclaimed prophet. In her time, the religion was not perceived as a real religion by true Christians. She said that God didn't condone false prophets, and they held their founder as a prophet, but no other religion believed he was.

God had told me that this would happen; still, I was surprised that it did. The Word of God had been written for centuries before this false religion came along She told me of other religions that people made up just to make money, and they cared nothing for God, or the people that tithed their hard earned money. I was sure that these people were in the bowels of the Earth.

God told me he was very disturbed that people had enabled the Catholic Church to flourish as much as it had. It had started as a good church, but there had been too many perversions committed by this church. He told me that the priest would take confessions weekly from their parishioners and absolve them of their sins. This upset him greatly. He said questioning. "Do these men think that they can put themselves as equals to me? I am the one and only true God. I am the only one who can absolve a man from his sins."

As a Catholic, you could sin all week, go to church, and a mere mortal man would tell you to say a few Hail Mary's and Our Father's, then you would be washed clean of your sins, blasphemy!

Then after being absolved by these blasphemers, the confessed sinners would repeat the same behavior the following week, confess, and the priest would absolve them time, and time again, only for them to once again commit the same sins.

He said, "Long ago, I should have rained fire and brimstone down on the church, for their church heads spend tithing money as if it were their own. That money belongs to the people that are the faithful. It is given by those for the purpose of maintaining the church and supporting the staff at a modest living. Before the hierarchy of the church should build themselves a mansion, a bowl of soup, and a dry warm place to sleep should be given to the downtrodden.

Then they take no wife, and their priest molests children. They are no better than Sodomites and Gomorrahns. I should have destroyed the church in the same manner as I did those people and their towns."

> Do you not know that your bodies are members of Christ himself? Shall I then take the members of Christ and unite them with prostitutes? Never! Do you not know that he who unites himself with a prostitute is one with her in body? For it is said, "The two will become one flesh." But he who unites himself with the Lord is one with him in spirit.
>
> Flee from sexual immorality. All other sins a man commits are outside his body, but he who sins sexually sins against his own body. Do you not know that your body is a temple of the Holy Spirit, who is in you, whom you have received from God? You are not your own you were bought at a price. Therefore honor God with your body."
>
> Corinthians 6:15–20 (NIV)

"How can you convert nonbelievers, when the church is a larger perversion than that of being a nonbeliever? It is better to not know the word and live as you will, than to know the word and still live as you will."

We stayed in Salt Lake for a few years. Even though it is a large city, religion caught on fairly fast.

We moved to Lake Tahoe from Salt Lake, trading one lake for another. We ended up in a home that was up the Truckee River a few miles. The river had been, in the past, one of the bigger tourist attractions in the country due to its dangerously fast waters and rapids.

One day, Cain and Abel were relaxing by the river with Sampson. The river had a higher water level than usual from the winter snow melt. Cain was a much better swimmer than Abel was, and when Abel slipped on a wet rock and fell into the river, he was swept away.

I wasn't too far from them, and when I heard Sampson bark, it sounded all too familiar, I knew something was wrong, and I ran with my heart in my throat.

I got to the river's edge just after Cain jumped in. I saw Cain reach down and pull Abel up out of the water, and they both held on to a branch that overhung the river.

I knew they were still in grave danger, but I breathed a sigh of relief, seeing that for the moment they were all right.

Just then the limb broke in between Cain and Able.

I watched in horror as Cain was washed downstream. At the moment the branch broke, Sampson lunged into the raging river and swam over to Able. He barked at Able until Able let go of the branch and grabbed a hold of Sampson's collar. Sampson battled the strong current though, and he and Able made it to the riverbank in seconds.

I still had my eye on Cain, who although a strong swimmer, was struggling against the torrent.

With Able exhausted, but safe on the bank, Sampson and I ran down the trail to aid Cain. We caught up to him just in time to witness him holding on to a big rock, his head lying against it, resting, spent. I saw a log approaching and was horrified to see it hit Cain in the back of his head.

The noise it made when it hit him was audible over the noise of the rapids. He let go of his hold on the rock and slowly sunk under water.

I went to jump in to save him, but Sampson jumped in front of me and growled. This shocked me as he had never done this before. He then turned and jumped in to retrieve Cain. Sampson must have known that I would be lost also if I tried a rescue.

I ran back to Able to see if he was all right, and upon seeing he was okay, I ran as fast as I could to see if Sampson had been successful.

I ran until I caught up to the log that had hit Cain, then I went back upstream thinking they must have been underwater when I passed them, but I never saw them again.

That day, we lost both Cain and Sampson. That was why Sampson growled at me. He knew it was suicide to jump into the torrent. He couldn't save Cain, but he could stop me from dying, and he did.

The only solace I could take from it was I believed they would both be in heaven with Mike.

As I said, we never found either body. They had probably been swept all the way to Lake Tahoe and sank in its cold depths.

I went back to Able who had recovered by now, and he asked where Cain was. All I could manage to do was to shake my head. Able started to cry and said, "Couldn't Sampson save him too?" Then I had to tell him that he tried, but he couldn't even save himself.

At this, Able crumbled to the ground in a heap and sobbed. I left him there for a moment then told him, "Let's go. We have to let your mother know what happened."

When we got to the cabin, Able sat on a bench on the porch while I delivered the bad news to Pam. When I told her, her reaction was very similar to Kay's reaction to Mike's death. The difference being Pam didn't see Cain slip away as Kay did with Mike. There was a body. There was a service for Mike. At least Kay had closure. Pam didn't get a body. We did of course, hold a service for him, but without a body, closure is difficult.

Pam and I went to the river's edge, and I asked God to care for our son and Sampson. When I finished, Pam threw a bouquet of flowers into the water, then all she said was I will always love you both, then said good-bye, turned, and numbly walked back to the cabin.

When Pam woke the next morning, she heard a voice in her head. All it said was, "Let him go." Naturally, Pam thought this meant to let go of Cain. She thought it odd that the day after Cain's death, God would ask her to let him go. Was she not supposed to mourn him at all?

She got her answer at dinner that night. Abel said, "You know that I have been wanting to go out on my own to help spread the word. I know this is not a good time. However, I was going to tell you before the accident. My time has come. I know this is terrible timing, but it is time I struck out on my own."

Before I could say anything, Pam said, "Yes, it is what the Lord wants. I heard him say, 'Let him go.' So if you are ready, I see no reason you should stay. It is God's will."

I was, to say the least, surprised. I expected her to say, "No, we just lost your brother, we're not going to let you go. Not right now." However, I am often surprised by what she says, and she did have a point. If God did tell her, that was good enough for me.

Not much was said through the rest of dinner. After we had finished the dishes, Pam began to mend clothes that Able would need on his trip.

While she did this, Able and I mapped out the course he would take and how to go about inserting himself into a community. Pam and I had taught the boys this from the beginning of their indoctrination into Christianity.

We talked all night about his plans for the future. None of us mentioned Cain the whole night. In a way, Able leaving helped us make it through the night without Cain. I can only surmise it was because we were keeping busy getting Abel ready for the rest of his life.

The next morning we ate a large meal, and after that Able and I went through a checklist to make sure he had everything he would need. It was unnecessary though, we had done it twice already. It was just busy work, something to keep him around for just a few more minutes.

Pam finally said, "If we don't let him go now, he might never leave." I couldn't believe Pam was encouraging him to leave, almost shoving him out the door. It was unlikely that we would ever hear from him, and even more unlikely that we would ever see him again.

We watched out the kitchen window as he walked up the road and eventually out of sight. Once he was gone, Pam dropped to her knees, sobbing and inconsolable.

She had grown up without a family of her own, and now she was alone with me again. Most people never experienced that type of loss once in their lives. Pam had now experienced that loss twice. I didn't know how to console her, even though I experienced the same loss for the first time also that day. It was a terrible experience.

Pam and I were alone again, and now we were in our seventies, but it was not time for us to rest. We had God's work to do, and would for the rest of our lives.

That night, Pam didn't say anything until we retired. While looking at the ceiling, she said, "I think it's time we moved on too. Let's wait three months to see if Cain's body shows up." I agreed to her proposal. It would also give us time to make plans for the trip.

Then she leaned over and kissed me good night. Neither of us slept that night. I know because I lay awake all night listening to her weep.

46

We were getting on in age and decided to work our way back up to the Pacific Northwest to see our old friends the Bartlett's. After all, we weren't getting any younger, and traveling was a little harder on us than it had been when we first began our journey.

I was wondering if the time machine was still there and in operable condition. It would be good to take a trip to see the gang again. It had been too long.

It took about two months to make it back to Everett, and the weather held good until we reached town and found the Bartlett's.

It was so good to see them again. They still lived in the same house, and had made the house where we had once lived into a museum. We decided not to resume living there again and took a place at a boarding house.

Martin helped us settle in, while Kay made a special dinner to celebrate our return.

Once we got settled in, the three of us went to the Bartlett's house. We ate a meal of venison roast with vegetables, the same feast they had fed us the first night we had arrived there so many years ago.

We talked late into the night. Most of the talking was done by Pam and Kay, which was a good thing. Pam seemed to be herself for the first time since losing both sons in the span of a few days.

We told them about the tragedy a few months before with Cain and Sampson. Now it was Kay's turn to comfort the mother who had lost a son.

Martin told me that he was sorry, and wished that he could have met them. Then he said he could hardly believe Sampson was gone also.

I told him that I believed Cain got stuck under a rock or some sunken debris and Sampson drowned by not giving up trying to save him. It was only conjecture, but Martin agreed that it had to be something like that.

He said Sampson was too strong for a river to take him without something extraordinary happening, and agreed that Sampson must have drowned trying to free Cain. "I believe he would have given his all to save Cain. He was not the kind of animal to give up."

I could only agree. I changed the subject by asking about Aaron. Martin said he has taken over at the seminary. It's quite famous around these parts. In fact, you are quite famous around here. They call you, *The man God asked to save our souls.* It's a big title, but it speaks the truth.

I said it sounds a little like blasphemy to me. I would never take the credit. I was just a tool for God.

I asked about the Moore's and how they were. Martin said they were still here, and would be excited to see us again. I agreed that it would be good to get together with them again also. Aaron went over to their house and brought them back. Martin, Kay, and the Moore's, kept us busy with conversation all night.

It was getting late, and I know Pam wanted to stay longer. Her friendship with Kay was something that the light never went out on. It was like they were long-lost sisters. I understood her desire to stay. I really wanted to talk more with Martin, but I told Pam we would have time for more talk tomorrow.

We had neglected to set an alarm clock that night, and we slept in until ten o'clock the next morning, and would have slept longer if Martin hadn't woken us with a gentle knock on the door.

We lay in bed and told him to come in. He opened the door and stuck his head inside. He apologized for the intrusion, and said that breakfast was being held for us in the dining hall of the seminary. I told him we would be there shortly, and he said he would go inform Aaron.

When we got outside of the boarding house, the whole town had turned out and lined the street. As we walked past them, they dropped to their knees as a gesture of reverence.

We thought it too much and pleaded with them to not kneel for us. Most of the faces in the crowd were unrecognizable to either Pam, or myself. I believed that was because we had been gone so long, that the people were very young when we were here before. Either that, or they had come from the surrounding area, so a member of their family could attend the seminary.

We made our way to the seminary, and were greeted by Pastor Aaron. He was very excited to see us, as was everyone else in town.

It made us a little uneasy eating with all the student body, as they would not take their eyes of us while we talked with Aaron, his parents, and the Moore's.

We had lively conversation though, since we had been gone for over thirty years, there was much to discuss. We had questions for them, and they had plenty of questions for us.

Aaron had decided to not hold classes that day, and elected it to be a day of celebration. He said that everyone was in awe of our arrival, and students would be so distracted that work would be hard for them to accomplish anyway, so he declared it a holiday.

We talked about our plans as to how long we would stay. It was a little odd, all the time it took us to get there, and we had not once discussed those plans as yet. Of course, everyone at the table had the opinion that we should stay, that we had done enough.

I countered that when it came to the Lord's work, there was no time to rest. Aaron said, "Perhaps we can make a compromise." He asked if I had heard about the space elevator that had recently been put in orbit. I told him I had, it's a great achievement, and it will help to communicate with other believers.

"That is exactly what I'm getting at." He said, "I mean no offense, but you're getting older. You could use a rest." Pam said she knew she could use a rest.

Aaron said, "The internet will be worldwide in a short time, and you could utilize it to reach far more people than you could by travel.

"Well, I guess that settles it. We will stay here for the time being. An online church just might be the right thing. I definitely could reach more people that way."

So a new chapter of our lives started. We decided to move back into our old home next to the Bartlett's. It was more comfortable than the boarding house, and it was nice to have our old neighbors back. I started my online overseas teachings, reviving the religions that were, at one time, prevalent in their prospective regions of the world.

We established communities all over the world of people who were God's faithful, no matter if they originally be Catholic, Buddhist, Christian, Orthodox, Muslim, or Jewish. If it was a religion that believed in a one and, in their eyes, a true God. Pam and I would learn about their religion and culture. Then Aaron, Pam, and I would choose about half of each graduating class from the seminary to be missionaries. We chose our candidates from the entire class, because every one of them volunteered.

We tried to bring back every religion we could learn about, taking heed of God's Word to be sure not to revive any false religions as we had not with some of the religions we had deemed false before. Making the decisions ourselves was a large responsibility, and we would not be able to revive every religion.

Also, I didn't know how long I had to complete my task. We decided to bring back the root of each religion. If once they were established, and a group wanted to go on their own, then they could do so. This was not a preferred method, but it made my work much less complicated, and I could move on to the next religion faster. After all, they have free will. They would need to learn how to make their own decisions, and I couldn't make them all anyway.

At first, I was concerned about how to go about the selection, but with Pam's knowledge of religions, choosing was not as hard as I believed it would be.

By the time I started my internet ministry, I was seventy-five years old. Pam had started to comment on my looking much younger than my age. I had noticed she also was not looking as if she was aging much either.

We had found the time machine to still be in the cave, and in good repair upon our return to Everett. We made our customary trips, traveling back in time for supplies and then forward to my time. Pam and I had relived this day so many times in the past, that we could tell when a knock on the door would happen, or stop Ali from spilling his glass of wine.

On one trip I said to Pam, "This time, we should start living an equal amount of time as the gang and let them live the life they were meant to live."

Pam agreed, she added she was also tired of having to explain ourselves every time that we traveled.

As I said, we hadn't aged physically very much in the last forty years, but there was a noticeable change in our appearance. It became tiring explaining ourselves every time we went back. Pam had told me that we were probably not aging as fast because we had been chosen by God. "Just as Moses and many others of the faithful lived for hundreds of years, we too will probably live for a long time. Eventually, they will catch up to us and even start to appear to be getting older than us. We will probably outlive them also."

I said that we would be going to a time when Dr. Simmons won't be in our lives. "What really troubles me though, is the thought that Dr. Simmons may not exist at all. It almost feels like murder. We won't have actually killed him though. We will just have prevented his birth."

Pam asked if it would hurt. I asked what she meant. She said, "When, or if, Jason ceases to exist, what will happen to him? Will he just disappear, or will it be like some kind of science-fiction thing where he slowly, and agonizingly fades away?"

I really hadn't thought about that aspect of the process. I told her I didn't know. I said, "I need to know though, as a scientist, and as a friend."

I told her I wanted to go to the week before he disappeared and stay until it happens. "I need to understand what happens to my friend."

47

We went back to 2100 and bought a weeks' supply of food. We already knew that Jason would be gone within the week. At what point during that week he would vanish was anybody's guess.

We got back to the machine, and I set the timer so we would arrive after the gang arrived. There was so much to carry. We decided to enlist the gang to help carry the supplies from the cave.

After we finished retrieving the supplies, Donna asked why we had brought so much. I let her know that we were going to stay for a week. The gang was happy to know we would be able to have some time to catch up on the separate lives Pam and I led from theirs.

That night, Pam and I told them about our lives and all we were accomplishing for the Lord. We had to explain to them once more how we had been reliving the same week over and over, and how we had told this same story time after time. They were, as usual, shocked to find that we had been coming back to the same week. Kim said, "You're having us relive the same day over and over? To what end are you doing this?"

I didn't know what to say. They had never asked this question before. I couldn't think of what to say. I couldn't tell them that they had become my lab rats, that I had come to see what would happen when they vanished, and that the ones left behind would not even remember that the other had ever existed.

I was stumbling for something to say when Pam said, "I will tell you what will happen."

I held my breath for fear of what she would say next.

She laid it out for all of them. They were all numb. Pam had not said who would vanish and how many of them would cease to exist, or who would be the first.

Then Jason asked who the first was. It felt odd that he asked that question in a past tense because in this time, it had not happened as of yet.

Pam lowered her head and sheepishly answered that it was him. "You will be the first Jason, it will be you."

Jason slowly slumped back in his chair then suddenly bolted upright in protest. "But I am alive. I exist. I know all of you. You all know me. You must be wrong." Then he asked, "When will it happen?"

I told him some-time this week.

"A week, I have only one week of life left? I guess I have arrangements to make. I'll have to find someone to take over my classes."

I said that it would not be necessary, that someone else would automatically be switched into his life. He said he didn't understand. I told him that if he didn't exist in this path of life, someone else would have filled the void long ago. He needed to make no arrangements.

I could tell he was rather upset about the news, and with good reason. We had just told him that he was going to, well, we still didn't know to where he would go; we just knew it would happen.

I said that it didn't mean that he would cease to exist altogether. I told him he may go down a different path in life. He said that he liked the path he was on and didn't care for another.

"Listen to me Jason, I know how hard this must be to take. The Lord knows how long I have struggled with this, but Pam and I decided that we had to let you live your lives the way you were meant to. None of us can change what will be, because what will be has already been put into motion. You can change what will happen in the future, but what has already been put in motion in the past will be. No one can stop it. Jason, you may not be a scientist in the future, but whatever you become is what you will wish to become in your new life."

He came back with, "If I still exist!"

There was nothing I could say to him for comfort. What do you say to a man you truly love who would just be a memory in a week? On top of that, only a memory to Pam and I; the others would not remember Jason at all.

Donna brought a glass of wine to Dr. Simmons to help him calm down. He thanked her for the gesture and quickly dispatched the glass. Donna stood by him with the decanter and filled his glass again. None of us were big drinkers, but when Donna finished filling Jason's glass, everyone else wanted a glass, including me.

Then Jason blurted out, "Take me with you. I can be of great use to you in the past."

"If we do that, you will only disappear in the past because you won't have started to time trip until you are the age you are now. If you go back in time, it won't change how you grew up. You will still become whatever you became. You would simply disappear in the past. You would still take the path you choose, and we never would have met, so you would have never made the trip back in time you are asking for."

I explained that it was not up to me to change things that were meant to be. He argued back that I had changed the past, and that it was my fault that he would be gone.

I told him this was God's will, that I only did what God had wanted.

He became enraged and began to yell at me. He accused me of making up the stories about talking to God. The wine was starting to slur his words. The others in the gang tried to get him to settle down, but he was understandably inconsolable.

It took some time for him to settle down, but we were finally able get him to do so. Jason had several glasses of wine and went to his room for the night.

Since I didn't know the exact date or time he would vanish, I put a camera in his room to monitor his sleep in case he went during the night; at least we would know what happened when the event took place.

Nothing happened though for the first three days, and then on the fourth day, while having dinner it happened.

Jason was beginning to think we were mistaken and had even started to make jokes about our revelation. I was glad to see Jason in a good mood again.

When the event happened, it was as I had hoped it would be, instantaneous. What took place after the event though, was one of the eeriest things I have ever experienced. Jason just vanished in midsentence. His plate and flatware vanished at the same moment he did. His chair was instantaneously transported to the wall, where it would sit if he had never been there.

The oddest thing that happened was the aftermath though. At the same moment he vanished, Ali began talking right where Jason had left off. Only the conversation and the mood of everyone changed at the same time Jason disappeared.

The change was so instantaneous that when Ali began talking, he had started in midsentence, as if he had been the one talking when the event happened. Pam and I alone heard him say, "And then I fell face first in a mud puddle." The gang, or what was left of them all laughed. Pam and I were dumbfounded. For some reason, we were the only witnesses when this anomaly took place. It had to be, because for them, the whole evening happened differently than it had for us.

We never said anything that night, but it was almost as if we had been watching a movie and suddenly another film started up. This night would haunt me for the rest of my life.

When we went to bed that night, we talked about the event and concluded that we would not tell the others about the incident. For their part, the gang acted as if nothing had happened, because for them, nothing had. It was kind of like refreshing the page on a computer had been commanded.

We prayed that whatever happened to Jason was not harmful to him, and that he was either living a good life, or that he was with God.

That night, we realized that we were not just reviving religion, we were changing humanity, and life in my time would never be the same.

That night, I had a dream. I flew to the lake that I had visited so many times in my dreams. When I landed, I was once again greeted by God's reflection in the water.

He began, "You are troubled about your friend Caleb?"

"Yes my Lord, can you tell me," I stammered for a moment then finished, "what happened to him? You see, I feel as if I killed him. It is not a good feeling."

"No, I can imagine that you do feel badly about this 'event,' as you have named it. Understand this. Your friend is fine. What you witnessed today was a correction. Your friend Jason just took a different path with his life. Because of you, he became one of my most powerful tools. Jason Simmons has brought many of my children to me. They were lost, and Jason put them back on the path. You have lost your friend, but in return, you have given me one of my greatest soldiers."

"He was a good man."

"Because of you Caleb, he became even greater. He added to my numbers exponentially. Instead of feeling bad, you should rejoice. Your efforts all these years are beginning to work. Take solace knowing that he will be beside me when it is his time."

"Thank you Lord, it is a great comfort for me to know that he is not only all right, but that he is also a good Christian."

"That is good, Caleb. Our time is over. Go now, and tell your wife that she can take comfort in this knowledge."

Then, as always before, and as always would be, I was pulled back to my life. Pam had already woken, and was tending to me in my stressed condition as she always did, and always would.

She asked, "What did I Am have for you tonight?"

I told her about my dream and that Jason was all right and that he would become one of God's greatest soldiers.

She smiled and said that it was a wonderful thing, and we should be happy. I had trouble with the idea, and Pam knew it. She told me that I needed to let go of my sadness and rejoice as the Lord said. "Things change throughout life.

Some for the good, and some for the bad. When we know they change for the good, we need to rejoice. Rejoice now Caleb, you are responsible for that soldier of God."

The next morning we got our things together and went to the cave, and back to the time we had come from. I had suffered a great loss, while God had gained a great soldier. I didn't know it at the time, but I would suffer many great losses over the years to come. I finally came to grips with loss, and tried to prepare as many as I could for what would come after their lives ended.

There was, of course, nothing I could do about death. It is, after all, unavoidable. Still, as many times as I would be around death in my life, it was something that I would never, or could ever get used to.

I know I felt comfortable getting back to 2285, and Pam was happy to be back so she could talk with Kay. It wasn't that she didn't have a good relationship with Donna, it was that her relationship with Kay was different; they were like sisters.

I have to admit I was becoming more comfortable talking to Martin, than I was talking to my contemporaries in my time. It had been so long since I had thought about physics in any manner, I had become, for a lack of better words, simple.

Once you get used to a certain lifestyle, it makes it more difficult to get used to living the life you once took for normal. I imagined it was somewhat similar to a war veteran returning home from a long deployment overseas, without the inherent dangers of course.

48

The years passed by, as I looked back on them, it seems they went in the blink of an eye. This happens when you get older. It helps to keep busy, and besides, idle hands are the devil's workplace.

As those years passed, Pam and I presided over funerals for the Moore's and the Bartlett's. This included Aaron and his wife. We were outliving everyone, but we were performing more christenings, than old friends we were burring.

My internet churches were full to the point I could no longer keep up with them, and I had to appoint others to oversee them grow. I had effectively made myself into an administrator, and was for the most part, not involved in the day-to-day workings of all the different religions that Pam and I had revived.

We were both getting old and tired, but I knew the devil was just waiting for us to give up. I was not about to let that happen.

About 160 years after the war, Pam and I sat down for dinner one night. Pam and I were now over 130 years old. After saying grace, I said to Pam that God had put it in my heart that we needed to tell the righteous to go forth and multiply the faithful.

I Am had told me in one of my dreams that people misunderstood his intention when he said people should multiply. God did not want the earth to be overpopulated. What he meant was to go forth and multiply the numbers of the faithful.

I Am told me that his intentions were misunderstood. He said, "Why would I destroy man because of his evil ways, then have them overpopulate it with more evil people?"

With man having free will though, he was able to interpret his words how they did.

God told me that he was saddened to see what had become of the earth. The population had gotten out of hand so much, that the world could no longer sustain it.

God said that when there is not enough to go around, people get desperate. When people get desperate, they will resort to any means available to survive. This of course, will naturally bring the evil out in man just to survive.

He said, "As you know Caleb, you found shortcomings in your time and tried to correct the injustice with no compassion from community leaders. I am sad that so many of my children had to suffer death in the prime of their lives. However, in order for some to live, the war had to be. If not, the population by your time would have been as high as twenty billion." He continued, "I created the earth to support about seven billion people. Any more than that, and the poisoning of the environment by humans would begin to kill the planet.

In Pam's time, there were activists that tried to tell the world's governments they were allowing the world to be destroyed, but it really wasn't the government's fault. The fault lies with humans, period.

They will do anything to survive, even if that means completely destroying the planet.

The only solution for there being enough to go around is less people.

That is the main reason the Chinese started the Great Attrition War. If people would not have created such large families, the earth would not have gotten so overpopulated, and religion would not have been put to an end."

Pam asked what we should do, or if there was a way of telling them.

"The problem with telling people to not have large families in this time, is basically the same problem that people had back in the pre-industrialized age. Families needed to be large to have hands to work the fields, or to make the family businesses succeed.

However, unlike before the industrial revolution, families can now maintain their crops with only a few members. While we no longer have all the mechanization that was available after the industrial revolution, there are other improvements that have been developed, such as irrigation and fertilization methods, which vastly improve crop sizes and a plant's yield.

"This makes a family of four or five large enough to be successful at providing food for said family. Thus, there is no longer a need for a large family of ten or more. That was necessary just for survival before mechanization came along. The need to have large families should have ceased at this point in time, and it has for the most part. However, there are still people that follow the word of the Bible too literally, and are still producing too many offsprings.

"God doesn't see the population as a problem now, because the war killed so many that the earth can once again support the people that are still alive, but he is concerned that if not kept in check, the population will come full circle, and the problem will repeat itself."

Again Pam asked what we should do.

I looked at her and smiled, then told her that we can only put the word out and hope that God will put this problem on their hearts. At any rate, it is all we can do, we can't force people to limit the amount of children they have.

After we ate, Pam said she wasn't feeling well, and she laid down to rest. While she rested, I did the dishes. When I finished, I went to check on her to see if she wanted anything.

She seemed to be sleeping, so I didn't bother her. I instead went online to see what was happening to the ministries. I checked around to as many as I could, and at two o'clock in the morning, I decided I had done enough for the day. I went over and woke Pam up so we could go to bed. She was quite startled when I awoke her, and told me she had been having a bad dream.

She said that she had dreamed about the day we lost Cain. She said that, although she had not witnessed the accident, it was a very vivid dream, and it was a horrible thing to see. Having witnessed the accident myself, I can tell you it was a horrible thing to see.

We prayed, said "I love you" to each other, kissed, and said good night. I didn't know it, but it would be our last night together. When I woke up the next day, I thought I would let Pam rest while I cooked some breakfast for us. When I finished, I walked upstairs to give Pam hers.

I walked to her side of the bed, put the tray on the floor, and tried to wake her. I touched her to wake her up. I realized right away that she had passed in the night.

I fell to my knees protesting to God that I still needed her. I shouted to God, "How can you do this to me? Have I not done your bidding faithfully? What more do you want from me?"

I fell to the floor and wept for what must have been hours. Finally, one of my aides came to check on me when I didn't answer my e-mails.

When he saw what had happened, he picked me up in his arms, carried me down the stairs, and laid me on the couch.

He then went to my computer and e-mailed an associate the news, requesting that they bring over the necessary people, but not too many.

Within a few minutes, there were five people in the house. There were two women who went upstairs to tend to Pam, and the others tended to me. A woman named Julie, who was the Bartlett's granddaughter, cleaned the kitchen. She had brought food with her, and began to cook a pot of stew. It was to feed everyone who came to help, but she brought me the first bowl. I declined, but she was insistent and got me to eat some.

What would I do without my darling Pam? I already felt so lost, and it had only been a few hours. The next few days would be very hard on me.

Pam had asked that she be buried some place where I also would make my final resting spot. The voice in my head said, "Take her home." Why was it always so vague? Did God mean her home or mine?

After I thought about it a bit, I realized he must mean my home. To take her back to her time would involve too much explaining, and how would I get there when I died? I would have to trust that God would provide.

My property was only about twenty miles from Everett. I could bury Pam in this time, and make sure that in my will there would be a provision for me to be laid to rest beside her.

The day came to bury Pam, and thousands of people came for the service. There were twice as many people for her funeral as there was for Mikes', all those years ago.

I didn't know the people who owned the property, but they knew who I was, and did not hesitate to allow me my request; it would be their honor to have Pam be laid to rest on their property. They even asked if it would be all right to have her buried by a tree close to the house so they could easily tend to her grave. I couldn't ask for any more. They said it was because of me that they had been saved.

They did ask why I wanted their property. I said I couldn't tell them. They didn't say another word, or ask any more questions.

We finished the service, and all of us went back to Everett, getting home just before dusk.

That night, I was alone in my house. I thought about this and realized that it had been many years since I had been alone. I would need to adjust to being alone.

49

After a few days, there was a knock on the door. I opened it to find a young woman with a suitcase.

I asked if I could help her. She responded that she had been sent by the seminary to be my housekeeper. I was a little stunned. She explained that her husband was a student at the seminary, and that they couldn't afford the tuition. "The president of the seminary had told us that we could live with you, and he would waive Jacobs's tuition in return for us helping you here at your home."

I thought about this for a moment. At first, I was a little upset that this decision was made without my being involved. This feeling lasted a very short time though, and I said, "Well, Jacob is your husband's name. What shall I call you?"

"I beg your pardon, sir," she said as she looked at her feet. I believe she was embarrassed that she had neglected that important bit of information. "My name is Beth, sir."

"Well Beth, hadn't you better come in?"

"Yes sir. Thank you."

"Please call me Caleb."

"Yes sir—I mean, yes Caleb."

"Pleased to meet you Beth, allow me to show you to your room." We walked to a room on the main floor, and I said, "This is it."

Every four years, I would get a new student. It didn't bother me, except I would just be getting used to having one couple living with me. When they would finish their stay, and move on to their assigned station, then I would welcome a new couple and start all over.

I always found his candidates to be acceptable.

This went on for years. I was now 268 years old. There were reports I had known of where other holy men who lived to 150 years old, but I was living longer than anyone else. Living this long was getting tiring. I found myself wanting to not wake up the next morning at times. I had to keep burying friends who lived a normal life span. There were still babies being born, and since the seminary had opened, there were more people moving to Everett all the time. I could no longer keep up with my overseas ministry, and the seminary took over those duties.

I was as busy as I cared to be with baptisms, marriages, and burials. It seemed that everyone wanted my blessings for whatever the event may be.

Even though I was keeping as busy as I wished, I felt as if life had no meaning for me anymore. For lack of a better way of saying it, I was bored!

I would pray to the Lord that something would happen to create my end. I was becoming depressed. So much was happening in my life, but it was happening around me, not to me.

I began to feel as if life held nothing for me. I realized that it had been a long time since I had visited Pam. I told my housekeeper that I would be visiting Pam, and that I would be late coming home.

It was an arduous journey, taking me four hours to make the trip; it took about two and one-half hours to make the trip when Pam was buried.

I got to the house and made my way to the grave site. It was still being maintained. The original tree had died, and the tree that was there now was the third tree that had been planted there. I was pleased to see that it was so well maintained.

At that moment, a man exited the house, and as he approached me, I realized that it was me. I thought about the date and realized it was two weeks before I would make my first time trip.

I was on the far side of the grave when he approached me. He stopped and said his name was Caleb Bronson. He stuck out his hand and asked what my name was.

I hesitated for a moment. He stuck his hand further toward me. I retreated a step.

He said, "I'm not going to bite." He asked if I was a descendant of Pam.

I answered that I was not. I then said, "I would shake your hand, but it would kill us both."

He dropped his hand, saying a little handshake would not hurt.

I simply replied, "The same matter cannot occupy the same space at the same time."

He had a strange look on his face, then he squinted his eyes and said, "What is your name sir?"

I looked him in the eye and said, "Caleb Bronson."

The look he gave me was that of astonishment. He said, "But that's my name."

I said I knew what his name was.

He said, "Are you telling me that you are me?"

I said, "I was always quick at catching on." Even now that I was 268 years old, I was still sharp as a tack.

He said, "That's why the headstone says simply, 'The Doctor.'"

"Yes, to have put my—our name on it—would have been giving you a clue," I said. "I'm sure you have many questions. I will tell you what I can, but I would like to talk to Donna first." He called for Donna, and when she approached us, she simple said, "Hello, Doctors."

Young Caleb was a little taken aback. Realizing that Donna recognized me, his mouth opened a little from shock.

Donna said, "Let's go inside and talk. Come on, gentlemen. Let's go." She said, "I would recognize you anytime."

We sat down at the table, and he looked at me, still stunned.

I had brought my journal with me and pushed it across the table to him.

He inquired as to its content, and I explained what it was. Again he looked stunned.

I asked Donna if I looked so silly when presented with an unbelievable fact. She replied that I had always looked that way, even when the news was not that earth-shattering.

I said I was tired and asked if I could go to sleep. They both said I could, and Donna escorted me to my room and helped me get in bed. It was odd to see myself so young and full of inspiration. Now I was just an old man who needed to be helped into bed.

That night, Caleb went through my journal. The next morning he started to grill me. Would I do anything different if I could change something? I told him in the end I would not change a thing, that I had a good life, and the only thing I would change if I could, would be to have Pam live longer, it had been over 130 years since she had passed. I finally said, "Enough of the past. You have a mission in the future. Did you read about the Second Attrition War?" He replied he had. I said, "This is your mission. I have restored religion. Your mission will be to stop the Chinese from creating the serum that will end humanity."

He asked if I knew how this would be done. I dropped my head. I had went through so many scenarios, and I kept coming back to the only idea that sounded like it would work. That was to go to China, find the inventors' parents, and kill one of them. "It goes against everything I believe in, but I have not been able to think of another way. I made a trip to the future and found the families' pertinent information. You will have to go to China in order to complete this task, but complete it you must, fore the human race will be depending on you."

I had just dumped on him the worst assignment that anyone could ever have been given, and I gave it to myself, but that was it. I would have asked him if he could think of any other way to do this, but I would just be asking myself, what was the sense of doing that?

That was the last task that I had to complete for our Lord. I went to bed that night assured that I had completed everything that the Lord had placed before me. We had beaten the devil back to his fowl labyrinth, and restored the Lord to his rightful place with man.

From this time forward, religion spread throughout the world.

My young self completed his task, eliminating the theater of mankind's doom by the Chinese. Since the poison to sterilize all women never materialized, the Second Great Attrition War never took place. However, he figured out a way to complete his task other than I had instructed him to.

I was pleased to know that he completed this task without having to kill anyone.

With religion coming back stronger than ever, even the Chinese loosened their policy on religion. People no longer felt that one race should be the ruler, and the races of the world began to intermingle.

While I slept that night, I had a dream. It was different than the others I had, because I was walking instead of flying. I knew I was on my way home to our Lord. I did pass that night, and was finally on my way to paradise.

Donna went to Everett and informed the president of the seminary that I had died. He put the word out about my death. People came from all over the country. It was a very large service, more than fifty thousand people attended.

Now that I have passed, and you have finished reading about my life, you are probably wondering if I really did go to heaven. Am I spending eternity with Pam, our sons, and all the friends we met along the way? What about Sampson? Is he with me in heaven?

I would like to give you the answer to those questions, but I would never deprive you of having your own magnificent journey through life. Remember this; life truly is a magnificent journey all by itself. Don't be afraid of what someone thinks or does. Don't allow someone to try and make you something you don't want to be. This would alter your journey, and the journey is what life is really about. Don't think about things like, I have to have the right shoes or the latest fashion. These are just things. You can't take them with you when your soul leaves the temporary vessel called your body. So live life like there is no tomorrow; there may not be one. By this I mean, live your life for God. In the end, nothing else really matters.

I'm sorry, I can't tell you whether or not I am in heaven. You have to decide for yourself if God is real. All I can say is I believe. I guess the best I can tell you is to just keep believing; you'll get your answer when your end comes. God bless you all. I'll see you later, on the other side.

50

My name is Dr. Caleb Bronson. I am at a loss for words as to how I should be presenting myself at this moment. I am the young version of my old self, who has just passed away, so I will simply refer to myself as I always have, since I am, once more, the only Dr. Caleb Bronson.

I have to start by echoing the sentiments of my old self when he began this journal that I will continue.

It seems odd that I should start keeping a journal at this point in my life. However, the path which I am about to embark on is not more important than the one my old self took. It is nonetheless something that was as important.

The difference between our missions is my old self went back in time to save man's very soul. My mission was to save man's very existence.

I too would have the honor of private audiences with our Lord. In my first encounter with God, it struck me that it wasn't necessary to kill one of the inventors' parents. Instead, I could locate the mother before she would meet the father, and court her. Taking her for my bride and preventing the birth of the inventor of the mankind-ending formula, preventing the tragedy from ever happening.

This pleased the Lord very much, as murder was very distasteful to him also. I asked why he never told this to my older self. He replied that free will prevented him from interfering. He also said that I would never have met Pam, and she was as important to reviving Christianity as I had been.

Unlike I did, God made no distinction between my young self and my old self. This was sometimes a little confusing to me, but I would eventually catch on and understand that there really was no distinction between the two of us, because in reality, we were one and the same. We were both just soldiers for our Lord, set on different paths.

So I began my own wonderful journey through life. My bride-to-be lived in North Korea. Her name was Wang Xiao Ling. She was a descendant of a naturalized Chinese couple that had been part of that government's political reeducation process. As such, she had been granted dual citizenship.

When I first met her, she had been planning on returning to China to live. This is where her husband-to-be, whom she knew nothing about at the time, lived. She would never even meet him, so I felt no remorse about breaking a couple up because they never would know each other.

Things worked out for Wang Xiao Ling and I we were married and lived a good life having two children. We named our children Joseph and Rebekah.

Although it was still illegal to practice Christianity in the countries that China possessed, the authorities had more important problems to handle.

With religion coming back stronger than ever, even the Chinese eventually loosened their policy on religion. People no longer felt that one race should be the ruler, and the races of the world began to intermingle.

This also brought about a change to how women were treated. There was an end to prostitution: any man that tried to enslave women in to that brutal trade was dealt with harshly. If you were convicted of being a pimp, you received an automatic death penalty. If caught as a customer of prostitution, you would receive life behind bars to regret your poor judgment.

When caught, a child molester would receive a public stoning. I understand that this sounds barbaric, but think of how this damages the life of the victim.

This greatly reduced the number of children that were abused and had their lives ruined as a result. Homosexuals were banished to the desolate island of Tasmania and allowed to live their sinful lives the way they desired. They were seen as hurting no one but themselves and would never be among God's chosen.

A scientist discovered a segment of DNA that could be detected in the amniotic fluid of a pregnant woman eventually, and through treatment, the fetus would be altered, and it prevented those perversions from occurring again.

Equality between the sexes finally came to pass; unfortunately, this didn't happen because it was the right thing to do, it happened because a new form of world commerce came into being.

You would earn credits instead of gold. Your earnings would be downloaded on to a chip that was activated by your DNA, so theft became a thing of the past. There were set prices for work done with no distinctions between sexes.

A certain amount and type of work was assigned a certain amount of credits, and they were distributed by a machine that didn't differentiate between sex or age.

This machine also promoted a person based on their performance alone. It was found that after the machine straightened out the sexist way the business world was run, women ended up heading 64 percent of the global companies.

It was also discovered that men did have as good a head for business as women; they had just become complacent.

After men realized the glass ceiling had been shattered, they buckled down, and while they never got back above 50 percent in charge, they came to realize that women were their equals, if not better, and there was an, as unknown before, harmony in the work place.

Blood lines were mixed, and about five hundred years after my death, there were no more countries. It was impossible to tell one race from another because of this. Instead of countries, we became one people, with one purpose, and that was to spread the word and worship God.

For the first time in world history, if you were to ask someone what race they were, they would say, "I'm a human being." There were no more lines to cross, no more color to be prejudiced about, no land to fight about, because the world belonged to everyone.

It reminded me of Ephesians 2:14–16:

> For he himself is our peace, who has made the two one and has destroyed the barrier, the dividing wall of hostility, by abolishing in his flesh the law with its commandment and regulations. His purpose was to create in himself one new man out of the two, thus making peace, and in this one body to reconcile them both to God with the cross, by which he put to death their hostility.
>
> Ephesians 2:14–16 (NIV)

After Wang Xaio Ling and I were married, we began to spread Christianity in our village, as my old self had done in the free world of the past.

By this time, Christianity was known throughout the world. It was easy to get a church started because it was a popular concept, despite its illegality.

Soon after we started the first church, others began springing up everywhere; it was like an avalanche, and nothing could stop the growth.

Wang Xiao Ling and I lived well past two hundred fifty years, and we were revered as the people that united the whole world. We knew that God had made this happen, and we told that to anyone that tried to treat us as if we were something special.

You're probably wondering if I am in heaven with all the good people I have met along the way and with my other self or did we both become one when I died.

Also, did I get meet all the people I never got to, the people that my other self knew and loved.

I'm sorry. I can't give you the answer to that question. All I can say is live your life for good, you will be much happier in the end.

What will happen to you is your decision to make in this life, so my advice to you is to live, but be righteous in your living.

Don't try to cheat yourself out of the journey; the journey is the most important part of life other than praising God. Be a good person and enjoy life; if you rush it, you may miss something miraculous, so take life in and enjoy the short time you have here.

Remember, eternity lasts a long time; take the right path.

God bless you all. I'll see you on the other side.